From The We
124 Shoreditch

Janet Frame   Photo by Anne Noble

Janet Frame was born in Dunedin, New Zealand, in 1924. Her works include ten novels, among them *Owls Do Cry, A State of Siege, Scented Gardens for the Blind* (The Women's Press 1982) *Living in the Maniototo* (The Women's Press 1981) and *Faces in the Water* (The Women's Press 1980); also four collections of stories and sketches, a volume of poetry and a children's book, *Mona Minim and the Smell of the Sun. To The Is-land*, the first volume of her autobiography, was published by The Women's Press in 1983, and won the James Wattie Book of the Year award in 1983. The second volume, *An Angel At My Table*, was published by The Women's Press in 1984. Janet Frame was awarded the CBE in the 1983 Queen's Birthday Honours List. She has been a Burns Scholar, won the New Zealand Scholarship in Letters and the Hubert Church Award for prose, was awarded an honorary doctorate in Literature by the University of Otago, and in 1980 won the Fiction Prize, New Zealand Book Awards for *Living in the Maniototo*.

Janet Frame

You Are Now Entering The Human Heart

Stories

The Women's Press

First published in Great Britain by
The Women's Press Limited 1984
A member of the Namara Group
124 Shoreditch High Street, London E1 6JE

First published by Victoria University Press,
Wellington, New Zealand, 1983

British Library Cataloguing in Publication Data

Frame, Janet
    You are now entering the human heart.
    I. Title
    823[F]   PR9639.3.F4

    ISBN 0-7043-2849-6
    ISBN 0-7043-3938-2 Pbk

Printed in Great Britain
by Nene Litho and bound by
Woolnough Bookbinding, both of
Wellingborough, Northants

To Piki, Jody Anne,
Derek, Jill, Christopher and Amy,
with love.

Contents

You Are Now Entering
the Human Heart

Keel and Kool

Father shook the bidi-bids off the big red and grey rug and then he spread it out again in the grass.

'There you are,' he said. 'Mother here, and Winnie here, and Joan you stay beside Winnie. We'll put the biscuit tin out of the way so it won't come into the photo. Now say cheese.'

He stepped back and cupped his hand over the front of the camera, and then he looked over his shoulder—'to see if the sun's looking too', he told the children who were saying cheese. And then he clicked the shiny thing at the side of the camera.

'There you are,' he said. 'It's taken. A happy family.'

'Oh,' said Mother. 'Were we all right? Because I want to show the photo to Elsie. It's the first we've taken since Eva — went.'

Mother always said went or passed away or passed beyond when she talked of death. As if it were not death really, only pretend.

'We were good weren't we Dad,' said Winnie. 'And now are you going fishing?'

'Yes,' said Father. 'I'm going fishing. I'll put this in a safe place and then I'm off up the river for salmon.'

He carried the camera over to where the coats were piled, and he stowed it in one of the bags carefully, for photos were precious things.

And then he stooped and fastened the top strap of his gumboots to his belt.

'Cheerio,' he said, kissing Mother. He always kissed everyone

when he went away anywhere, even for a little while. And then he
kissed Winnie and pulled her hair, and he pulled Joan's hair too
but he didn't kiss her because she was the girl over the road and no
relation.

'I'll come back with a salmon or I'll go butcher's hook.'

They watched him walking towards the river, a funny clumpy
walk because he had his gumboots on. He was leaning to one side,
with his right shoulder lower than his left, as if he were trying to
dodge a blow that might come from the sky or the trees or the air.
They watched him going and going, like someone on the films,
who grows smaller and smaller and then The End is printed across
the screen, and music plays and the lights go up. He was like a man
in a story walking away from them. Winnie hoped he wouldn't go
too far away because the river was deep and wild and made a
roaring noise that could be heard even above the willow trees and
pine trees. It was the greyest river Winnie had ever seen. And the
sky was grey too with a tiny dot of sun. The grey of the sky seemed
to swim into the grey of the river.

Then Father turned and waved.

Winnie and Joan waved back.

'And now we're going to play by the pine tree Mrs Todd, aren't
we Winnie,' said Joan.

'We'll play ladies,' said Winnie.

Mother sighed. The children were such happy little things.
They didn't realise. . . .

'All right kiddies,' she said. 'You can run away and play. Don't
go near the river and mind the stinging nettle.'

Then she opened her *Woman's Weekly* and put it on her knee.
She knew that she would read only as far as Over the Teacups and
then she would think all over again about Eva passing away, her
first baby. A sad blow, people said, to lose your first, just when she
was growing up to be a help to you. But it's all for the best and you
have Wonderful Faith Mrs Todd, she's happier in another sphere,
you wouldn't have wished it otherwise, and you've got her photo,
it's always nice to have their photos. Bear up Mrs Todd.

Mrs Todd shut her eyes and tried to forget and then she started to
read Over the Teacups. It was better to forget and not think about
it.

Winnie and Joan raced each other through the grass to the pine tree by the fence, Joan's dark hair bobbing up and down and getting in her eyes. 'Bother,' she said. Winnie stared enviously. She wished her own hair was long enough to hang over her eyes and be brushed away. How nice to say bother, and brush your hair out of your eyes. Eva's hair had been long. It was so funny about Eva, and the flowers and telegrams and Auntie May coming and bringing sugar buns and custard squares. It was so funny at home with Eva's dresses hanging up and her shoes under the wardrobe and no Eva to wear them, and the yellow quilt spread unruffled over her bed, and staying unruffled all night. But it was good wearing Eva's blue pyjamas. They had pink round the bottom of the legs and pink round the neck and sleeves. Winnie liked to walk round the bedroom in them and see herself in the mirror and then get into bed and yawn, stretching her arms above her head like a lady. But it would have been better if Eva were there to see.

And what fun if Eva were there at the picnic!

'Come on,' said Joan. 'We'll play ladies in fur coats. I know because my Mother's got a fur coat.'

'I'm a lady going to bed,' said Winnie. 'I'm wearing some beautiful blue pyjamas and I'm yawning, and my maid's just brought my coffee to me.' She lay under the pine tree. She could smell the pine and hear the hush-hush of its branches and beyond that the rainy sound of the river, and see the shrivelled-up cones like little brown claws, and the grey sky like a tent with the wind blowing under it and puffing it out. And there was Joan walking up and down in her fur coat, and smiling at all the ladies and gentlemen and saying oh no, I've got heaps of fur coats. Bother, my hair does get in my eyes so.

Joan had been Eva's best friend. She was so beautiful. She was Spanish she said, a little bit anyway. She had secrets with Eva. They used to whisper together and giggle and talk in code.

'I'm tired of wearing my fur coat,' said Joan, suddenly. 'And you can't go on yawning for ever.'

'I can go on yawning for ever if I like,' said Winnie, remembering the giggles and the secrets and the code she couldn't understand. And she yawned and said thank you to the maid for her coffee. And then she yawned again.

'I can do what I like,' she said.

'You can't always,' said Joan. 'Your Mother wouldn't let you. Anyway I'm tired of wearing my fur coat, I want to make something.'

She turned her back on Winnie and sat down in the grass away from the pine tree, and began to pick stalks of feathery grass. Winnie stopped yawning. She heard the rainy-wind sound of the river and she wondered where her Father was. And what was Mother doing? And what was Joan making with the feathery grass?

'What are you making, Joan?'

'I'm making Christmas trees,' answered Joan graciously. 'Eva showed me. Didn't Eva show you?'

And she held up a Christmas tree.

'Yes,' lied Winnie, 'Eva showed me Christmas trees.'

She stared at the tiny tree in Joan's hand. The grass was wet with last night's dew and the tree sparkled, catching the tiny drop of sunlight that fell from the high grey and white air. It was like a fairy tree or like the song they sang at school — Little fir tree neat and green. Winnie had never seen such a lovely thing to make.

'And Eva showed me some new bits to Tinker Tailor,' said Joan, biting off a piece of grass with her teeth. 'Boots, shoes, slippers, clodhoppers, silk, satin, cotton, rags — it's what you're married in.'

'She showed me too,' lied Winnie. 'Eva showed me lots of things.'

'She showed me things too,' said Joan tenaciously.

Winnie didn't say anything to that. She looked up in the sky and watched a seagull flying over. I'm Keel, I'm Keel it seemed to say. Come home Kool come home Kool. Keel Keel. Winnie felt lonely staring up into the sky. Why was the pine tree so big and dark and old? Why was the seagull crying out I'm Keel I'm Keel as if it were calling for somebody who wouldn't come. Keel Keel, come home Kool, come home Kool it cried.

Winnie wished her Mother would call out to them. She wished her Father were back from the river, and they were all sitting on the rug, drinking billy tea and eating water biscuits that crackled in your mouth. She wished Joan were away and there were just Father and Mother and Winnie, and no Joan. She wished she had long hair and could make Christmas trees out of feathery grass. She wished she knew more bits to Tinker Tailor. What was it Joan had said? 'Boots shoes slippers clodhoppers.' Why hadn't Eva told her?

'You're going to sleep,' said Joan suddenly. 'I've made three Christmas trees. Look.'

'I'm not going to sleep. I'm hungry,' said Winnie. 'And I think Joan Mason that some people tell lies.'

Joan flushed. 'I *have* made three Christmas trees.'

'It's not that,' said Winnie, taking up a pine needle and making pine-needle writing in the air.

'I just think that some people tell lies.'

'But I'm not a liar, Winnie,' protested Joan anxiously. 'I'm not honestly.'

'Some people,' Winnie murmured, writing with her pine needle.

'You're not fair Winnie Todd,' quivered Joan throwing down her Christmas trees. 'I know you mean me.'

'Nobody said I did. I just said — some people.'

'Well you looked at me.'

'Did I?'

Winnie crushed her pine needle and smelt it. She wanted to cry. She wished she had never come for a picnic. She was cold too with just her print dress on. She wished she were somewhere far far away from the river and the pine tree and Joan Mason and the Christmas trees, somewhere far far away, she didn't know where.

Perhaps there was no place. Perhaps she would never find anywhere to go. Her Mother would die and her Father would die and Joan Mason would go on flicking the hair from her eyes and saying bother and wearing her fur coat and not knowing what it was like to have a mother and father dead.

'Yes,' said Winnie. 'You're a liar. Eva told me things about you. Your uncle was eaten by cannibals and your father shot an albatross and had a curse put on him and your hair went green when you went for a swim in Christchurch and you had to be fed on pineapple for three weeks before it turned black again. Eva told me. You're a liar. She didn't believe you either. And take your Christmas trees.' She picked up one of the trees and tore it to pieces.

Joan started to cry.

'Cry baby, liar, so there.'

Winnie reached forward and gave Joan a push, and then she turned to the pine tree and catching hold of the lowest branches, she pulled herself up into the tree. Soon she was over half-way up. The branches rocked up and down, sighing and sighing. Winnie peered down on to the ground and saw Joan running away through the grass, her hair bobbing up and down as she ran. She would be going back to where Winnie's mother was. Perhaps she would tell. Winnie pushed me over and called me names. And then when Winnie got down from the tree and went to join the others her Mother would look at her with a hurt expression in her eyes and say blessed are the peacemakers. And her Father would be sitting there telling them all about the salmon, but he would stop when she came up, hours and hours later, and say sternly I hoped you would behave yourself. And then he would look at Mother, and Winnie would know they were thinking of Eva and the flowers and telegrams and Auntie May saying bear up, you have Wonderful Faith. And then Mother would say have one of these chocolate biscuits, Joan. And Mother and Father and Joan would be together, sharing things.

Winnie's eyes filled with tears of pity for herself. She wished Eva were there. They would both sit up the pine tree with their hands clutching hold of the sticky branches, and they would ride up and down, like two birds on the waves, and then they would turn into princesses and sleep at night in blue pyjamas with pink round the edges, and in the daytime they would make Christmas trees out of feathery grass and play Tinker Tailor — boots, shoes, slippers, clodhoppers.

'Boots, shoes, slippers, clodhoppers,' whispered Winnie. But there was no one to answer her. Only up in the sky there was a seagull as white as chalk, circling and crying Keel Keel Come home Kool, come home Kool. And Kool would never come, ever.

My Cousins
Who Could Eat Cooked Turnips

For a long time I could never understand my cousins in Invercargill. They were good children, Dot and Mavis, they folded up their clothes before they went to bed at night, and they put their garters on the door-knob where they could find them in the morning, and they didn't often poke a face at their father when he wasn't looking.

They had a swing round the back of the house. They let us have turns on it, waiting respectfully at the side, and not saying your turn's over you're only trying to make it last, only one more swing and then it's ours. No. They waited respectfully.

They had a nice trellis-work too, with dunny roses growing up it, you could almost touch the roses if you were swinging high enough. Their mother was our Auntie Dot and their father was Uncle Ted, who was a captain and wore Khaki, and sat at the head of the table, and said sternly eat what you're given, what about the starving children in Europe.

There were always children starving in Europe. Sometimes people came to school, thin women with pamphlets, and told us about Europe, and then after the talk we put our names down for a society where we went and sat on a long form and had a feast once a term.

Actually I didn't think my cousins were of the same family as us, they couldn't have been I thought. They were very clean and quiet and they spoke up when visitors came to their house, aunts and uncles I mean, and they didn't say dirty words or rhymes. They were Cultured.

But for a long time I could never understand them, for instance they could eat cooked turnip.

Now where we lived there were turnips in the garden, some for the cow and some for us. We used to go into the garden, pull up a turnip, wash it under the garden tap and then eat the turnip raw.

But if it came cooked on the table, even at Auntie Dot's, we said no.

At home Dad would say eat your turnip. Nancy eat your turnip. Billy eat your turnip, you too Elsie.

'But we don't like it cooked.'

'Do as I say, eat your turnip.'

Well what could we do in the face of such grim coercion? But we didn't eat it all, and we didn't like it, it didn't seem to have the good earthy taste raw turnip had, and we weren't eating it outside down the garden with the cow looking approval over the fence and the birds singing in the orchard and people hammering and dogs barking and everything being alive and natural uncooked.

It was different inside, the hot room and the chairs drawn up to the table and everybody quiet as if something important and dreadful were about to happen, like a ghost or the end of the world, and my Father sitting at the top with his knife and fork held the proper way and his eyes saying elbows off the table.

eat your turnip eat your turnip

No we just couldn't manage to like cooked turnip that way.

And then one week-end we went to Auntie Dot's. We had new fancy garters and new fleecy-lined nighties and we travelled first class on the train because Dad was on the railway and had a free ticket. Auntie Dot met us at the station, and how *are* you all, I got your letter Mona, little Elsie's shooting up isn't she, yes they're so shy at that age, where's Mavis come on Mavis. Auntie Dot was big, with smothering brown eyes and hair. She wore shoes like baskets and a hat with a cherry in front, that bobbed whenever she moved her head, a little for Auntie Dot, here's your cherry Auntie Dot, I've picked the dust off it, I meant to tell you it was loose, thank you child you're a credit to your mother, I hadn't noticed it had fallen.

Uncle Ted drove us home in the car, Mavis and Dot and Elsie and Billy and I in the back and the others in the front. Nobody talked in the back, we didn't ever talk to our cousins. Mavis had on a pink frilly dress with a cape collar and Dot had on a pink frilly dress with a cape collar, and both together the girls looked like lollies, and when they turned to us and smiled shy smiles, they looked like little pink lollies waiting to be licked. Mavis and Dot had lace too. I could see it round their petticoats, and I knew they had fancy garters, and remembered to myself what my Mother had said to us

be sure you hang your garters on the door-knob

be sure you fold your nighties

be sure you say can I help with the dishes

and do eat your turnip this time.

When we got to the house with its swing and its clothesline that twirled round and round, and its dunny roses on the trellis-work, we wanted to go home. Each time we came to Auntie Dot's we were visitors to an alien world. Auntie Dot's kitchen smelt like seed-cake and leather. There was a clock with a different kind of ticking on the mantelpiece and when the hour struck, a little bird popped out to say hello, it was all so sad and strange, the seed-cake and the little bird and the teapot with a knitted cosy, and the green gnome sitting on the sideboard, and our Mother far away and high up, talking about things we didn't understand. And then going out on to the lawn and standing with our arms hanging as if they didn't belong, staring about us at the swing and the clothesline that twirled round and round, and the different kinds of flowers in the garden. And then coming inside to tea and seeing the table all white and ready, and hearing the grownups talking again, really is that so just fancy they were saying importantly and deliciously, but it seemed sad too, really is that so just fancy, over and over again, and it got sadder when we sat down to tea and saw the turnip.

Cooked turnip. Vitamins said Uncle Ted. Roughage.

(really is that so just fancy)

For a long time I could never understand my cousins. That night they sat there in cold blood, eating cooked turnip. Perhaps it was our new nighties, perhaps it was the swing, perhaps it was the little bird that popped out to say hello, but I looked at Billy and Elsie, and Billy and Elsie looked at me, and that night we sat there too, in cold blood, eating cooked turnip.

And then we understood. And after tea I said to Mavis I've got a new nightie, it's fleecy-lined, we put our fancy garters on the door-knob when we go to bed, we've got a cow at home. Our clothesline isn't like yours it doesn't go round and round. I don't suppose you know what this word means, and I whispered a word in her ear, and Mavis said I do too. I know lots of words.

Mavis and I were very good friends. In the morning we got up and played on the swing, and my Mother looked out of the window and laughed and waved to me, and she didn't seem far away any more, and everything was all right again. And we played house together, Mavis and I, and we drank tea out of little china cups, and we said really is that so just fancy, and we swung, all day we swung as high as the dunny roses.

Swans

They were ready to go. Mother and Fay and Totty, standing by the gate in their next best to Sunday best, Mother with her straw hat on with shells on it and Fay with her check dress that Mother had made and Totty, well where was Totty a moment ago she was here?

'Totty,' Mother called. 'If you don't hurry we'll miss the train, it leaves in ten minutes. And we're not to forget to get off at Beach Street. At least I think Dad said Beach Street. But hurry Totty.'

Totty came running from the wash-house round the back.

'Mum quick I've found Gypsy and her head's down like all the other cats and she's dying I think. She's in the wash-house. Mum quick,' she cried urgently.

Mother looked flurried. 'Hurry up, Totty and come back Fay, pussy will be all right. We'll give her some milk now there's some in the pot and we'll wrap her in a piece of blanket and she'll be all right till we get home.'

The three of them hurried back to the wash-house. It was dark with no light except what came through the small square window which had been cracked and pasted over with brown paper. The cat lay on a pile of sacks in a corner near the copper. Her head was down and her eyes were bright with a fever or poison or something but she was alive. They found an old clean tin lid and poured warm milk in it and from one of the shelves they pulled a dusty piece of blanket. The folds stuck to one another all green and hairy and a slater with hills and valleys on his back fell to the floor and moved slowly along the cracked concrete floor to a little secret place by the wall. Totty even forgot to collect him. She collected things, slaters and earwigs and spiders though you had to be careful with earwigs for when you were lying in the grass asleep they crept into your ear and built their nest there and you had to go to the doctor and have your ear lanced.

They covered Gypsy and each one patted her. Don't worry Gypsy they said. We'll be back to look after you tonight. We're going to the Beach now. Goodbye Gypsy.

And there was Mother waiting impatiently again at the gate.

'Do hurry. Pussy'll be all right now.'

Mother always said things would be all right, cats and birds and people even as if she knew and she did know too, Mother knew always.

But Fay crept back once more to look inside the wash-house.

'I promise,' she called to the cat. 'We'll be back, just you see.'

And the next moment the three Mother and Fay and Totty were outside the gate and Mother with a broom-like motion of her arms was sweeping the two little girls before her.

O the train and the coloured pictures on the station, South America and Australia, and the bottle of fizzy drink that you could only half finish because you were too full, and the ham sandwiches that curled up at the edges, because they were stale, Dad said, and he *knew*, and the rabbits and cows and bulls outside in the paddocks, and the sheep running away from the noise and the houses that came and went like a dream, clackety-clack, Kaitangata, Kaitangata, and the train stopping and panting and the man with the stick tapping the wheels and the huge rubber hose to give the engine a drink, and the voices of the people in the carriage on and on and waiting.

'Don't forget Beach Street, Mum,' Dad had said. Dad was away at work up at six o'clock early and couldn't come. It was strange without him for he always managed. He got the tea and the fizzy drinks and the sandwiches and he knew which station was which and where and why and how, but Mother didn't. Mother was often too late for the fizzy drinks and she coughed before she spoke to the children and then in a whisper in case the people in the carriage should hear and think things, and she said I'm sure I don't know kiddies when they asked about the station, but she was big and warm and knew about cats and little ring-eyes, and Father was hard and bony and his face prickled when he kissed you.

O look the beach coming it must be coming.

The train stopped with a jerk and a cloud of smoke as if it had died and finished and would never go anywhere else just stay by the sea though you couldn't see the water from here, and the carriages would be empty and slowly rusting as if the people in them had come to an end and could never go back as if they had found what they were looking for after years and years of travelling on and on. But they were disturbed and peeved at being forced to move. The taste of smoke lingered in their mouths, they had to reach up for hat and coat and case, and comb their hair and make up their face again, certainly they had arrived but you have to be neat arriving with your shoes brushed and your hair in place and the shine off your nose. Fay and Totty watched the little cases being snipped open and shut and the two little girls knew for sure that never would they grow up and be people in bulgy dresses, people knitting purl and plain with the ball of wool hanging safe and clean from a neat brown bag with hollyhocks and poppies on it. Hollyhocks and poppies and a big red initial, to show that you were you and not the somebody else you feared you might be, but Fay and Totty didn't worry they were going to the Beach.

The Beach. Why wasn't everyone going to the Beach? It seemed they were the only ones for when they set off down the fir-bordered road that led to the sound the sea kept making forever now in their ears, there was no one else going. Where had the others gone? Why weren't there other people?

'Why Mum?'

'It's a week-day chicken,' said Mum smiling and fat now the rushing was over. 'The others have gone to work I suppose. I don't know. But here we are. Tired?' She looked at them both in the way they loved, the way she looked at them at night at other people's places when they were weary of cousins and hide the thimble and wanted to go home to bed. Tired? she would say. And Fay and Totty would yawn as if nothing in the world would keep them awake and Mother would say knowingly and fondly The dustman's coming to someone. But no they weren't tired now for it was day and the sun though a watery sad sun was up and the birds, the day was for waking in and the night was for sleeping in.

They raced on ahead of Mother eager to turn the desolate crying sound of sea to the more comforting and near sight of long green and white waves coming and going forever on the sand. They had never been here before, not to this sea. They had been to other seas, near merry-go-rounds and swings and slides, among people, other girls and boys and mothers, mine are so fond of the water the mothers would say, talking about mine and yours and he, that meant father, or the old man if they did not much care but Mother cared always.

The road was stony and the little girls carrying the basket had skiffed toes by the time they came to the end, but it was all fun and yet strange for they were by themselves no other families and Fay thought for a moment what if there is no sea either and no nothing?

But the sea roared in their ears it was true sea, look it was breaking white on the sand and the seagulls crying and skimming and the bits of white flying and look at all of the coloured shells, look a little pink one like a fan, and a cat's eye. Gypsy. And look at the seaweed look I've found a round piece that plops, you tread on it and it plops, you plop this one, see it plops, and the little girls running up and down plopping and plopping and picking and prying and touching and listening, and Mother plopping the seaweed too, look Mum's doing it and Mum's got a crab.

But it cannot go on for ever.

'Where is the place to put our things and the merry-go-rounds and the place to undress and that, and the place to get ice-creams?'

There's no place, only a little shed with forms that have bird-dirt on them and old pieces of newspapers stuffed in the corner and writing on the walls, rude writing.

'Mum, have we come to the wrong sea?'

Mother looked bewildered. 'I don't know kiddies, I'm sure.'

'Is it the wrong sea?' Totty took up the cry.

It was the wrong sea. 'Yes kiddies,' Mother said, 'now that's strange I'm sure I remembered what your Father told me but I couldn't have but I'm sure I remembered. Isn't it funny. I didn't know it would be like this. Oh things are never like you think they're different and sad. I don't know.'

'Look, I've found the biggest plop of all,' cried Fay who had wandered away intent on plopping. 'The biggest plop of all,' she repeated, justifying things. 'Come on.'

So it was all right really it was a good sea, you could pick up the foam before it turned yellow and take off your shoes and sink your feet down in the wet sand almost until you might disappear and come up in Spain, that was where you came up if you sank. And there was the little shed to eat in and behind the rushes to undress but you couldn't go in swimming.

'Not in this sea,' Mother said firmly.

They felt proud. It was a distinguished sea oh and a lovely one noisy in your ears and green and blue and brown where the seaweed floated. Whales? Sharks? Seals? It was the right kind of sea.

All day on the sand, racing and jumping and turning head over heels and finding shells galore and making castles and getting buried and unburied, going dead and coming alive like the people in the Bible. And eating in the little shed for the sky had clouded over and a cold wind had come shaking the heads of the fir-trees as if to say I'll teach you, springing them backwards and forwards in a devilish exercise.

Tomatoes, and a fire blowing in your face. The smoke burst out and you wished. Aladdin and the genie. What did you wish?

I wish today is always but Father too jumping us up and down on his knee. This is the maiden all forlorn that milked the cow.

'Totty, it's my turn, isn't it Dad?'

'It's both of your turns. Come on, sacks on the mill and *more on still.*' Not Father away at work but Father here making the fire and breaking sticks, quickly and surely, and Father showing this and that and telling why. Why? Did anyone in the world ever know why? Or did they just pretend to know because they didn't like anyone else to know that they didn't know? Why?

They were going home when they saw the swans. 'We'll go this quicker way,' said Mother, who had been exploring. 'We'll walk across the lagoon over this strip of land and soon we'll be at the station and then home to bed.' She smiled and put her arms round them both. Everything was warm and secure and near, and the darker the world outside got the safer you felt for there were Mother and Father always, for ever.

They began to walk across the lagoon. It was growing dark now quickly and dark sneaks in. Oh home in the train with the guard lighting the lamps and the shiny slippery seat growing hard and your eyes scarcely able to keep open, the sea in your ears, and your little bagful of shells dropped somewhere down the back of the seat, crushed and sandy and wet, and your baby crab dead and salty and stiff fallen on the floor.

'We'll soon be home,' Mother said, and was silent.

It was dark black water, secret, and the air was filled with murmurings and rustlings, it was as if they were walking into another world that had been kept secret from everyone and now they had found it. The darkness lay massed across the water and over to the east, thick as if you could touch it, soon it would swell and fill the earth.

The children didn't speak now, they were tired with the dustman really coming, and Mother was sad and quiet, the wrong sea troubled her, what had she done, she had been sure she would find things different, as she had said they would be, merry-go-rounds and swings and slides for the kiddies, and other mothers to show the kiddies off too, they were quite bright for their age, what had she done?

They looked across the lagoon then and saw the swans, black and shining, as if the visiting dark tiring of its form, had changed to birds, hundreds of them resting and moving softly about on the water. Why, the lagoon was filled with swans, like secret sad ships, secret and quiet. Hush-sh the water said; rush-hush, the wind passed over the top of the water; no other sound but the shaking of rushes and far away now it seemed the roar of the sea like a secret sea that had crept inside your head for ever. And the swans, they were there too, inside you, peaceful and quiet watching and sleeping and watching, there was nothing but peace and warmth and calm, everything found, train and sea and Mother and Father and earwig and slater and spider.

And Gypsy?

But when they got home Gypsy was dead.

The Day of the Sheep

It should not have rained. The clothes should have been slapped warm and dry with wind and sun and the day not have been a leafless cloudy secret hard to understand. It is always nice to understand the coming and going of a day. Tell her, blackbird that pirrup-pirruped and rainwater that trickled down the kitchen window-pane and dirty backyard that oozed mud and housed puddles, tell her though the language be something she cannot construe having no grammar of journeys.

Why is the backyard so small and suffocating and untidy? On the rope clothesline the washing hangs limp and wet, Tom's underpants and the sheets and my best tablecloth. We'll go away from here, Tom and me, we'll go some other place, the country perhaps, he likes the country but he's going on and on to a prize in Tatts and a new home, flat-roofed with blinds down in the front room and a piano with curved legs, though Tom's in the Dye Works just now, bringing home handkerchiefs at the end of each week, from the coats with no names on.

'Isn't it stealing Tom?'

'Stealing my foot, I tell you I've worked two years without a holiday.' You see? Tom striving for his rights and getting them even if they turn out to be only a small anonymous pile of men's handkerchiefs, but life is funny and people are funny, laugh and the world laughs with you.

She opens the wash-house door to let the blue water out of the tubs, she forgot all about the blue water, and then of all the surprises in the world there's a sheep in the wash-house, a poor sheep not knowing which way to turn, fat and blundering with the shy anxious look sheep have.

'Shoo Shoo.'

Sheep are silly animals they're so scared and stupid, they either stand still and do nothing or else go round and round getting nowhere, when they're in they want out and when they're out they sneak in, they don't stay in places, they get lost in bogs and creeks and down cliffs, if only they stayed where they're put.

'Shoo Shoo.'

Scared muddy and heavy the sheep lumbers from the wash-house and then bolts up the path, out the half-open gate on to the street and then round the corner out of sight, with the people stopping to stare and say well I declare for you never see sheep in the street, only people.

It should not have rained, the washing should have been dry and why did the sheep come and where did it come from to here in the middle of the city?

A long time ago there were sheep (she remembers, pulling out the plug so the dirty blue water can gurgle away, what slime I must wash more often why is everything always dirty) sheep, and I walked behind them with bare feet on a hot dusty road, with the warm steamy nobbles of sheep dirt getting crushed between my toes and my Father close by me powerful and careless, and the dogs padding along the spit dribbling from the loose corners of their mouths, Mac and Jock and Rover waiting for my Father to cry Way Back Out, Way Back Out. Tom and me will go some other place I think. Tom and me will get out of here.

She dries her hands on the corner of her sack apron. That's that. A flat-roofed house and beds with shiny covers, and polished fire-tongs, and a picture of moonlight on a lake.

She crosses the backyard, brushing aside the wet clothes to pass. My best tablecloth. If visitors come tonight I am sunk.

But no visitors only Tom bringing cousin Nora, while the rain goes off, she has to catch the six o'clock bus at the end of the road. I must hurry I must be quick it is terrible to miss something. Cousin Nora widowed remarried separated and anxious to tell. Cousin

Nora living everywhere and nowhere chained to number fifty Toon Street it is somewhere you must have somewhere even if you know you haven't got anywhere. And what about Tom tied up to a little pile of handkerchiefs and the prize that happens tomorrow, and Nance, look at her, the washing's still out and wet, she is tired and flurried, bound by the fearful chain of time and the burning sun and sheep and day that are nowhere.

'But of course Nance I won't have any dinner, you go on dishing up for Tom while I sit here on the sofa.'

'Wait, I'll move those newspapers, excuse the muddle, we seem to be in a fearful muddle.'

'Oh is that today's paper, no it's Tuesday's, just think on Tuesday Peter and I were up in the north island. He wanted me to sell my house you know, just fancy, he demanded that I sell it and I said not on your life did you marry me for myself or for my house and he said of course he married me for myself but would I sell the house, why I said, well you don't need it now he said, we can live up north, but I do need it I've lived in it nearly all of my life, it's my home, I live there.'

Cousin Nora, dressed in navy, her fleecy dark hair and long soft wobbly face like a horse.

'Yes I've lived there all my life, so of course I said quite definitely no. Is that boiled bacon, there's nothing I like better, well if you insist, just the tiniest bit on a plate, over here will do, no no fuss, thank you. Don't you think I was right about the house? I live there.'

What does Tom think? His mouth busies itself with boiled bacon while his fingers search an envelope for the pink sheet that means Tatts results, ten thousand pounds first prize, a flat-roofed house and statues in the garden. No prize but first prize will do, Tom is clever and earnest, the other fellows have tickets in Tatts, why not I the other fellows take handkerchiefs home and stray coats sometimes why not I and Bill Tent has a modern house one of those new ones you can never be too interested in where you live. Tom is go-ahead. In the front bedroom there's an orange coloured bed-lamp, it's scorched a bit now but it was lovely when it came, he won it with a question for a radio quiz, his name over the air and all —

Name the planets and their distance from the sun.

Name the planets.

Oh the sun is terribly far away but of course there's only been rain today, pirrup-pirruping blackbirds, how it rains and the sheep why I must tell them about the sheep.

Nora leans forward, 'Nance you are dreaming, what *do* you think about the house?'

'Oh, always let your conscience be your guide.'

(Wear wise saws and modern instances like a false skin a Jiminy Cricket overcoat.)

'That's what I say too, your conscience, and that's why we separated, you heard of course?'

Yes Nance knows, from Nora herself as soon as it happened Dear Nance and Tom you'll hardly believe it but Peter and I have decided to go our own ways, you and Tom are lucky you get on so well together no fuss about where to live you don't know how lucky you are.

No fuss but lost, look at the house look at the kitchen, and me going backwards and forwards carrying dishes and picking up newspapers and dirty clothes, muddling backwards and forwards in little irrelevant journeys, but going backwards always, to the time of the sun and the hot dusty road and a powerful father crying Way Back Out Way Back Out.

'Oh, Oh I must tell you, there was a sheep today in the wash-house.'

'A what?'

'A sheep. I don't know where he lived but I chased him away.'

'Oh I say, really, ha ha, it's a good job we've got somewhere to live, I in my house (even though I had to break with Peter) and you and Tom in yours.

'We *have* got somewhere to live haven't we, not like a lost sheep ha ha. What's the matter Tom?'

'74898, not a win.'

The pink ticket thrust back quickly into the envelope and put on the stand beside the wireless, beside the half-open packet of matches and the sheaf of bills and the pile of race-books.

'Well, I'm damned, let's turn on the news, it's almost six.'

'Oh it's almost six and my bus!'

'So it is Nora.'

Quick it is terrible to lose something for the something you miss may be something you have looked for all your life, in the north island and the south island and number fifty Toon Street.

'Goodbye and thank you for the little eat and you must come and see me sometime and for goodness sake Nance get a perm or one of those cold waves, your hair's at the end of its tether.'

Here is the news.

Quick goodbye then.

Why am I small and cramped and helpless why are there newspapers on the floor and why didn't I remember to gather up the dirt, where am I living that I'm not neat and tidy with a perm. Oh if only the whole of being were blued and washed and hung out in the far away sun. Nora has travelled she knows about things, it would be nice to travel if you knew where you were going and where you would live at the end or do we ever know, do we ever live where we live, we're always in other places, lost, like sheep, and I cannot understand the leafless cloudy secret and the sun of any day.

A Note on the Russian War

The sunflowers got us, the black seeds stuck in our hair, my mother went about saying in a high voice like the wind sunflowers kiddies, ah sunflowers.

We lived on the Steppes, my mother and the rest of my family and I, but mostly my Mother because she was bigger than the rest. She stood outside in the sun. She held a sunflower in her hand. It was the biggest blackest sunflower in Russia, and my mother said over and over again ah sunflowers.

I shall never forget being in Russia. We wore big high boots in the winter, and in the summer we went barefoot and wriggled our toes in the mud whenever it rained, and when there was snow on the ground we went outside under the trees to sing a Russian song, it went like this, I'm singing it to myself so you can't hear, tra-tra-tra, something about sunflowers and a tall sky and the war rolling through the grass, tra-tra—tra, it was a very nice song that we sang.

In space and time.

There are no lands outside, they are fenced inside us, a fence of being and we are the world my Mother told us we are Russian because we have this sunflower in our garden.

It grew in those days near the cow-byre and the potato patch. It was a little plant with a few little black seeds sometimes, and a scraggy flower with a black heart, like a big daisy only yellow and black, but it was too tall for us to see properly, the daisies were nearer our size.

All day on the lawn we made daisy chains and buttercup chains, sticking our teeth through the bitter stems.

All day on the lawn, don't you remember the smell of them, the new white daisies, you stuff your face amongst them and you put the buttercups under your chin to see if you love butter, and you do love butter anyway so what's the use, but the yellow shadow is Real Proof, O you love early, sitting amongst the wet painted buttercups.

And then out of the spring and summer days the War came. An ordinary war like the Hundred Years or the Wars of the Roses or the Great War where my Father went and sang 'Tipperary.' All of the soldiers on my Father's side sang 'Tipperary,' it was to show they were getting somewhere, and the louder they sang it the more sure they felt about getting there.

And the louder they sang it the more scared they felt inside.

Well in the Russian War we didn't sing 'Tipperary' or 'Pack Up Your Troubles' or 'There's A Long Long Trail A-Winding.'

We had sunflowers by the fence near where the fat white cow got milked. We had big high boots in winter.

We were just Russian children on the Steppes, singing tra-tra-tra, quietly with our Mother and Father, but war comes whatever you sing.

The Birds Began to Sing

The birds began to sing. There were four and twenty of them singing, and they were blackbirds.

And I said what are you singing all day and night, in the sun and the dark and the rain, and in the wind that turns the tops of the trees silver?

We are singing they said. We are singing and we have just begun, and we've a long way to sing, and we can't stop, we've got to go on and on. Singing.

The birds began to sing.

I put on my coat and I walked in the rain over the hills. I walked through swamps full of red water, and down gullies covered in snow-berries, and then up gullies again, with snow-grass growing there, and speargrass, and over creeks near flax and tussock and manuka.

I saw a pine tree on top of a hill.

I saw a skylark dipping and rising.

I saw it was snowing somewhere over the hills, but not where I was.

I stood on a hill and looked and looked.

I wasn't singing. I tried to sing but I couldn't think of the song.

So I went back home to the boarding-house where I live, and I sat on the stairs in the front and I listened. I listened with my head and my eyes and my brain and my hands. With my body.

The birds began to sing.

They were blackbirds sitting on the telegraph wires and hopping on the apple trees. There were four and twenty of them singing.

What is the song I said. Tell me the name of the song.

I am a human being and I read books and I hear music and I like to see things in print. I like to see vivace andante words by music by performed by written for. So I said what is the name of the song, tell me and I will write it and you can listen at my window when I get the finest musicians in the country to play it, and you will feel so nice to hear your song so tell me the name.

They stopped singing. It was dark outside although the sun was shining. It was dark and there was no more singing.

The Pictures

She took her little girl to the pictures. She dressed her in a red pixie-cap and a woolly grey coat, and then she put on her own black coat that it was so hard to get the fluff off, and they got a number four tram to the pictures.

They stood outside the theatre, the woman in the black coat and the little girl in the red pixie-cap and they looked at the advertisements.

It was a wonderful picture. It was the greatest love story ever told. It was Life and Love and Laughter, and Tenderness and Tears.

They walked into the vestibule and over to the box where the ticket-girl waited.

'One and a half in the stalls, please,' said the woman.

The ticket-girl reached up to the hanging roll of blue tickets and pulled off one and a half, and then looked in the money-box for sixpence change.

'Thank you,' said the woman in the black coat.

And very soon they were sitting in the dark of the theatre, with people all around them, and they could hear the sound of lollies being unwrapped and papers being screwed up, and people half-standing in their seats for other people to pass them, and voices saying can you see are you quite sure.

And then the lights went down further and they stood up for 'God Save the King'. The woman would have liked to sing it, she would have liked to be singing instead of being quiet and just watching the screen with the photo of the King's face and the Union Jack waving through his face.

She had been in a concert once and sung 'God Save the King' and 'How'd you like to be a baby girl.' She had worn a long white nightie that Auntie Kit had run up for her on the machine, and she carried a lighted candle in her hand. Mother and Father were in the audience, and although she had been told not to look, she couldn't help seeing Mother and Father.

But she didn't sing this time. And soon everybody was sitting down and getting comfortable and the Pictures had begun.

The lion growling and then looking over his left shoulder, the kangaroo leaping from a height. That was Australian. The man winding the camera after it was all over. The Eyes and Ears of the World, The End.

There was a cartoon, too, about a cat and a mouse. The little girl laughed. She clapped her hands and giggled and the woman laughed with her. They were the happiest people in the world. They were at the pictures seeing a mouse being shot out of a cannon by a cat, away up the sky the mouse went and then landed whizz-thump behind the cat. And then it was the cat's turn to be shot into the sky whizz-thump and down again.

It was certainly a good picture. Everybody was laughing, and the children down the front were clapping their hands.

There was a fat man quite close to the woman and the little girl. The fat man was laughing haw-haw-haw.

And when the end came and the cat and mouse were both sitting on a cloud, the lights were turned up for Interval, and the lolly and ice-cream boys were walking up to the front of the theatre, ready to be signalled to, well then they were all wiping their eyes and saying how funny how funny.

The woman and the little girl had sixpence worth of paper lollies to eat then. There were pretty colours on the screen, and pictures of how you ought to furnish your home and where to spend your winter holiday, and the best salon to have your hair curled at, and the clothes you ought to wear if you were a discriminating woman, everything was planned for you.

The woman leaned back in her seat and sighed a long sigh.

She remembered that it was such a nice day outside with all the spring flowers coming into the shops, and the blue sky over the city. Spring was the nicest of all. And in the boarding-house where the woman and little girl lived there was a daffodil in the window-box.

It was awful living alone with the little girl in a boarding-house.

But there was the daffodil in the window-box, and there were the pictures to go to with the little girl.

And now the pictures had started again. It was the big picture, Errol Flynn and Olivia de Havilland.

Seven thousand feet, the woman said to herself. She liked to remember the length of the picture, it was something to be sure of.

She knew she could see the greatest love story in the world till after four o'clock. It was nice to come to the pictures like that and know how long the story would last.

And to know that in the end he would take her out in the moonlight and a band would play and he would kiss her and everything would be all right again.

So it didn't really matter if he left her, no it didn't matter a bit, even if she cried and then went into a convent and scrubbed stone cells all day and nearly all night. . . .

It was sad here. Some of the people took out their handkerchiefs and sniffed in them. And the woman in the black coat hoped it wasn't too near the end for the lights to go up and everybody to see.

But it was all right again because she escaped from the convent and he was waiting for her in the shelter of the trees and they crossed the border into France.

Everything is so exciting and nice thought the woman with the little girl. She wanted the story to last for ever.

And it was the most wonderful love story in the world. You could tell that. He kissed her so many times. He called her beloved and angel, and he said he would lay down his life for her, and in the end they kissed again, and they sailed on the lake, the beautiful lake with the foreign name. It was midnight and in the background you could see their home that had a white telephone in every room, and ferns in pots and marble pillars against the sky, it was lovely.

And on the lake there was music playing, and moonlight, and the water lapping very softly.

It is a wonderful ending, thought the woman. The full moon up there and the lights and music, it is a wonderful ending.

So the woman and the little girl got up from their seats because they knew it was the end, and they walked in the vestibule, and they blinked their eyes in the hard yellow daylight. There was a big crowd. Some had shiny noses where the tears had rolled.

The woman looked again at the advertisement. The world's greatest love story. Love and Laughter, Tenderness and Tears. It's true, thought the woman, with a happy feeling of remembering.

Together they walked to the tram-stop, the little girl in the red pixie-cap and the woman in the black coat. They stood waiting for a number three car. They would be home just in time for tea at the boarding-house. There were lots of other people waiting for a number three car. Some had gone to the pictures too, and they were talking about it, I liked the bit where he, where she.

And although it was long after four o'clock the sun seemed still to be shining hard and bright. The light from it was clean and yellow and warm. The woman looked about her at the sun and the people and the tram-cars, and the sun, the sun sending a warm glow over everything.

There was a little pomeranian being taken along on a lead, and a man with a bunch of spring flowers done up in pink paper from the Floriana at the corner, and an old man standing smoking a pipe and a schoolboy yelling 'Sta-a-r, Sta-a-r.'

The world was full of people and little dogs and sun.

The woman stood looking, and thinking about going for tea, and the landlady saying, with one hand resting on the table and the other over her face Bless those in need and feed the hungry, and the fat boarder with his soup-spoon half-way up to his mouth, The Government will Go Out, and the other boarder who was a tram-conductor answering as he reached for the bread, The Government will Stay In. And the woman thought of going up stairs and putting the little girl to bed and then touching and looking at the daffodil in the window-box, it was a lovely daffodil. And looking about her and thinking the woman felt sad.

But the little girl in the pixie-cap didn't feel sad, she was eating a paper lolly, it was greeny-blue and it tasted like peppermints.

Snowman, Snowman

1

People live on earth, and animals and birds; and fish live in the sea, but we do not defeat the sea, for we are driven back to the sky, or we stay, and become what we have tried to conquer, remembering nothing except our new flowing in and out, in and out, sighing for one place, drawn to another, wild with promises to white birds and bright red fish and beaches abandoned then longed for.

I never conquered the sea. I flew at midnight to the earth, and in the morning I was made into a human shape of snow.

'Snowman, Snowman,' my creator said.

Two sharp pieces of coal, fragments of old pine forest, were thrust in my face to be used for my eyes. A row of brass buttons was arranged down my belly to give me dignity and hints of fastenings. A hat was put on my head, a pipe in my mouth.

Man is indeed simplicity, I thought. Coal, brass, cloth, wood—I never dreamed.

A passing bird, a half-starved grey sparrow said to me, 'You are in prison.'

But that was not so, it is not so now. I helped to conquer the earth, but because I did not arrive here with the advance armies, I have never seen the earth except in this whiteness and softness, and although I remember a time when I was not a snowman, the habit of being a man, a creature of coal, brass, cloth, wood, has begun to persist; yet it does not seem to have deprived me of my freedom. Even in the few moments after I was born I knew how to live, and for me it is easy, it is staying in the same place without any more flying, without trespassing or falling over cliffs or being swept down to sea and swallowed by the waves; never diving or dancing; staying the same, never influenced by change as human beings are; not having to contend with the invasions of growth which perform upon human beings in the name of time and change all the eccentric acts of whitening strands of hair, shrinking pink skin to yellow leather over bones gone porous, riddled with early-nesting sleep, stopping the ears, making final settlement concerning their quota of tumult; at last bandaging the eyes injured with seeing. Partly snow, partly man, I am preserved, made safe against death, by my inheritance of snow, and this I learned from the Perpetual Snowflake on the window sill.

Let me explain. It is the window sill of the house of the Dincer family—Harry, his wife Kath, and their daughter Rosemary. I belong to them. I stand forever now in their suburban front garden looking out upon the street of the city. Rosemary created me. I have learned something of her life from the Perpetual Snowflake who has explained to me the view, the situation, the prospect of my immortality and its relation to the swiftly vanishing lives of people.

I have a strange sensation of being, a mass chill and clumsiness, a gazing through pine-forest eyes upon a white world of trees drooping with snow, the wind stirring milk-white clots and curds of my essence in street and garden, for my immortality does not mean that I contain myself within myself, I breathe my essence in a white smoke from my body and the wind carries it away to mingle it with the other flakes of the lost armies that flew with me to earth, and that still fall—see them paratrooping in clouds of silk—but they do not recognise me, they float by without acknowledging my snowman-being rooted here in the white world with my limbs half-formed by the caprice and modesty of my creator who can scarcely know the true attributes of a man, who chooses coal, buttons, hat, pipe, as his sole fuel weapon and shroud.

Am I common property? On my first day, although Rosemary Dincer made me to stand in her front garden, people in the street kept pointing to me and saying to each other, 'Look, a snowman, a snowman.'

Children came in the gate and touched me or struck me or threw stones at me, as if I belonged to them. One man looking over the hedge at me remarked, 'You won't be standing there so proudly for very long. Look at the sky!'

I looked at the sky and I felt lonely at the sight of the white whirlpool of the still-conquering armies, and I wondered if there were other snowmen, or do we exist singly and what is it that prompts people to make us?

Even Rosemary's making of me had caused her father to utter the strange observation, 'A snowman at your age! Surely not!' which called forth the reply from his wife, Rosemary's mother, 'Why not? It is not only children who make snowmen, anyone who has the chance makes a snowman, all up and down the town people are making snowmen!'

Why?

'Your time is limited, Snowman,' someone remarked, looking over the hedge at me.

'How do you like your first day on earth, Snowman? Do you feel at home? Are you learning to see with those coal-black pine-forest eyes?'

That is the Perpetual Snowflake with his questions.

'Of course I can see. Everything is outlined clearly against the snow—trees, this tree beside me in the garden, the street, cars, people, buildings, everything is whole and contained within itself. The world is a remarkable place.'

'I doubt if you will ever learn to see, Snowman. Trees, cars, streets, people, they are but the dark print upon the white page of snow. Your coal-black pine-forest eyes are no use until you are able to read the page itself, as men read books, passing beyond the visible obstructions of print to draw forth the invisible words with the warmth of their passionate breathing.'

'But my breath is ice. And I am the white page. I have no passion. Is that why I shall live forever?'

He does not answer. Perhaps he is asleep.

Two doors away a little boy began to gather the snow to mould it into the shape of a man, but he grew tired of making a snowman, with the result that he abandoned it, and it stood half-formed, eyeless, faceless, with none of the salient emblems of humanity. A few moments later the child's father appeared with a tin of rubbish, last week's relics of Christmas—paper wrappings, tinsel, discarded angels, which he emptied over the body of the snowman, and drawing matches from a box in his pocket, he lit a fire, he made a fire of the neglected snowman, and from where I stood I could see the flames rising from the snow and a smoke or mist blurring the garden, and for an age I stared with horror at the flames and I could not turn my coal-black pine-forest eyes away from them, and even from where I stood safe in the Dincer garden I could feel my cheeks burning as if they sought to attract the fire. Soon the half-formed snowman disappeared and the tinsel, the paper wrappings, the discarded angels, were transformed to black ash. I sensed an assault on my own being, but I could not discover traces of it though my cheeks were wet not with tears of rage or sadness but with a stealthy nothingness of wet as if in some way I were being drained of my life, and I knew although I could not seem to make the effort to consider the significance of it, that fire was my enemy, and that should fire flow or march against me in its crimson ranks of flame I should be helpless and without courage and my urge to escape would lead only to my swifter dissolution.

'Your first day on earth and already you consider death?'

'Oh no, oh no.'

My confidence returned. Oh the ease, the simplicity of static living! What wonders I observe with my coal-black pine-forest eyes! Is it not taken for granted that I shall live forever?

'Snowman, Snowman, a germ cell like a great sleeping beast lies curled upon the Dincer doorstep, tethered to past centuries, and every time Harry Dincer comes staggering up from the King's Arms he trips over the lead of the sleeping beast. Harry is a telephonist. He saw an advertisement in the daily paper, a picture of a man wearing headphones, listening to the world in conversation. "'Ullo Marseilles, Paris, Rome," the man was saying, and Harry was filled with a desire for a similar chance to eavesdrop on the world's conversations, therefore he becomes a telephonist; but they have never put him on the Continental Circuit. He cannot speak the languages.

'So he goes to the King's Arms and gets drunk and staggers over the lead of the sleeping beast.'

'I can see nothing on the front doorstep but a small mat for wiping feet, and yesterday's footprints dark with mud and soot.'

'You will understand, Snowman. Tomorrow and the next day it will be clear to you.

'It is a matter of age. Of sickness, accident, time, of the assaults people make one upon the other. They are organised and trained to kill because the growth of centuries has entangled them in the habit as in a noxious weed which they are afraid to eradicate because in clearing the confusion between being and being, the thick hate-oozing stems, the blossoms feeding upon the night-flying jealousies and hungers, they face each other set in an unbearable clearing of light and proper original shade, with the sky naked in its truth, and what protection is there for them now as they crouch in fear of the new light, with none of them brave enough to stand tall, to welcome the eradication of death? Or they kill on impulse because, loving too much, they isolate the act of love and thus extend it to encompass the memorable loneliness of death; they choose to make one visit to the altar of possession, imagining that wherever and whenever they return, the scene will be unchanged. They find it has vanished, Snowman, as soon as the killing is over. And the stained glass is not pictures in beautiful compartments of colour: it is blood.

'You will understand, Snowman. Tomorrow and the next day it may be clear to you. You will learn part of the meaning of the people who made you, of the street and the city. You will know that Harry Dincer is deeper and deeper in despair because he is unable to say "'Ullo Paris, Rome, Marseilles," to communicate over thousands of miles in a foreign tongue, that although he is a telephonist with his own headphones more select and private than ears, he will never be given permission to work on other than his allotted circuit. "My headphones." He brings them from work at night and polishes them. Has skin-to-skin conversation failed him so sadly? "My headphones. I've heard famous people talking in private. Conductors of orchestras, stars of show business and television, so many stars I couldn't count them if I tried."'

'We heard rumours of stars in the sky on our journey to earth. Are people stars?'

'You will understand, Snowman, tomorrow and the next day and the next day. You will know the child who made you, and her mother, and their house and their car, their gondola shopping bags, their television sets, all of which may seem to you, a snowman, to be irritating trivialities, but when you learn to consider them it will be of their deeper layers that you think. You will have noticed how buildings emerge from the earth—houses, the shops at the corner, plants, your neighbour tree that is burdened with snow. All these things—even televisions and gondola shopping bags, are anchored to the earth or to people upon the earth, and when you find the point of anchorage, the place which most resists the ravages of the tides of forgetfulness and change, there you will also find the true meaning of the objects, their roots, those hairy tentacles which embrace the hearts of people or merely cling there, like green moss to a neglected stone that no one will ever want to overturn to observe the quick-running life beneath it.

'Tomorrow and the next day you may understand.'

'Is it necessary? I am only a snowman.'

Who is the Perpetual Snowflake? I never knew him before though our family is Snowflake. On my first day on earth I have known pride, fear, curiosity, and now sadness for I cannot ever return to the lost fields of snow that are not on the earth, that have no houses no cities no people. I cannot go back to be among my sisters and brothers far in the sky, lying in our cold-white nightclothes while a calm wind ties down the corners of the sky, arranging the covers of cloud over our white sleeping bodies. I have been made Man. I am an adventure in immortality. Is it not a privilege to be made Man?

It is night now. There is a golden glow from the street light stretching its golden beak across the white street. It says no word but a quiet humming sound issues from it, as a life-signal.

I close my coal-black pine-forest eyes and sleep.

2

There is a clock in the city. It keeps time. That is remarkable, isn't it? When the snow came the clock stopped suddenly because the hands (which grasp) had frozen, and workmen climbed ladders to reach the clock's head, and they burned small fires day and night behind its face to warm it, with the result that it soon kept time once again. Time can be rejected, refused or kept. The chief problem is where to keep it as there is not much space on earth for invisible property. It is easier for people to put shopping into gondola shopping bags than to put time into a convenient container.

I am worried. My back aches. I have a feeling of rigidity, my roots seem so far from my head, there is no communication between them as there was on my first day on earth when I could say to myself, My one foot is in place, and know that it was so. Now I do not seem to have control of my knowing, it has floated from me like the smoky breaths floating from the people in the street when they open their mouths. The Perpetual Snowflake has confused me by trying to explain the earth when I know there is nothing to explain. The earth is covered with snow. It has always been covered with snow.

I feel so strange. He has told me that people eat dead animals and that before they choose which part to eat they mark and map the carcasses in blue or red pencil, the latitude and longitude of death. The lines are joined. Everything is named and contained and controlled. Today I seem to feel like an animal that is being killed slowly, but I have not the certainty of knowing the boundaries and labels of my own body, and if I see red marks in the snow I expect they will be not red pencil but blood. I experience the same heaviness which overcame me yesterday shortly after I was born. My head sinks deep into my shoulders, my laughter is invisible and does not show on my face or in my eyes.

I frown.

I have a feeling of anxiety because no one has yet taken my photograph, yet it seemed a promised event of importance when I heard Kath Dincer say to her husband, 'We'll take a photograph of it while it lasts. We must at all costs get a photo of the snowman!'

Large grey drops of water are running down my face.

'Mummy, the snowman's crying!'

A child walks by with her mother. They are going shopping, around the corner to the greengrocer's. The little girl is tightly parcelled in woollen clothing, bright red, with a cap fitting close to her head and brown boots zipped on her feet. Her face is rosy. She belongs to the snow, all the children belong to the snow, see them sliding, scuffing, throwing snowballs, hear them shouting with their voices leaving their mouths and forming into brilliant piercing icicles suspended in the clear air!

The children dance; their footmarks have the same delicacy as those of cats, dogs, birds.

I perceive that all children are the enemies of their elders, and that the snow possesses a quality which causes all pretence of love between them to be discarded.

'Mummy, the snowman's crying!'

The little girl points to my tears which are not tears.

'Stupid, he's not crying. He's only a snowman.'

'But he's crying!'

'It's only snow, love.'

'If I hit him will he cry?'

'Don't be silly. He'll fall to pieces.'

Now that was strange. Would I fall to pieces?

'Come here won't you, I don't know what the snow does to you, you can't go into other people's gardens like that. The snowman doesn't belong to us.'

'Who does the snow belong to, Mummy?'

'Don't be silly, love, I suppose it's everybody's.'

'Then the snowman's ours!'

'Don't be silly, stupid, it belongs to the person who made him.'

Everything is very confusing. Do I belong to Rosemary Dincer because she made me, and to Kath because Rosemary belongs to Kath and to Harry because Kath belongs to Harry, and who does Harry belong to, does belonging describe a circle which starts again at Rosemary or does it extend to all people and everybody belongs to everybody else on earth? Who decides?

'What is around the corner, and in the houses, and who are the people and how do they accommodate time when he is their guest?'

'Around the corner there is a gas man, a wood louse, an empty carton, a man's ear, a desolation, a happiness, shops and people.'

'I mean what is there in its rightful order. Surely there are no ears

lying on the pavement and no one is sweeping out a desolation
with the night's dust from the floor of the grocer's!'

'Oh you want facts the usual way, as people arrange them
through habit? You want a human focus? You prefer me to abolish
the gas main and the empty carton and present the complete man
instead of his Ferris wheel of a left ear; you wish to play parlour
games like join the dots and name the important objects in the
picture.

'It is what is known as a built-up area. With fifty square yards
you have a population of hundreds. Now there are instruments to
measure the sound of planes, cars and other machines, but not to
measure the enormous sound of people living, their hearts beating,
their digestions working or refusing to work, their throats being
cleared to make way for mighty language, their joints creaking,
bones grinding, hair, skin and fingernails growing, and the roller-
coaster movement of their thoughts. Why, even the measurement
of a man's heart beating is a wearisome business, with one person
appointed as a special listener, and listening so solemnly to the
wild echoes within. What hope is there of hearing a man's heart,
recording the storms, the sudden darknesses and flashes of
lightning, the commotions of unseen life? No one really listens to
the beating of a heart. He merely listens to the listening of the
stethoscope which in its turn has been eavesdropping and
transmitting the most secret nameless sound which no one has ever
heard distinctly, nor is anyone certain that the secret sound is not
itself merely listening and transmitting another murmur which is
yet more remote, and so on, to the centre, the first sound that
cannot be heard apart from that other insistent murmur like the
inland sea. And to think that Harry Dincer lives in despair because
he is not qualified to put on his polished headphones and get in
touch with Paris, Rome, Marseilles!

'People live here in the street of the city, in a constant
commotion. Their lives are bustled and stirred and tasted like a big
Christmas pudding packed with cheap good-luck tokens, little
bells and fairy shoes that look as if they are made of silver, but they
feel too heavy in the hand and they are perhaps poisonous. Life
here, Snowman, is a big dark mess. Of course you are only a
snowman and do not need to take account of the lives of people. See

that house on the corner? The people living there have such a struggle to persuade the postman to deliver the letters addressed there, for the house is neither in one street nor in the next, and the owners are always painting heavy black numbers on the gate, and the numbers get larger each time they are painted, for it is so important for people to know where they live, and to let others know, to have their places defined and numbered. The family who live in that house have a passion for looking alike and that is quite natural for it is a family, yet the likeness is so startling that if you look from either of the two sons to his father you have the confusing impression that your eyes have telescoped time, that your glance at the son has caused him to arrive in a twinkling at middle age, to abandon his career as an apprentice accountant or an industrial designer and become his father, the homeworker, sitting in the little top floor room under the neon strip light sewing men's trousers and overcoats, with the whirr-hum of the machine penetrating the house and the sounds from the radio, Music While You Work, coming through the open window into the street; always a noise of work, an occupational murmur; it is the modern fairy tale, Snowman, it is not the old grandmother who sits in the attic spinning, but the father, the homeworker, weaving spells into overcoats.

'It is also strange that if you glance from either of the sons to his mother you experience the same feeling of the concentration of time, with the son becoming his own mother, the mother being transferred to the son. The face of mother, father, sons, has each changed from an individual right and possession to a family concern. Instead of saying proudly of mother and son, "Look, you can see the likeness," you feel a sense of uneasiness, of the massing of hidden determined forces which will destroy every obstacle in order to retain their right-of-way within the deep genetic groove.

'This family has a new car. The two boys spend Sunday mornings inside the new car, with the hood up, studying it; or sitting in the driver's seat or the back seat; standing, looking, touching. Sometimes they drive slowly round the block followed by the three West Indian children from next door, dressed in their Sunday best, bunched and frilly as daffodils.

'You are startled, Snowman? Daffodils? There's nothing to fear,

Snowman. I have my own story, you know. I cannot tell the length of time I have been away from the sky and it is months or years since snow fell like this, reaped summer wheat into lily-white flour and all the cars huddled in the streets, look, like barracuda loaves of bread without any crust, only crisp snow for tasting by the saw-toothed wind, oh Snowman you need not fear daffodils for they mean nothing these days, they are forced, compelled, the pressure is put on them. People stamp and trample on everything, including other people, and everything rises dazed, dazzling, complete, from the earth. And so round and round the block the boys go in the new car, and the children follow laughing and screaming with their black eyes shining. Oh no who need be afraid of daffodils?'

Sunday morning is a separate season. In the afternoon the people watch television, that is except for the West Indian family who hold a Church Service in their upstairs rooms with their friends and relations coming from far and near, the women and children resplendent in brocades, flocked nylon, satin, the men in carefully pressed suits with bright shirts and polished shoes. They open all the windows of the room, the pianist begins to play, the congregation begins to sing, and you can hear the hymns even from where you are standing in this garden. They are not sung in a tone of weariness and complaint, as people sing when they are trying to catch up with God on the Grand March but are suffering from stones in their shoes and blisters on their feet: they are sung with gaiety and excitement as if God were outpaced, as if the congregation were arriving before him, to make everything comfortable with provisions and shelter in preparation for the long long night.

'At this time of year they sing carols: "From the Eastern Mountains Pressing On They Come." "Away in a Manger." "Oh Little Town of Bethlehem." The children from the Council Flats around the corner, the boys of twelve and thirteen set free on Sunday, with nowhere to go and nothing to do, stand outside the house mimicking the singers, adopting special piercing voices, as they mimic everything, for boys of that age, Snowman, are not people at all, they make noises like engines and lions and airplanes whenever they pass in a gang along the street, all making the noise at once, interrupting it sometimes with fragments of human language which no one listens to, and do you know, Snowman, I can never understand how without talking to one another, with only animal, machine, engine cries and disturbances of sound, these boys can yet decide so unanimously where they are going, and they swagger along in the direction of the Park or the Green or their favourite café as if one of them had said clearly in human speech, "We'll go here, eh?"

'On Sunday afternoons the man in the house opposite watches television. He comes from Barbados. He bought the house a few months ago and moved into the vacant flat on the ground floor, and at first whenever his student friends came to see him the white people occupying the top floor would lean from their window, popping back and forth like cuckoo clocks trying to arrange a regular rhythm. "Blacks," said the people on the top floor, and gave notice. Those on the second floor stayed. Myra, her husband Ken, their daughter Phyllis. People have names. Ken is short and muscular with his bones arranged firmly and squarely as if to support unusual or surprising turns and somersaults of flesh—like those steel jungle-gyms in children's playgrounds which are always crowded with children swinging on them and climbing and hanging from them, their knees gripping the bars, arms dangling, faces growing redder and redder.

'People passing say warningly to each other, "Look at them. The blood will go to their head." You see, when people grow up they learn to be afraid of what is happening inside their own bodies, and they become anxious and suspicious if their blood travels suddenly from here to there, or if their hearts, tired of staying in their accustomed places, quite naturally "turn over"; and thus they are resentful of the way children seem so unconcerned when they dangle from jungle-gyms and their blood goes to their heads. Why? the adults wonder. Why can't they learn that blood going to the head is not a simple healthy matter like an impulsive excursion to the seaside?

'Myra is stout with dark hair and eyes and an ordinary face, as most faces are, with its lines and pouts and puckers and its tired middle-aged skin layered with Cake Makeup, Invisible Foundation, Fairy-Spun Face Powder. Every afternoon Myra

dresses carefully and goes to the telephone box at the end of the
street to make a call. To whom? I don't know, and Ken doesn't
know. See the telephone box? The directory has H to K missing
because last weekend some people known as *youths* tore pages
from the directory and smashed the mirror on the wall and tried to
wrench the telephone from its stand. People have such a hate and
love for telephones. "'Ullo Paris, Rome, Marseilles. Hold the line
a minute, I have got through to your heart. SOS Save our Souls."

'Snowman, I heard of a man who sent to a mail-order firm for a
radio transmitting and receiving set. When he assembled the kit of
tiny parts he found that he could send or receive only one message,
SOS. He listened day and night, and he never found out who was
sending the message or why he himself should be sending it, for he
didn't need to ask for help, he was not in despair, not bankrupt or
crossed in love; his life was happy.

'He got up one morning, washed, dressed, looked out of his
window at the world and shot himself.'

'I am sure it is interesting. But I am only a snowman.'

'Phyllis is very thin. She wears mauve eyeshadow and mauve
lipstick and the expression on her face implies that she can't
understand or didn't hear clearly or interpret correctly the sound of
the world about her. She works in a dusty cut-price store a
threepenny bus ride away although while she was at Secondary
Modern she dreamed of being a secretary, a receptionist, the
manageress of a *boutique*. She spends her time amongst pieces of
timber, wallpapers, paraffin cans, last year's boxed Christmas soap
and cheap perfumes, dented dust-covered cans of Mulligatawny
and Cream of Kidney Soup; pots, brooms, double toilet rolls; prices
slashed. Even the sweets displayed in the opened boxes in the
window beside the bathcubes and the plastic dishes and the free
offer tube of toothpaste with shampoo riding strapped to its back,
are all covered in dust. The liquorice allsorts are shrunken and
crippled with age.

'On Friday nights Phyllis goes with her Indian girlfriend to the
pictures or the youth club, and on Fridays when the knocker
downstairs is rattled and banged and Myra opens the living-room
window to see who is visiting, she has to make her observations
very carefully, for usually if she looks down and sees someone with

dark skin she exclaims, "Not for us! It's for upstairs or downstairs."

'But on Friday nights when the young Indian girl comes for Phyllis, Myra has to make sure to let her in, but she finds it so difficult especially on these murky winter evenings to know whether the caller has Indian skin or West Indian skin or European skin, it seems all the same when the light has gone.

'A West Indian woman and her husband live now on the top floor. He works as a conductor for London Transport. There is a new baby, Cynthia. For months the young woman, Gloria, sat up there at the window every day staring down at the street, only venturing outside to shop at the grocer's or the butcher's around the corner, and then she would walk slowly and carefully, leaning backwards, with her baby safe as a coconut inside her. Then suddenly two faces appeared one day at the window, that of Gloria and of a tiny baby in a white shawl, but Gloria withdrew the bundle quickly and did not let Cynthia see out of the window for many many weeks, as if she were preparing her by first explaining to her the curious ways of people in the world. And during that time Gloria did not go out, even to the grocer's or the butcher's, but stayed inside with Cynthia, and the curtains were drawn across the window, and one evening when Gloria's husband came home from issuing tickets on the one-seven-six Catford to Willesden, Willesden to Catford, he brought a bundle of lace which Gloria made into curtains, and now there were two pairs of curtains to protect Cynthia and her mother from the world, and though it was summer with the world banging singing screaming echoing and the voices and radios loud in the street and the cars hooting and dogs barking and jet planes shuddering the sky, there was no sound at all from the room with the double curtains, and the window stayed shut, and no faces looked out. The husband went to work in the morning and came home at night. The district nurse called sometimes, propping her bicycle against the fence, staying ten or fifteen minutes in the house, then coming out, saying nothing, going immediately to her bicycle, unlocking it, putting her bag in the basket over the handle bars, cycling down the road, disappearing round the corner, and who knows if she did not then reach the edge of the world and drop into darkness with the shining steel spokes of the back wheel of her bicycle spinning blindly like a star?

'Suddenly one day the double curtains were drawn aside. There were two faces at the window, Gloria, and her baby sitting up in the cot which had been moved to the window. Gloria took the tiny black hand, held it high, and waved it merrily at the world.

'Cynthia knew now, you see. All the while, in the secretive room behind the double curtains, her mother had been teaching her, preparing her, and now everything was arranged for Cynthia to consider the world outside. If you look up there now, Snowman, you will see the baby's face staring from the window. She still hasn't learned to wave by herself, but she laughs and cries at what she sees, and this morning with you here in the garden, and with the world all sheet and tablecloth and napkin, she cannot understand, she does not know that if she came outside to tread on the snowy tablecloth she would leave footprints in common with all other creatures living or dead who touch the snow: birds, cats, branches of trees, people, the old man with the shovel, the child with the stones and the snowballs, and Cynthia's own father on his way to work with the one-seven-six to Willesden.'

It has begun to snow again. Reinforcements. I am feeling safe though my newest white coat obscures my sight. Children keep running into the garden and stealing from me—one has taken a brass button; or they prop me up with more snow as if I were in danger of falling. Sometimes they make strange menacing remarks about what will happen to me *after*. After what? Am I the only snowman in the world now?

'Others are appearing in the city. Perhaps they are your distant relations. Some are seven feet tall and others are only three feet tall. Some wear uniforms and carry weapons such as swords, umbrellas, sticks, newspapers. And all have been made by children or by those whom others regard as children. Living in the house by the telephone box there is a middle-aged woman who is four feet high and has the understanding of a child. She is employed to clean the house belonging to the Indian doctor and it is she who every morning polishes the brass plate outside his door and erases the rude remarks A Wog Lives Here, Go Home Black, with a drop of

Cleanic upon a bright yellow cloth. It is marvellous, Snowman, the way Cleanic can remove all trace of an overnight scar; it ought to be more used by human beings when they suffer attacks from those who love them so much that they must write their love as insults upon the heart of the loved. Have human beings hearts of brass?

'Snowman, Snowman, after the woman whose real name is Dora but whom everybody calls Tiny, had polished away the insults, and had cleaned the surgery and the other rooms in the house and had shopped at the grocer's for her mother, and had walked home up the road, carrying her little bag of private possessions and family food, she went outside to the back garden of her home and made a snowman. She made him exactly her own size, to fit, eye level with eye, mouth with mouth and heart with heart. The two matched perfectly.

'Then as soon as she had finished making him she stared at him with her head on one side and a serious expression on her face. She decided to push him over and get rid of him. No. She decided to keep him there in the garden forever. So she laid a ring of pebbles around him as a sign that he belonged to her and that no one was to touch him, and she went inside to her lunch. In the afternoon on her way to work she stopped everyone she met and explained that she had made a snowman.

'"I made a snowman. He's mine."

'No one disputed that. Apparently if you make a snowman he belongs to you, and although children might pluck out his eyes and carry off his bright buttons and plunge his hat over his head so that he cannot see, no one will try to steal the whole snowman because he belongs to the person who made him.

'Later in the afternoon when Tiny returned from work she became angry with her snowman, at the way he stood in the garden, not speaking or smiling or moving, just submitting to the perpetual collision of fresh flakes upon his body. Tiny's anger increased. She began to cry, not simple crying with tears running down her cheeks but a moaning complaining cry without tears. Then seizing the garden shovel which had helped her to make her snowman, Tiny battered the snowman over the head, and his eyes fell out, his body broke in two, he sank within the charmed pebbled circle, making no protest, soundlessly. Tiny put away the shovel in its correct place in the garden shed and she went inside to watch television while she knitted the palm of the right hand of the gloves she is making to protect herself from the everlasting cold.

'Another of your relations was a three-inch-high snowman standing upon a cake in a shop window. He wore a red woollen cap, smoked a red pipe, and of course wore buttons, little red round ones placed in a row down his fat belly. I believe that he was different from your other relations because no one saw him being made and when people passed him they did not make the remarks which you find so fearful—about the day *after* or "what will happen soon," or "let him wait a few days and he won't be so proud." He was taken from the shop, shut in a dark box, carried to a strange room and placed in the centre of a table laden with food. The room was hung with decorations, glittering trees and lights and angels, in fact it was such a dazzle that the snowman may have imagined that he had arrived in heaven except that the angel at the top of the tree gave him no welcoming smile, her face seemed made so that she could not smile, it was a face with a small split of red like a cut, while the lights twinkling round her gave her skin a yellow colour blotched with shadow which made her two tiny black specks of eyes look like mouse dirt dropped in porridge, and that is no way for an angel to appear; therefore your distant relation couldn't have arrived in heaven, though it may have been a matter of opinion, as the people in the room were in the happiest mood, snatching kisses from one another, drinking sparkling wine, unwrapping presents given as a sign of their love. Snowman, it was a typical scene of human happiness.

'Now a snowman, though he is made of snow, is in some respects human. Imagine the feelings of a snowman when he observes that when people are in their happiest mood they are likely to seize and devour each other. I do not mean to make you afraid when I tell you that one of the guests walked over to the table, grasped your distant relation, and treating him as if he were an article of food, began to bite, chew and swallow him, while the party continued as if nothing unusual had happened. And later, when the rejoicing was over, the men took their women to bed and because they were again so happy they seized and devoured each other and the eating continued all night yet nobody disappeared like your poor three-inch-high snowman. It seems that people who have lived on the earth for so many centuries have used much of their cunning to discover this marvellously secret way of concealing the fact that they are continuously eating and being eaten by those whom they love.'

Why should I be afraid? There are grey envelopes flapping in the sky and the trees are writing their destinations against the sky, and pinned to the corners of the clouds are the red-footed storks so eager to be flying south to sit upon a golden pyramid and sharpen their beaks on the golden stone. I remember this, though I am only a snowman. I like to look up at the sky. And then I look out at the street and think of what the Perpetual Snowflake has told me of the people, and I wonder to myself, Where are the heroes driving through the streets in their chariots? I thought the earth was filled with heroes, with happiness, and so it is, oh yes, I have a feeling of happiness, there's just a soft settling of new snow brushing my cheeks, and white fellow-snowflakes disguised as dragonflies tickling my nose, and a passing child had made two hands for me and enclosed them in furry red and yellow mittens. Each day I live someone adds to me or subtracts from me, therefore perhaps I am more human than I realise? Then I must be happy, as human beings are, for in spite of the story of the three-inch-high snowman and the Christmas party, it cannot be true that people eat each other. They eat only vegetables and fruit and other animals who do not speak their language, and birds, and fish. People do not drink each other's blood. They drink wine, beer, milk, tea, coffee.

'Snowman, Snowman, there is a great gale of fear blowing in the snowflakes, for when it snows the earth is obscured and people are unaware of the divisions between street and pavement and they become afraid for they have always known where to walk. The obliteration of the earth enhances the need to touch it, to feel the shape of it, to be guided by it, knowing its hard and soft places, its corners, hollows, ravines, hills brushed by stars, valleys with lion-winds raging with their golden manes indistinguishable from the mountain grass, oh Snowman, all recognition has been wounded.'

'I am only a snowman. I am surely and permanently anchored in

a small suburban front garden. Here is Rosemary Dincer, my
creator. I belong to her. Why is she crying?'

'She went to the Modern Jazz club where she met a University
student on holiday who promised to ring her and make a date but
when he rang her mother answered the phone and said, "Do you
know how old she is, she's only thirteen," and he said, "Oh. Tell
her I'm sorry." And that was the end.'

'The end? Do people cry when it is the end?'

'People do not cry because is is the end. They cry because the end
does not correspond with their imagination of it. Their first choice
is always their own imagining; they refuse to be deterred by
warnings; they say I choose this because although the price is high
the thing itself is more precious, durable and beautiful. The light
of imagined events is always so arranged that the customers do not
see the flaws in what they have chosen to buy with their dreams.
Rosemary brought so much happiness from her meeting with the
University student and from the cinema date which followed, and
then the concert, and then the excursion up the river, her visit to
his home, his visit to her home. . . . Now it is the end.'

'I thought the end was death. Is Rosemary dead?'

'Rosemary is not dead. There are other places where people may
find the end: the edges of cliffs, the corners of streets, the lines of
boundaries, the conjunctions of sentences, the disappearance—I
should say the melting—of dreams. There is the view which
suddenly comes to an end not because it is the end but because an
obstacle stands or takes root there and will not be displaced.
Rosemary's age is blocking the path of her dreaming. There are
other powers which produce and arrange obstacles. Daylight,
Time, Chance, Fear, the sudden closing of two blades of scissors,
crocuses, a broken wall with grass growing through the cracks—
like the wall over the road which the man who bought the house
takes care to inspect each evening, peering into the joints of the
brick for signs of decay. On his first morning as a tenant he heard
two housewives talking outside: "A coloured man has bought this
house. It will go to rack and ruin."'

'Rack and ruin, Snowman, is a sleepy quiescent stage before
death; it allows waiting weeds and insects to nest and flourish, and

the once solid bricks to move, shudder, breathe decay, split, crumble and fall.

'After one energetic day of trowelling damp concrete into the crack in the brick the man gave up. He had grown wise. A woman passed him with her face going to rack and ruin and no amount of trowelling could have hidden the decay. So why should he care what people were thinking? If some people thought of his race as a forerunner of death, well let them. It was flattering, in a way, for death is impersonal in these matters whether it is a question of the decay of a brick wall or of a human face.'

'But snowmen do not decay? A fresh overnight fall of snow and we are new. Is Rosemary dying then?'

'It is a human habit to provide remedies for grief because even if tears are a common and usual sign of unhappiness they must never be allowed to become emissaries of death, to claim more than brief significance. "Things" are the remedy most used by people to cure grief, disappointment, discomfort, celebration by tears and laughter, in order to return to a deathless Eden—a level of uncluttered garden—vegetable state with drops of dew shining like mirrors between the separate lives, with the sun cradled in the leaves, the misty morning webs and traps making the air glimmer with deceiving lightness, with the earth safe and solid underfoot.'

'Safe and solid underfoot?'

'You have never seen it that way, Snowman. Snow is a mass camouflage. No people would accept a government which performed the world-wide deceptions of snow; or perhaps they would be unable to resist the comfort of its beautiful treachery? I have seen the earth before and after snow. You may see it too when you become an old-fashioned Perpetual Snowflake talking to next year's old-fashioned snowman.

'But I was telling you of remedies. "Things" are an effective and popular remedy. Most people begin using them very early in their lives. I don't know how it began and I'm not going to travel back until I reach the beginning, not simply for your sake, Snowman, for I may discover the real nature of the beginning, and that may frighten me, and you. Besides, I may not recognise it when I reach it, for the beginning like the end is never labelled. What should I do if I reached the beginning and thought that I had arrived at the

end? What should I do? Both the beginning and the end demand
such drastic action that I should be forced to decide immediately,
and what if I made a mistake? There are responsibilities which
even I am not prepared to face.

'Now Rosemary's life is full of things. A tape recorder, a piano,
plenty of clothes—winkle-picker shoes, a white raincoat, slacks,
chunky jerseys; a duffle bag, a school case with her initials in gold
upon it; a share in the family car, television, a caravan in Sussex.
She is given pocket money each week. Next year she will go for a
skiing holiday on the Continent. The difficulty of things or objects
as remedies is that the supply of them depends upon income and
that is not earned according to the tally of grief. There may be a
time when there is no money left, and no more things, and no more
remedies, and the tears will keep running down little girls' cheeks
for ever and ever, or until the little girls grow up and trowel cement
upon their faces to hide the rack and ruin.

'Tonight Harry and Kath will decide what to give Rosemary in
order that she may be able to bear the disappointment of being too
young. I myself do not know what happens inside people when
they long for the companionship and adventure of another, and are
given instead a box of chocolates with separate handmade centres,
or a new dress or the top of the pops gramophone record. I suppose
they get used to the comfort of things, and may even approach the
state of holding a thrilling conversation with one of the handmade
centres. Things are really much more convenient to human beings
than their own kind; things can be thrown out when they are not
wanted; they can be destroyed, torn to pieces or burned without
questionings of conscience; the only effective way of destroying
people is to equate them with things—handmade centres or the
cheap song embedded in the groove.'

A blackbird shadow came across my face. There was the sudden
heavy sigh of snow when the tree by the hedge moved in the wind, a
white soft dollop of a melted sigh that shifted along the branch, fell
to the earth, and vanished in the concealing softness.

Now it is night, deep blue with butterscotch light under the clear
folded sky, and the giants are trampling the snow, walking with
two or three swift paces across the earth, for it is night, and fairy

tales have come to rest, and now I will sleep. Is it the fault of my coal-black pine-forest eyes that I dream of white squirrels brushing their tails over me, or is it only the wind blowing down the reinforcements of snowflakes, the new armies that will keep control of the earth and conceal the truth forever?

3

'Children are ripe for smiling. Those living in the Council Flats around the corner have sallow faces and streaky hair and their clothes have chopped hems, but they go hand in hand, Snowman, hitting each other and grasping and hugging and then suddenly running away. You will not know how it feels to be a child walking with your elder sister and to have your elder sister suddenly begin to run and run until she disappears around the corner leaving you alone in the street with the buildings so tall beside you and fierce dogs with black noses parading up and down, and cars and lorries growling by, and stern-looking women in purple hats and blue aprons, out sweeping their share of pavement, and telling you to mind, mind, and what else are you doing but minding? People learn the technique of vanishing when they are so young. They rock into and out of sight and when they are gone, when you cannot see them, then perhaps they are dead or drowned in the rain barrel. Vanishing is always magic. Now you see me, now you don't, people say, laughing, and their laughter is cruel.

'Has my sister gone away forever? the little girl thinks. Or is she just around the corner, up the street where I cannot see her?'

'How can she know?

'People vanish and never return, people vanish and return, but each vanishing brings unhappiness. And then when people finally vanish, when they are dead, they are brought determinedly within sight, captured, enclosed, while everyone persists in saying that they are gone and will never return. It is very confusing and contradictory, Snowman.'

Another morning. My overcoat changed, clean and white, the snow blinked from my eyes. I am pleased that the technique of

vanishing does not concern me. I am so permanently established
here that I would not believe vanishing was possible if I did not
observe it happening each day—around corners, into the sky,
behind doors, gates, hedges; the smiles, greetings, alarm, anger,
vanish from faces; even the visiting wind wearing his cloak of
snow, a generous gift from the night sky, has played vanishing
tricks with yesterday's carpet and all the footprints, ridges, patterns
impressed upon it. The morning earth is freshly decked from floor
to ceiling with new white upholstery, white cushions, covers, wall
hangings, the earth is a vast white room with the wind and his
brothers lounging in every deep chair, drinking snow-tasting tea
out of the grey and white china clouds. It is very civilised and
ceremonious, I am sure.

'Just think. In a few days it will have vanished, we'll never know
it was there.'

That is a passer-by speaking. What does he mean? Who are
people to make such menacing remarks about snow?

'That man lives across the road with his wife, his daughter, his
mother-in-law and her husband. People live in clusters like
poisonous berries. The mother-in-law is the head of the house
because she wears a purple hat and a blue apron and sweeps their
share of the pavement and carefully closes the gate when the
postman and the milkman have left it open. She makes strangled
cries to children in danger in the street. Her face is almost
overshadowed now by the thrusting bone-shape which will
command it when it is a mean-nosed skeleton with dark worked-
out mines for eyes. It is strange to think that she resembles most of
the other middle-aged women in the street, yet they are not related,
but all possess domineering bones impatient to be rid of the tired
webbing flesh with its yellow-ochre tint which appeared gradually
as the cloudy colours of time were poured into the smooth golden
morning mixture; people do not stay young, milky, and
dandelion.

'Mrs Wilbur belongs to the Church and for Jumble Sales, Special
Evenings, Harvest and Christmas Festivals, she displays a poster
inside her front window, ALL ARE WELCOME. She goes to church
for the company of God and of people, for the socials and meetings
and "drives". In the evening she watches television with her

husband, and during the day she has her shopping and cleaning and polishing, and her granddaughter Linda to look after while her mother, Dorothy, goes into town. Yet I don't think I answer your question, Snowman. Who are these people? Their being is more elusive than separate handmade centres or the pop song swatted like a fly into the surface of the record. The young couple have a son who boards at a special school and is home during the holidays. He is Mark, that is, a stain or blot or saint. He is always afraid that his mother will vanish, and he screams for long periods in the day and the night, and when she takes him to the shops his cry is Carry me, Carry me, but Dorothy is sharp and stern for the people at the special school have told her to treat Mark as if he were an ordinary child of seven, not to give him cause to believe that he is different, not to "give in" to him—giving in is a kind of balloon collapse where people see their power escaping from them into the air and being seized by others who have no right to it—but to accept him "as he is", to be calm, casual, unobtrusively loving.

'"I can't carry you. You're seven! I mean, you can walk, Mark love, it's only to the shops and back."

'"Carry me, carry me!"

'"Don't be silly. Take my hand."

'"Carry me, carry me, carry me!"

'At the sound of the little boy's cries people living near open their windows and front doors and look out.

'"It's Mark Wilbur."

'They say his name aloud, pleased with the certainty of it, for if he is Mark Wilbur then he can't be any of their own children, can he, the ones who go cheerfully to school each morning, who can speak intelligibly, who play with other children and stand up for their share of everything, who will perhaps (like Rosemary) pass their eleven-plus and go to grammar school.

'"It's Mark Wilbur. Home for the holidays. The little girl is rather sweet isn't she?"

'That is Linda, four. One numbers people for so long then one ceases to number them, but when people die they are always given their correct numbers. Ron Smith, forty-four, suffered a heart attack. Peter Lyon, seventeen, was in collision with a van driven by Herbert Kelly, fifty-five. It is a kind of code, a time-attention and

bribery. Linda has fluffy brown hair. She wears billowy clothes
and velvet hair ribbons. She is allowed to help grandma put out the
empty milk bottles in the morning although she cannot quite
reach the window sill where grandma places them, beyond the
contamination of the street. Linda is so good. She behaves. When
Mark is home he smashes the milk bottles deliberately. Actions
which are carried out deliberately are so hard to forgive, even by a
mother who knows her child is different. And grandma busy
dusting or sweeping in her purple hat and blue apron, does not
always understand.

' "I was looking out the window, Dorothy, dusting the sill, and I
saw him snatch the milk bottle from Linda and smash it. He did it
deliberately." Dorothy is silent. There is no defence for deliberate
misbehaviour, therefore she slaps Mark across the ears or the face
while Linda watches smiling, feeling so good and well-mannered
in her billowy dress and velvet hair ribbon. Mark begins to scream.
He will not stop screaming. His mother drags him inside. The
people close their front doors and windows.

' "She'll be glad when he goes back to that special school."

' "Carry me, carry me!"

'You must admit, Snowman, that there is something to be said
for riding in a chariot, and who can blame the child for insisting
upon what is perhaps the first right of his life? Yet now he must
wait so many years before anyone will again carry him, and then
what a solemn expensive duty it will be! I think that if I were
human I should want to be carried, like Mark Wilbur. Every
morning Mark's father climbs into his vermilion car that is
balanced like a clot of blood upon the snow, and he addresses the
car, "Carry me, carry me," and no one punishes him or tells him
not to be ridiculous, that he is old enough to carry himself.

'And when people are asleep they cry "Carry me, carry me" to
their dreams and their dreams carry them and no one complains,
for dreams are secret. Yet for the real pomp and pleasure, the final
satisfaction of their lifelong desire, people must wait until they are
dead.

'Carry me. It is the prerogative of the dead, Snowman. You
know, don't you, what has happened in the house two doors away
on this side of the street? Are you too busy being flattered by the

children who lick your hand to see what you taste like and find you taste like soot—how can snow taste like soot?'

'I am no more than a snowman. People are not my concern, I do not even know my creator. All I know is that she is thirteen, goes to Grammar School, and fell in love with a University student who wore a long striped scarf. Her father is a telephonist who cannot get through to Paris, Rome, Marseilles. Her mother has a blouse shop, subscribes to the *Amateur Gardener* and the annual *Flower Arrangement Calendar* and has two geraniums growing in pots outside the back door.'

'If you know as much as that, Snowman, then you easily complete the picture, play the human game with the human focus. I wanted to tell you that Sarah Inchman is dead; she died one night and you never knew because you are not yet able to read the signs or join the dots.'

'Why should I? I am only a snowman. I shall live for ever. I do not care if Sarah Inchman is dead. What were the signs which my coal-black pine-forest eyes refused to interpret?'

'The other day the doctor made two visits to the house, the second visit outside his normal hours, and when he was leaving Thomas Inchman came to the door with him and walked bareheaded through the snow to the car. You ask what is strange about that? When Thomas Inchman stands bareheaded and without an overcoat or gloves far from his front door and in the freezing air with snow on the ground and threats of snow in the sky, then it is a sign that he is in distress. He seemed more helpless perhaps because he is going bald and the blue light cast upon his head from the sky and the snow seemed to draw the blue veins nearer his scalp so that his head seemed fragile and in great danger like a baby's head with the fontanel not closed and no one to protect it. He stood there beyond the time it would usually take for him to say, "Thank you, Doctor," and for the doctor to answer, "Right. Call me if there's a change for the worse." While Thomas Inchman seemed helpless in the blue light the doctor seemed self-possessed; he wore a heavy tweed overcoat and a warm brown hat made of furry material and his gloves were fur-lined and his Indian skin showed warm and brown and alive and his hands held the rich brown leather briefcase in a secure grip. He drew up the collar of his overcoat as if enticing the forces of life closer to him, and he smiled sympathetically at Thomas Inchman, yet at the same time there was a flash of triumph in his glance. He climbed into his car, started the engine, and was away with the powerful car moving effortlessly through the snowy street where only the same morning other cars had been abandoned.

'When the doctor had visited for the third time and Thomas had once again watched him drive away, he returned to the house and drew the curtains in the ground-floor front room, not closing them casually with gaps of light shining between them but sealing them as if they were made of an impenetrable metal which only a desperate strength would cleave in order to admit the murky snow-filled daylight.

'People passing in the street may not have realised that Sarah Inchman was dead, but if they had stopped to take notice they would have sensed the disorganisation of the household. Robert's car stood outside. Robert is the son. Robert came home only at weekends. Why was he home now, in daylight when people who should be at work were at work and the only movement of traffic was of heavy lorries trying to get through to Peckham, of salesmen passing with their cars stacked with samples, rag-and-bone men on their rounds, men from the Water Board making their strange probing inspections through the snowfall. All these were legitimate travellers but not sons arriving home in broad daylight when their usual practice was to come on Friday evening after dark.

'If you did not guess, Snowman, by seeing Robert's car, you would surely have known if you had seen Robert, for the wind was bitterly cold, the flakes were falling, and Robert was clad in a heavy overcoat, and why should he not be? When the doctor drew his overcoat closer to his body he was confidently enticing the forces of life; when Robert turned up the collar of *his* coat he seemed to be trying to repel the forces of death, his coat seemed to be worn with no thought for outward weather, and his reliance upon it was not born of his need to escape from the snow. With the collar turned up, all the buttons buttoned, the lapels drawn close together, he had a total appearance of helplessness. The coat was black-and-white-checked tweed. Woven with snowflakes? The enemy had penetrated the weave and lay snug on Robert's back.

'Yesterday Thomas Inchman kept coming to the front door of his home, walking out, still not dressed for the weather, and peering up and down the street as if he were waiting for someone. His son came and went, came and went, shuttling his car back and forth from here to there with the restlessness brought on by grief. If you had observed all these incidents, and the house with the feverish hanging light shaped like a crystal ball burning behind the impenetrable curtains, and if you had not divined the nearness of death, surely you would have known when darkness fell (like an axe) and a sprightly little black van drew up outside the Inchman house. The writing on the side of the van was almost concealed in the gloom of night.

'FUNERAL SERVICE AND FURNISHINGS.

'In this part of the world, Snowman, dying is meant to be a discreet matter like taking tea but the untidiness of death makes itself visible in the clothes of the bereaved, in the daily routine—yesterday's milk not opened or even collected, the television silent, the beds unmade. In spite of people's desire for death to be a neat occasion—what is neater than dying?—there are always slovenly obtrusions which mar the effect.

'The funeral will be held tomorrow. Everything will be in order. The undertaker in the sprightly black van will have arranged everything. All is quiet now in the Inchman house. There was a time when members of the family died and were abandoned, and their relatives packed their bundles and fled over the plain or desert to reach the friendly oasis by nightfall, where, seeming to forget the dead, the little group would make their meal and then huddle together looking up at the stars that were wild beasts—lions, bears, wolves—prowling the shifting cloudfields where even the white grass and trees never stay and the cities of fire are trampled by the restless sparking hoofs. And the family would fall asleep and in the morning they did not weep for the dead for the dead had no share in the living but were alone, already becoming a part of the plain or the desert with the shadows of the wings of the vultures wheeling over the earth like great broad blades of a windmill set in motion by winds blowing from beyond the frontiers of death to draw new forces of life from the mingled grass and sand and dead human flesh.

'The dead are not abandoned here, Snowman. It is not the fashion to abandon them until it is certain that they are decently covered and imprisoned. Yet the urge to escape from them is always overwhelming. Sarah Inchman has been taken to the chapel mortuary. Thomas and Robert have gone to stay with Sarah's niece and her family in Lewisham. If you looked carefully inside the house you would notice the telltale marks of flight, of haste, which would differ only in surface detail from the traces left by the bereaved tribe in the desert or the plain; you would sense the same underlying urgency to escape from the presence and the place of the dead.'

'But I am only a snowman. Death is no concern of mine, but the world grows more depressing each day that I live. Why should I who am destined to live forever be troubled by this finality which touches every human being? I am only a snowman with a head and belly full of snow. I have no means of wandering in plains and deserts or in the rooms of houses where the dead have lain. I am pleasurably heavy and sleepy, I will forget death, I am in a blue daze, tasted by rosy children, my limbs amputated and replaced by mischievous schoolboys. Soon I shall be photographed. Life is soft white bliss and the snow is falling away from my face with my laughter.'

4

'It is night. Here in the city the light has blue shadows under its eyes and stays up late and wanders restlessly from street to street picking up the shadows standing lonely on corners and in alleyways. The eyes of city light are bloodshot with watching. People depend so much upon the light to reveal to them the shadows and the dust which they have been careless in not sweeping away or laying shrouds against, and other people's faces which demand the most brilliant searchlight beams in order that their identity may be established. When you are walking in the street it is so important to know who passes close to you. When you are sitting at night in the same room or sleeping in bed side by side it is important to be able to recognise your companion. There are many strangers about, Snowman. Who knows? And there is also death by accident or intention in the dark. In the streets of the city they have built arcs of light which shine like gorse bushes in bloom, seen through the red haze of a bush fire; the street lights burst upon the street beneath them in thorns and blooms and twigs of red-and-gold light that stabs and changes—like a drug administered—the aspect of all colour. Tonight, Snowman, you are not snow, you are sunset; sunset and dragons.'

'It is the first time you have mentioned the sun.'

'Your nature as a snowman will reveal the sun to you soon enough. Let us talk of the night and the dragon-light which shines on you. Yet it is no use, Snowman, when events happen they appropriate the time to themselves, stealing days, months, years when a few minutes would be enough to satisfy them but there is no stopping them—what are we to do?'

'I need do nothing. I am only a snowman. It is people who are in danger.'

'One might say that a person takes a few seconds to die, and there can be no objection if someone wishes to claim a few seconds from the store of time, one might almost say it is a reward for dying, to sleep at last with a few seconds gathered like a posy of flowers upon one's breast, but the notion is false and people realise it, for it is death which takes the few seconds, and once death takes a handful of time there is no amount of minutes, days, years which will satisfy his greed; in the end he takes a lifetime. I wanted to talk to you about the night and the street lights, but I notice that the death of Sarah Inchman is at large prowling for more time, turning our attention to the Inchman house as surely as the wind turns the weather vane. Robert has come home tonight. He is aware of the prowling death of his mother, therefore he has secured the windows and fastened the chains across the front and back doors. He is sitting by the fire trying to read his book of science fiction but he is thinking about his mother and her clothes. What will he do about her clothes?

'Dr Merriman held up the globe of the world in all its blues browns greens reds and spun it lightly with his fingers. He withdrew his hand. The world continued spinning, faster and faster. Dr Merriman smiled. My God, he thought. He knew and the others in the room knew. The holtrime, the wentwail, the sturgescene had . . .

'Why were her clothes such a drab colour? The clothes of the one or two women he had brought home had been as bright as bird-of-paradise plumage, and his mother's clothes too had seemed full of colour. Where were all the blues and greens and pinks that she wore in the weekend when he came home? Why could he not find the bright clothes she had worn? Had he dreamed them? If that was so then was he also enchanted in looking at the rest of the world?

> *The fenew is cardled. The blutheon millow*
> *clane or hoven. In all the dolis gurnt plange*
> *dernrhiken ristovely; Kentage, merl,*
> *the fenew is cardled, onderl,*
> *pler with dallow,*
> *dimt, in amly wurl.*

'Why was it that as soon as his mother died her clothes seemed drab, brittle, that burnt brown colour like beetle shells found in the grass in September?

'Like a collapsed armour?

'The fenew is cardled. Dr Merriman twirled the hollow globe faster and faster.

'That is science fiction, Snowman. Soon there will be a visitor from outer space.'

'But I am such a visitor or am I old-fashioned?'

'No, Snowman, you are just as modern as the little green man with black horns. But now that the death of Sarah Inchman has ceased her prowling and has entered her son's thoughts for the profit to be had from his dreams, we can talk once again of the night and the street lights, but most of the people in the street are asleep now, and the lights in the houses have gone out and there is no more gunfire from the television sets. The fresh evening fall of snow, like a cat set before a saucer of milk, has lapped up all the wheel and foot marks and the street has a sunken smooth appearance and with few cars and people braving the snowfall only the wind and the wandering animals and the deaths in search of extra time have the pleasure of making patterns on the snow, while you, Snowman, are growing plumper and plumper and your brass buttons are covered with new snow and your coal-black pine-forest eyes are hooded with snowy brows.

'What a drifting careless life of snowflakes flying heedlessly without effort or decision. And I am remembering as a snowflake myself the time when I too was a visitor from beyond the earth. I remember how some of my companions alighted upon a cold stone doorstep and they seemed to vanish into it, while others died before they arrived on earth. There was a movement of their bodies, a sparkle through the white shadow of their secret crystal skeleton, a sudden falling away of their flesh, now a sweetness, now a trace of salt in the air as the released bones crinkled, snapped starlike, disappeared. I remember—but Memory like Death has a way of seizing time. Do not be alarmed, Snowman, if soon the snow changes colour. Now it lies with breathing space for each flake, but within the next few days the flakes may be churned together, one may smother its neighbour while a grey or black liquid oozes from their bodies, and people will say it is the snow bleeding in its true colour, black blood.

'I am warning you what to expect, for this evening I feel the touch of a wind that is an enemy of snow, that does not breathe the penetrating freezing breath which is the delight of snowflakes. Tonight there is a warm wind blowing from the south from the world where the olive trees grow, their grey shadows falling like flakes upon the grey stone, where the red earth crumbles like the hot ashes of a fire, and yellow flowers bloom in the dried river beds; where the eucalyptus trees lean above the stone fountain and the soft dust stirs about the feet of the people walking; a world of salt marshes, hills of salt, beanflowers, almond blossom, tiny pine trees with sticky purple flowers and small syrup-oozing cones; spotted poisonous toadstools that collapse when you touch them, clouding your face with a yellow mist, toadstools with tall extravagant stems the result of spurted growth which makes people afraid for they cannot accept the outrage of such furious vegetable growth, believing it should happen only in fairy tales. And when their own children growing up, change and develop as if overnight, people utter such cries of panic, "He's growing too fast, he'll outgrow his strength, it's not healthy, it's dangerous!''

'I feel the warm wind, Snowman, although it has not yet reached us here in the street of the city. It is fresh from blowing beneath blue seas above blue skies filled with shadowy houses and people and trees and fishing boats that, like people, make their coughing sounds at morning, cough-chug, cough-chug. There is herb-smell in the wind, and the sound of new green frogs, the population explosion of ponds.

'And the sad-looking cow with the rubbed scabbed shoulders and the too-small tethering-rope, has calved and swings and rocks her udder like a bagful of sea.

'It is all in the warm wind blowing from the south. Even if you pleaded with me, Snowman, I should not be able to delay its arrival here. People plant trees against the wind yet it always sneaks in twos and threes of breath through the gaps in the branches and between and beneath the leaves. People have found no way to refuse the wind's gift of blowing; they have discovered only how to establish its direction and force and how to adjust their lives, like sails, to let the wind carry them to the place they most desire to reach before dark. Oh Snowman I have desired to reach so many places! As a Perpetual Snowflake I am powerless and diminished. You never saw me in the height of my life when a thousand snowflakes leaned upon me and found shelter near me. How quiet it is now, you can hear only the city murmur that is not the sound of people but a murmuring like the sea washing the land.

'People live on earth, and animals and birds; and fish live in the sea but we do not defeat the sea for we are driven back to the sky or we stay.

'It is a question of reptiles hatching deep in the warm sand; of flayed shredded brown weed; crushed spiral houses and tall blue-bearded shells; and an old mapped tortoise in the Galapagos Islands that woke one morning to find himself famous. The embezzlements of living—that is the sound of the sea and of the city . . .'

'White flying squirrels brushing my face . . .'

'You are dreaming, Snowman.'

5

'I have learned to recognise the people in the street. I know the milkman, and the meter reader, and the window cleaner, and the postman who is limping with his sore foot. "I'll have to go on the National Health," he said, "or visit the Board." What does he mean?'

'The Board is not part of a forest but is a room with rows of seats facing a counter which has been divided into cubicles the average height of a person sitting. If you wish to claim a grant from the Board you go to one of these cubicles and answer questions about your income, property, age, occupation, and so on. You will understand, Snowman, that the cubicles have been constructed to ensure privacy, and it seems to have been calculated that personal secrets do not rise above the head of those who possess them, not like warm air which travels to the ceiling or like smell which penetrates the air and the walls and furniture and clothing; it has been assumed that personal secrets have a discretion of their own, that they will roam within the cubicle but never dream of escaping. Nevertheless the people who are being interviewed have not so much trust in their own secrets, for they whisper the details, glancing around them for fear something has escaped.

'"Speak up please, no one can hear you. You're in a cubicle to ensure privacy."

'The whispering continues.

'That is the Board, Snowman. It can be of little interest to you for it is no relation to a pine forest and it is not more ancient than coal, it is a way of getting money when you have no work, and incidentally of stabling and training secrets so that they do not rise above a man's head.

'Now here is the rag-and-bone man, the totter, sitting in his chair-sized cart surrounded by old striped mattresses stained with rust and blood, by twisted bed ends, fireplaces wrenched at last from their cavern in the wall to make room for the gas or electric heater, blackened fenders, iron bars, bundles of rags. The totter's piebald horse jerks to a stop, the driver rings his brass bell like a priest summoning the communion of refuse; then he cries out but you cannot understand what he has said for surely the purpose of his cry is to distort its meaning and arouse fear in those who are listening. "What is he saying?" they wonder. "Is it Bring Out Your Dead? Any old Rags? Old Rags, Old-Ways, Old-Ways, Gold Rags Rays Racks God-racks All Ways? And why does he never mention the bones?"

'There is his brother walking up and down the street to collect the refuse in his sack. The two look like twins and the small lithe horse with its coat of grey and white seems like a third member of the family. One might imagine that the three are interchangeable and that from time to time the brothers take their turns between the shafts of the cart.

'Now they have disappeared around the corner. When it snows people do not put out their old clothes and bedsteads and extracted fireplaces with the roots of the wall still clinging to them. People in snowstorms have other matters to think of; snow fills people's minds and the world, there is no room for nameless iron bars or mattresses stained with the residue of sleep and love when the concern is the residue of sky. Look at the earth now with its fat layers of wadding, the padded gates and fences with not an iron bone protruding, and the heavy-headed roofs that will soon discard their weight of snow when the fitted grey slates of their skulls begin to shift and slide. The pipes are frozen in the houses. The water has stopped in its tracks. I fear that the black blood is beginning to flow. Look, there's a blackbird sitting on an iced twig, singing!'

'I am afraid, though I am only a snowman.'

I slept and woke. I tried to think of the pleasures of being a snowman, to anticipate the delight of being photographed, but I could not ignore the small trickle of black blood flowing through the hedge into the gutter. People passing noticed it and remarked upon it, pointing to it and speaking in tones of excitement and dismay which left me unable to tell whether they were announcing disaster or victory. I was standing staring with my coal-black pine-forest eyes when I saw a woman walking from house to house with a basket of flowers and I shuddered and bowed my head for I knew they were daffodils.

'Look, Snowman, at the children crowding around her, screaming with pleasure, even the little Italian children from next door who cannot yet speak the language of this country although Salvatore can say Hello, Goodbye, and Milk. "Milk mama, milk." He can say bread too which was once yellow in a field, like daffodils, but you need not be too afraid, Snowman, for perhaps they are not real daffodils; it will be many weeks before daffodils can calculate the arrival of their moment and take their place in the dance. Snowdrops are in bud, but snowdrops are made of snow.'

'Why does everyone seem so pleased at the sight of the daffodils? Listen!'

'Lovely daffodils, early daffodils, bring yourself good luck and buy a bunch of lovely daffodils from a Gypsy.'

'Some will buy the flowers because they rely on their personal sense of time and will not wait until it agrees with the season, and it is those people who can experience spring in winter which may be agreeable, I do not know, yet it is the same people who will dread seeing others surrounded by daffodils with crowns of violets in their hair, while their own hearts are heavy with snow and their eyes cannot keep from gazing at the never-ending shroud wrapped about the world and the dark tomb waiting to admit the dead. All who believe in daffodils while snow falls around them are living uneasily beating lives, their rhythm is the lost note which cannot or will not join the chord because although it will gain security and strength by being with other notes it will at the same time forget the sound of itself, and therefore it stays alone in strange hollow places where there is no other music. The loneliness is the price and the reward.'

'Who are the gypsies to sell early daffodils, real or artificial, when there is snow on the ground, when snowmen are in charge of the earth?'

'The gypsies are all people who are out of step with usual time and place, and it is they who are a nuisance, an uneasiness to those who set their hearts by the clock, who stay and divide each day by twenty-four hours and get no surprising untidy scrawl of blossom in the remainder column; for primroses push their way through rusting iron, and new grass is a carpenter's tool, hammer, chisel, axehead, and snowdrops are the first white steel pylons erected to carry the message.

'Gypsies come and go and baffle like the delinquent swarm of bees that does not keep to the seasonal rhyme or rhythm but follows its own signals and smokes itself out of the secret hollow trees.'

Although the gypsy seemed in the distance to be an old woman, when she came nearer I saw that she was young. I am learning to guess ages in people, and lately I have longed for a sign that time is noticing me, and each night I have considered every inch of my body, saying to myself, 'Has time been here, here—how shall I know?' I stared at a baby in its pram yesterday. Then I looked away at the sky or the street or the shifting ledge of snow on the branch of the tree, and when I looked again at the baby I saw that its red fur cap now framed the face of its mother, and beyond that face like a shadow which is given a shape in darkness by a vivid beam of light shining upon it, was the face of the mother's mother, and then her mother before that, and if I had stared long enough I should have seen the dark space where the first signs of life were imprinted. I am envious of people and their association with time, of the way they can look into each other's eyes and see backward to the first empty darkness or forward to the final sun-blistered collage of light. How does a mere snowman recognise the effect of time upon himself?

The gypsy passed close to me and looked at me.

'When snow falls,' she said, 'there is always a snowman.'

A daffodil dropped from her basket and she did not see it fall, and I thought, that is strange, it is only when people are walking to hell that they can afford to drop flowers in their path. A child picked up the daffodil and stuck it in my hat. I slept with a daffodil in my hat—how brave of me! I could not smell it and it was stiff and shiny and it hurt where the stem thrust into my head. Rosemary was on her way home from school.

'Oh, a daffodil in the snowman's hat!'

She ran to me, withdrew the daffodil, and sniffed it.

'Plastic,' she said. 'They're everywhere.'

I looked about me to see if she spoke the truth but I could see no others in the street or in the sky. When the daffodils come will they be everywhere?

The woman next door looked over the fence.

'Plastic,' she echoed. 'But they're useful for wall vases or the back of the car. They melt, though, if you put them near the fire.'

I remembered vividly the snowman with a fire burning in his head, and the way he sank into the earth and disappeared. Was that death? Had Sarah Inchman died because she leaned too close to a fire?

'What are the signs of death?'

'The signs of death are without nobility or dignity or beauty, they are as shameful as the assenting chalk marks on the rust-red sides of a loaded cattle-truck after men have learned that a cattle-truck will hold more people than cattle, that it will accommodate the whole human race in its journey to the desert over drains and dust and broken stones and dandelions where the milk is sucked by little black flies, while babies with their bones pushing like soft white mushrooms through their flesh, and grown men and women with their bones rising like sharpened axes know nothing of the thin blue trickle of milk flowing through the stem of the dandelion.'

'Dandelion milk, mushrooms?'

'People must share the world and the streams which flow through it but if the dead have lain in the streams then to drink from them is death.

'Look at the icicle, Snowman, look above your head at the melting icicle!'

I saw the glistening silver rod wedged between the snow-covered slates of the roof and the spouting slowly begin to move, with its spine breaking, to shudder and writhe while its sharp point which as a weapon might have plunged and driven through my heart, began to disappear and drops of water fell upon the path to mingle with the stream of black blood which was growing wider and swifter and now was surging out into the street, so that even the curious frightened people staring at it were forced to acknowledge the fact of the wound.

Harry Dincer came to his front door. He held a shovel which he thrust before him as if he were angry. I imagined that he had come to help me win some obscure battle, that because his daughter Rosemary had created me, he felt obliged to protect me. His face was flushed, his eyes were streaked with red; he had been down at the King's Arms again drinking away his despair at never being able to say 'Ullo Rome, Paris, Marseilles. He plunged the shovel

into the snow and began to clear great masses of snow not caring
how he mishandled or crushed it, lurching it forward along the
path and into the street to the gutter where it was heaped in a grey
sweating mound, like a new grave.

'But you have never seen a grave, Snowman. Sarah Inchman's
grave is new, in a Garden of Rest where plastic flowers in shaded
alcoves await the fire. The funeral was conducted by tall men in tall
black hats and the wreaths were arranged high on the roof of the
polished black car—all as a pretence of being able to see into the
sky, the conjurer's approach, Snowman, to the magic moment
when the jaw drops and the accusing eyes are quickly pressed shut
in case they spy and tell. Children sometimes joke to a tall man, "Is
it cold up there?" You, Snowman, who came from the sky, you
know how often during the festivals of death you must have seen
the polished black chimney pots parading among the clouds and
the brittle stars to get a peep at the other world.'

When Harry Dincer finished the attack with his shovel he came
over to me and I thought for a moment that he would demolish me
also. I had no way of defending myself.

'Our snowman,' he said. 'I forgot about you. It won't be long
now will it? We'll take your photo as soon as we can, while we have
the chance.'

He looked at the sky.

'More snow today,' he said wisely.

'Hi Harry!'

That was the man next door who also works in the telephone
exchange but who is allowed on the Continental Circuit and can
get through to Rome, Paris, Marseilles almost any time he cares to.

'Hi Max. Never known it to last so long have you?'

'Looks like more tonight, what's up with the weather? Last
winter was mild as mild. You been working hard?'

Harry was silent for a few minutes. ''Ullo Rome Paris Marseilles.

'Couldn't sleep,' he said. 'Racket next door. Thought I'd clear
my share of snow.'

'I wonder what the Council think they're doing, drifts
everywhere.'

'How's the job Max?' Harry tried not to show his envy. 'Still on the Continental Circuit?'

'Sure.'

Harry's eyes filled with longing. Anyone could have told what he was thinking: What really happened when you put on the headphones and began to talk in a different language? To people so far away? And why did they keep showing that advertisement in the newspapers, 'Ullo Rome, Paris, Marseilles, men up to fifty-nine with or without experience. Why fifty-nine? What happened when you were sixty that gave you no hope of ever getting through to Rome, Paris, Marseilles? Max was fifteen years younger than Harry—thirty-seven—and the bald patch on the back of his head was so carefully darned with crisscross strands of hair that you didn't notice it unless you took special care to see it.

'You are learning, Snowman.'

Harry made a sudden wrench with his shovel, but I need not have been afraid for he did not attack me.

'See you Max,' he called, and went inside.

It snowed and I slept.

6

'There is talk of simplicity. Snow has made the world simple as deceit is simple, a soft mask concealing the intention and truth of hills and plains and cities, the toil and thrust and rock and stone and grass growing like green ribs to accommodate the sky's breath. A dust-sheet on the restless furniture of the world. You ought to be proud, Snowman, to have so changed the face of the earth, to have reduced it to such a terrible simplicity that people are blinded if they gaze upon it.'

Another morning. I am used to morning, to watching the light stealing red-rimmed through the smoke above the chimneys and the white walls of the buildings. I am used to children snatching my arms and my buttons or pipe and replacing them; to the sinister remarks made by people who stop to stare at me. I am used to the comings and goings of the Dincer family. I wonder if Rosemary has forgotten her grieving over the University student.

'Oh, that disappointment about her age?'

'Disappointment! But you said it was the end, you said it was a kind of death!'

'Language wanes, Snowman. Feelings wane. Death comes to be no more than a disappointment, and grief over events must be strictly rationed and the size of the ration is controlled by distance in time and space—the attentions of the heart are measured by the pacing of the feet and the movements of the hands of the clock. The massacre of a race of people is only on the level of a disappointment if it is beyond the range of the stay-at-home feet controlled by the stay-at-home heart beating in time with the familiar clock. When a man puts a telescope to his snow-blinded eye he can see streams of oil flowing and fields of wheat trampled by cloud-shadows driven by the wind, but he can't see the tiny distant ration of his own Care. But no, wait, what is that fluttering speck in his snow-blinded eye? It is a fly, disappointment and death, Care and Love crawling close to his own skin, the source of their lifeblood. Why should they travel to face the flood and the earthquake, the dark camp where the children's bones push soft as mushrooms through their flesh, and the men and women sharpen their gaunt axes upon the human stone?'

'Now Rosemary is walking sedately home from school. Her manner of walking comes easily to her for she has practised it during the years she was at Primary School, and now when she walks as a Grammar School girl she is preparing for the time when she will be a University student. As she walks she flings her long striped University scarf over her shoulder. Don't believe that people live in the present, Snowman. There is haste for tomorrow and the need to know how to behave when tomorrow comes. Walking like a University student is simple; and dressing like one; and later living and behaving like a wife, a mother, a career woman; knowing the clothes to wear, the smile to adopt, the opinions to discuss and agree or disagree with, the people to make happy or unhappy from the limited ration of Love and Care. But what is the correct behaviour for Death? Whom will Rosemary imitate in order to die? There is no clue for her except in her own sleep and dreams, for one imitates one's own death, and when the time comes Rosemary cannot borrow her grandmother's way of dying or her grandfather's or her Uncle Phil's or Sarah Inchman's.

'Now Rosemary is outside the gate. She sees Doris, a girl of her own age, walking on the opposite side of the road. As they go to different Grammar Schools and are not yet used to the strangeness, they like to spend their after-school hours, weekends, and holidays working delicate but swiftly fading patterns into their former Primary School friendship by embroidering their anxieties and new experiences. Now they call out and wave and smile at each other, and forgetting her Grammar School dignity Rosemary runs to talk to Doris. Her feet crunch upon the hardened snow. She slips and falls in an ice-filled trough of snow. The heavy lorry has no time to swerve or stop.

'And that, Snowman, is death.

'See how there is no concentration, no tension, only diffuseness, untidiness. There is no rigid drop of death congealed upon the surface of living, no stain that one may point to and try to erase. It is this elusiveness of death, the vacuum created when it happens that cause details, incidents, emotions of living people to flood in filling the emptiness and crowding the untidiness with a further disarray. From up and down the street, from beyond, around corners, out of front and back doors people come running toward the scene all with their contribution of irrelevance. One woman has a tea towel in her hand, another a shopping bag, the man over the road is still holding his half-sewn overcoat, the school children carry their cases and satchels. In a way they seem like refugees from the vague unimportant outer circle trying to reach a clarity and significance at the dark still centre. But where is the centre, the perfect stain of the moment? They cannot find it. Curtains are drawn aside. Those who have not chosen to join the crowd are staring from their windows, and one has telephoned 999 which is easier to contact than Paris, Rome, or Marseilles. Police ambulance fire. The lorry driver is sitting in the snow, quietly and sadly, as if his home were the snow and the snow were his doorstep where he sits in the evening looking out upon the world. The spectators seem to realise the driver's right to that small area of snow, for they avoid it and make detours about it. But the walls of the lorry driver's white house are made of glass and he can see out and the people can see in and their eyes are full of pity. They say, "What will we do, What will we do?"

'One man from the crowd is standing on guard beside Rosemary. He has felt for her pulse. He has placed his hand on her forehead, not because it will help or explain her condition but because his mother used to touch his own forehead when he was a child and felt sick. Everyone is staring at him, trying to read the expression on his face.

'Listen, Snowman.'

Like a dog yelping, I thought it was a dog and then I saw the navy coat and her in a heap.

They've rung for the ambulance.

Who rang?

I don't know. Someone, I don't know.

Is the ambulance coming?

I think so, someone rang for it.

Has someone called the ambulance?

Is there someone seeing to everything?

I suppose so, I should think so, definitely so.

I suppose the ambulance is on its way?

More than likely. Someone will have rung for it.

They're waiting for the ambulance. It shouldn't be long.

Did someone ring for it?

I think so, someone rang for it.

Who rang for it?

Someone who saw it happen.

Did you see it?

No, I was just turning the corner when I heard the screeching noise and a funny thing I was thinking how slippery the snow was just there. . . .

There?

Yes, just there, and someone screamed.

Look at the lorry driver.

Yes, just sitting there.

He's ill with shock. They've been trying to get him to move but he won't.

He just stays there.

Her parents are at work aren't they? Her mother runs that
little blouse shop down at the Green.

I believe so. Maisy's.

There's someone coming, it looks like an ambulance.

I think it is. Someone rang for it, someone over there.

I suppose it was the man who's standing near her.

Did he ring for the ambulance?

Someone said it was him. They say he says she's dead.

The girl Dincer isn't it?

Yes, she goes to Grammar School, her mother keeps the blouse
shop down at the Green.

Daisy's?

No, Maisy's. She owns it with her sister.

Didn't her father sell you that old television that never went?

It was the tubes, and such a lot of interference.

We had a man in two weeks ago, I'm getting tired of it.

Look the lorry driver's getting up. Someone's helping him into
that house. I wonder how he'll face her parents?

I can hear a bell ringing. It's the ambulance. It's taken ages.

Someone must have rung for it.

I think someone did.

There's the Dincer car with Mrs Dincer driving.

And here's the ambulance. Look they're getting out the stret-
cher. Look, the man's shaking his head.

Isn't it awful with everyone staring, like a circus. They should
tell everybody to go away, some people have no respect for
privacy.

Look he's shaking his head again.

They're covering up her face. I guessed it. She must be dead.

There's a blanket over her face.

Did they say she was dead?

Someone said. They said that man said who put that coat over
her to start with.

Look he's talking to the Dincers. I won't be able to walk past
there today or ever.

There's blood on the snow. It's a funny green colour. The police make a fuss don't they, they have to.

They're clearing the snow, putting things in order.

All the same I can't walk past there.

Did the Dincers go in the ambulance with her?

I didn't see. More than likely. I wonder who rang for the ambulance?

Someone must have rung.

They've taken the lorry driver to hospital too.

Why have the police put lanterns there, as if it's night?

They always do. It's dark early but in a few weeks the days will be longer, have you decided about this year?

No, we're waiting, though they say book early but there's always room when the time comes.

I wouldn't be too sure though. It's their only daughter too.

She goes to Grammar School.

Did they really say she was dead?

It looks like it. You could tell really though couldn't you? Who was that man in the brown coat who took charge? He doesn't live in the street.

He looks like a foreigner. A total stranger.

He had his wits about him. Did you see it happen?

No, I was just coming around the corner when I heard the scream.

They say she ran over to meet her friend, the girl Miller. Doris Miller. They've taken her away too.

Have they?

Yes, that woman who rang for ambulance took her inside.

Did that woman ring for the ambulance? I thought it was the man in the corner house. I had the impression it was him.

Him? No, it was that woman. They say she rang for the ambulance. And then she was out there talking to the ambulance men as if she'd rung.

Then she must have. She'd ring 999 I suppose and they'd get through. I suppose that's how the police came.

Are they leaving the lanterns there? It's not dark.

It will be. The snow makes it darker. I've never known it to snow for so long, not in the city, all night and all day and the Council have had to bring in casual labour to deal with it.

Yes, men with beards and tramps. Hear the bell?

Yes, perhaps it's the ambulance on the way to King's.

No, it will have got there ages ago, it must be another ambulance.

Perhaps there's been another accident.

More than likely. They shouldn't have these heavy lorries in the snow.

It was stupid of her to run across of course. She wasn't exactly a child. She goes to Grammar School.

Her mother has that blouse shop down at the Green.

Maisy's?

No, Daisy's.

The police must have rung for her.

Or the hospital when someone rang for the ambulance.

Who rang for the ambulance?

Wasn't it that man who was standing near her, the one who took charge. I've never seen him before.

A perfect stranger.

Well someone rang anyway. Her father's a telephonist. They'd get through to him quick enough.

Yes they'd ring the exchange.

The ambulance people?

No, the police or the woman who rang the ambulance.

Didn't the man ring?

Well someone rang anyway but I don't suppose they could do anything for her.

I saw the man shaking his head.

They put a blanket over her face, one of those grey blankets.

They shouldn't have done that in full view. It let us know she was dead, they shouldn't have let everybody see she was dead, they should have taken her in the back of the ambulance as if she were ill or something and would recover.

I don't suppose they thought at the time.

But it let everybody know she was dead, and it makes things worse to know. It would have been better to read about it afterward in the paper, as if she had died in hospital.

But they couldn't keep it from people, they couldn't keep it from the parents, not with them standing there.

It doesn't seem right though. To think she was lying there dead
   all the time!
I couldn't go past there.
They're measuring. Why are they measuring?
It's to do with the inquiry.
They'll want witnesses.
Yes, they'll ask over the BBC. You hear them in the morning
   before the eight o'clock news.
Well I didn't see it thank goodness.
Neither did I, I was just turning the corner. I heard it though.
Don't.
Whoever rang the ambulance must have seen it for them to
   ring the ambulance.
Yes, I wonder who rang the ambulance?

I am only a snowman. What must a snowman do? I will sleep; there
is news of other seasons.

7

'I saw a fiercely burning light flying beyond the clouds, and the
shadow of it passed across my body, and tears ran down my cheeks.
I shivered, and my flesh seemed to drop from me and soak into the
snow at my feet, and then I think I fell asleep for two days, and
when I woke it was morning. Just as I was waking a wind shook
loose one of my coal-black pine-forest eyes and blew it onto the
pavement where a black cat sneaked up to it, pounced at it and sent
it flying under the hedge into the deep snow and there it lay until a
little dog bounded along, scratched at the snow and finding my
coal-black pine-forest eye he put it in his mouth where it was held
prisoner until the little dog ran home to his owner and dropped my
coal-black pine-forest eye at his feet.
   'Coal, good boy,' she exclaimed, and taking it into her sitting-
room she placed it upon an interesting mound of other coal-black
pine-forest eyes. You have not explained what happened then,
Perpetual Snowflake. I do not find my partial loss of sight very
distressing; one coal-black pine-forest eye will serve me as well as
two.

'While I was asleep I dreamed I was a snowflake again, a tiny flat Peter-Paul tissue of snow with zigzags of air, like melting lace, binding the edges of my body, and I was tucked up in the sky under a soft blanket of cloud and there was no thought of conquering the earth or the sea and no idea that I would ever be a snowman witnessing the comings and goings of people upon their curiously snow-white earth.'

'Yes, you slept, Snowman, for two days. If you were being affected by time you would discover that as you grew older you would spend more of your life sleeping. I believe time is affecting you, Snowman, accumulating like layers of snowstorms upon your life. People long to shut their eyes. They yawn. They shade their faces from the snow. In old age they curl up like leaves and sleep beneath drifts of snow and have no care.

'But I had meant to tell you that you have been photographed, you have had what they call your "likeness" taken.'

'My likeness? Taken?'

'Oh there is only one of you, no part of you has been stolen, although keeping alive is a matter of greed more than of loneliness. There is one of each creature because that creature devours all others, it roams through the world with its magnetic mouth seizing the tiny filed brightnesses which are the commencement of others of its kind. You think that you observe other creatures—you have seen many people in the street, little dogs, birds flying or perched here on your tree (your tree!) with their feet plodged in a smooth spreading of snowflake sauce. But if you observe with your invisible eye you will know that to each creature there is only one— himself. The wind blowing from life and death puffs one being to the size of the world. The sky fits him like a skin, and the surface of the earth is only as wide as the soles of his feet or the grasp of his claws, and his wing-span is east and west, north and south, and his head is forever burned by the neighbouring flames of the sun. Strangely enough, Snowman, this proud lonely greed is a condition of love as well as of hate, for the self does not know where to stop, it devours friend and enemy.'

'But I am only a snowman. I have been photographed. Has it changed me to have had my likeness taken?'

'A snowman, and afraid of change!

'While you were asleep Rosemary was buried, and yesterday, the day of the funeral, Harry looked out of the window and catching sight of you he exclaimed to his wife, "We never took a photo of it. We promised to make a photo of it while it lasted. I think we ought to take a snap of it now, Kath. Before the warm weather comes and there is a thaw."

'"Yes, the snow's going," Kath said. 'Be quick, Harry, we don't want to be seen taking photos at a time like this, it will make people wonder."

'"If we don't take it now it will never get taken, you know how snowmen vanish, one moment they're in front of you large as life the next moment they've vanished."

'Harry found his camera, came into the garden, focused, clicked the shutter, and your photograph was taken. I assure you it won't hurt you, Snowman. It's just a flat impression of you, not as important as the shadow which remains by your side here in the garden and which changes its shape according to the light in the sky, now it grows corpulent with morning, now it braves the decapitations of noon and ends a starved evening shape with its fingers clawing at the sky.'

As he spoke of the sky I looked up and with my one coal-black pine-forest eye I saw such a dazzle and it was an icicle starred like a frozen wand and I could see a pink and light and deep-blue world enclosed in it, and all the colours of the rainbow were gathered inside, knocking on the glass walls to get free, and then I heard a sharp crack, a sun-groan, and the colours burst suddenly from the icicle and water ran down my face onto my shoulders and down my body to my feet where it changed to black blood.

'What does it mean? Is it a sign because I have been photographed?'

'You need not be afraid of having had your photo taken. The photo failed. It did not come out.'

'It did not come out?'

'No, it was misty and blurred, and everything which was not covered with snow appeared white in the photograph while everything white, including yourself, showed as a black shape encircled by a jagged rim of pale light. Solid brick, wood and stone were rendered unsubstantial, became part of a landscape of nothingness, while everything covered with snow—you and your fellow snowflakes who are so sensitive to the prospect of daffodils and fire and sun and warm winds from the south, who are unable to resist even the lightest breath of wind, all that is fragile became strong and bold, as certain as stone and steel, capable of withstanding ordeal by season and sun. That was your photograph, Snowman. It was a failure, it did not "turn out", and yet your photo was "taken" and no one will ever be able to explain the nature of what the camera discovered within you to represent your body as pillar of black stone in a garden where the branches of a black sword were growing from the earth beneath a sky full of prowling glossy black tomcat clouds; where the solid buildings melted into nothingness, doors, fences, gates, cars, including ambulances, and people dancing or resting or dead, all dissolving before the light-bribing eye of the camera. I hope you are not disturbed when I tell you that your photograph suffered the humiliation of most projects that fail—projects of light, conscience, time, discovery—it was burned quickly on the fire. It flared and crumpled enveloped in a translucent white flame which changed the photo from a cloud of light to a black brittle substance curled at the edges like a stale crust thrown out for the drooling mumbling pigeons—hear them?—that have lost the desire to fly and only potter about in people's heads making white messes in the attics of thought.

'But I wonder, Snowman, I can't tell you precisely what you lost through the burning of your photograph. I have said it is so necessary to be careful in one's observations, to question the actions of people because they do prefer most of all to be comfortable whether in the matter of truth or of toilet. And projects are considered failures because it might take too much time and energy to prove they are successes. Would you rather have an image of yourself as black stone (it might even be marble!) or as white nothingness? I myself am impressed by this bewitching process which extracts stone from snow, swords and knives from trees, and sets the sky wailing with old dark toms padding in and out of the winds that are huddled and tangled, like thorn hedges, about the borders of night.'

'How will the point of view of the photograph affect the death of Rosemary? She did not melt or change to snow, at least not when I looked at her with my coal-black pine-forest eyes. Is there a means of photographing death which changes it to life, as objects are changed in the photograph?'

'But the objects were not changed, Snowman. You are still a snowman. It was the view of them—have you ever heard people speak of a view? When they choose where to live they often say, "It must have a good view." People like to look at the sea; it flashes and shuffles the silver cards, it winks with enticement, with light, with promise. It deals out peace and speckled flowers pink and blue and rakes in the losses, deep deep, and the losses are secret and no one ever learns the extent of them.'

'I know of the sea. People live on earth, and animals and birds, and fish live in the sea but we do not defeat the sea for we are driven back to the sky or we stay and become what we have tried to conquer . . . .'

'That is true, Snowman. The victor has a habit of assuming the identity of those he has vanquished. It is a habit of people also, and animals and birds and bright red fish.'

'Do I understand the sea because I have arrived on land? Is that a focus where the true balance of knowing is brought into view?'

'You forget or you do not realise, Snowman, that most photographs "turn out", that is, most objects appear as they appear to everyone everywhere. The moment when the picture seems to fail or where the process is arrested before the picture is developed is one of the most exciting moments in the life of a human being. The damp blurred distorted film, the unexpected "failed" view of the familiar, bring the danger of happiness, and you may know that happiness is a great danger in the lives of people, and that they are prepared from birth to fight and overcome it, to protect themselves from it with shields, hoods, specially fitted secret claws and stings.

'Rosemary is dead. Her death is no real concern of ours because we are made of snow, but if we were flesh and blood we might be tempted to colour and retouch her death and place it beside other events instead of giving it a startling isolation upon a blank page.

'No photograph can alter the fact of Rosemary's death but it is likely that the focus of Kath and Harry has been altered. Violent happenings, sudden griefs upset the development of the scene often subjecting it to so much violent overexposure that the result is a view of nothingness. If this happens in the Dincer family, Harry will feel his body falling apart, like straw, or shredded like the weave of sacking. His hair will change to white cotton floating away on the wind and when he clenches his fist the flesh of his hand will melt. He will be a true snowman. The same changes will occur in his wife. Nothing will finally become nothing. And then when all creatures and objects are cleaned of their parasitical identity, why, then the rhymes will have reason. If all the world were paper, if all the seas were ink, if all the trees were bread and cheese—what a marvellous freedom of view that would be, Snowman!

'Kath and Harry may experience a little of this changed world but it is likely that their landscape will emerge in conventional form with death as a recognisable creature, perhaps a member of the family, and with the space in the snow where Rosemary lay after the accident, cleared and new snow scattered there to make it seem as if nothing had happened, as in those photographs which are arranged and retouched with people blotted from the scene if their presence is likely to cause embarrassment to themselves or to others. Memory is quite a useful agent for retouching scenes made complicated or dangerous by grief or happiness, and when people have photographs of others whose eyes reveal too much love or hate it is a convenient trick to make them unrecognisable by concealing their eyes with a strip of tape, as in official photographs of people in prison or in places for the insane. People with too much emotion in their eyes are usually prisoners under sentence and often halfway to losing their reason.'

'Snowman, Snowman, the sheet of snow is wearing thin. Were the season a good housewife she would halve the snow and "turn" it to give the worn places a rest from wear, and she would darn the holes with tiny snow-stitches, and then once again spread the sheet over the earth and the snow would appear brand-new; but the season is not a thrifty housewife; the snow is wearing thin, and there is no

one to change top to bottom or inside to outside. Grass is poking
through the holes in the material; the flannelette has lost its fleecy
lining. The linen is dirty, for the season has slept too long in it.
During the next few days if you look high in the sky you will see the
first white cleaned clouds being unparcelled and set adrift. Are you
afraid to look now in the sky? Remember, Snowman, although
your photograph did not turn out, they have the negative of you
where your appearance is very strange because neither you nor
your shadow can be identified unless the negative is held up to the
light; therefore you are preserved, for a time. I think you are
beginning to understand that when a positive and not a negative
snowman faces the light the result may mean death. Is that why
you are afraid to look high in the sky?'

'But I am only a snowman. Why should I be concerned about
death? It happens only to people—to old women and to Grammar
School girls attacked by lorries. Yet I confess that I am afraid. It is
strange that people do not last, that they change, not as snowmen
change with their flesh peeling from their body and being replaced
with new snowfall but a change which like a touch of iron that has
been dipped in burning time and is itself impervious to the force
and fury of years, brands the visible human body and no less
indelibly the secret individual life which accompanies it. As a
snowman, have I thoughts inside my head? What does the inside of
my head resemble? Is it like a white barn with rafters, and white
mice scampering along the beams and nesting in the corners? What
is my head? Is it a stone?'

'Yes, it is a stone. While Rosemary was making you she found a
large white stone upon which she packed layers of snowflakes; that
is your head. Does it help to know what your head is made of? To
know that before the city was conquered by the snowstorm your
head stood bald and white on top of a gatepost? Your head was a
decoration polished in its circular shape because people admired it
that way. It must not make you depressed to learn that your head
has been used as an ornament, for it is a custom common among
human beings and often persists after their flesh and face and hair
and eyes have been added, and no one would guess that a smooth
white circular stone was hidden inside.

'I cannot tell you the exact moment when you were born,

Snowman. I cannot say, When your right hand was made, then you became a snowman. Or, As soon as your stone head was covered with flakes, then you were a snowman. Or that you have been living since Rosemary had the idea of making you. It is the habit of people to look at the beginning of life in order to determine the moment of birth, but as a Perpetual Snowflake I am not so prejudiced, I know that seed is shed also at the moment of death, and that many people are still not born although they possess bodies with limbs in place and heads with thoughts in place.

'Look at the gap in the sky! It is the sun!'

8

When I looked up at the sky I could see nothing. Yet I felt my body shuddering and the familiar tears ran down my cheeks, and then in a sudden gust of wind something whirled about me, up and down, then out the gate, onto the pavement, into the pool of black blood, then toward me again, round and round my feet and then up to my head where flip-flop-flap it settled and the gust of wind vanished. I was grateful for the shelter upon my head because I was afraid to look too long at the sky in case I saw the sun, though I scarcely knew how I should recognise it.

'My head is protected now. I have shelter. I cannot even see the sky now.'

'You are not the only one to seek shelter from a newspaper; it is common practice. People use it to protect themselves from the weather, others use it to hide from history or time or any of those inconvenient abstractions which man would destroy if only they had a visible shape for him to seize and defeat. Oh these abstractions, Snowman, they are among the most intrusive companions. They are never satisfied unless they have built a nest on the tip of a man's tongue, in the keys of his typewriter, in the hollow of his pen-nib—all favourite places for abstractions to breed and overpopulate the world of words. Even in my talking to you I cannot help mentioning them. Time, I say. Time, History, change. But Time is surely not an abstraction, I think he is a senile creature who is blind because his eyes have been gouged out by an historic fire; his flesh is covered with fur and he licks the hours and swallows them and they form a choking ball inside him. Then Time dies. Time. Death. It is no use, Snowman. The proper place for abstractions is in a region of the mind which must be entered in nakedness of thought. Certain abstractions are powerful and may be lethal yet the way to approach them is not to carry weapons of personification but to act as soldiers do when they surrender, to discard all the known means of defence and retaliation and walk naked toward the hostile territory. Surprising things may happen then, Snowman. We may see abstractions in their truth.

'Truth, death, time, it is no use. How grateful I am that we are made of snow! People need to burn off the old words in the way that a farmer destroys the virgin bush to put the land to new use with controlled sowing and harvesting. I will not say, though, that all such farmers are successful. Their enthusiasm wanes, the crops fail, noxious weeds take the place of the former harmless ones, there are downpours, droughts. And there are always the earliest settlers who yearn for the time when the land was covered with familiar bush and the streams were not dammed to create inexplicable hydro works, and the tall known trees were starred with centuries-old white clematis. But Snowman, Snowman, perhaps words do not matter when it is only a question of surviving for one season. Then the word *Help* is vocabulary enough. Snowmen and Perpetual Snowflakes have no need of words. Snowman, Snowman, look at the gap in the sky. It is the sun.'

'I can see nothing while I wear this torn newspaper over my head. I can see only words in print as you have explained to me. Not *Help help*, but said Mrs Frank Wilkinson in charge of the unit I suppose they have seen some deaf and dumb people on buses and in the street and felt sorry that nobody could talk to them the boys admitted breaking into a prefab for food my girlfriend is a nurse and he made her stand in the snow waiting for me to come home before he would let her in made as new suspects arson her behaviour seemed quite out of character the role of the church is to provide this not to bribe them into attending they want real religion choice of two modern suites for happy holidays licensed bar dancing not guilty are you hard of hearing you lovers' dream home gas death two sides to him you've had your last chance I'm going to sentence you snowdrops are flowering and crocuses are showing in some places so get ready for spring planting if digging hasn't been done get it over quickly leave large lumps for the weather to work on we can still expect frost and snow fire destroys home heater blaze carpet linoleum were destroyed he woke to the smell of burning planned with you in mind luxury in the sun on the sands by the sea the summer of your dreams stretch black threads or the new nylon web over primula or polyanthus buds before the birds get at them planting can start soon for fruit trees fruit bushes roses he's finished his lunch when someone rang to tell him it's your shop on fire an unknown young boy discovered the fire he was walking past the shop when he thought he saw smoke or steam in the window monster sale end of season. . . .'

I was beginning to wish that I did not know how to read my newspaper shelter. It seemed full of references to fire and sun and spring, and I thought it strange that human beings should also be afraid of fire and sun and spring, so afraid that they had to keep writing of them in newspapers in order to dilute their fear. Two sides to him? What did it mean? And the picture of the sun puzzled me. I could see the caption clearly—FOLLOW THE SUN—and at first I was foolish enough to believe that if I looked at a picture of the sun it would have the same effect upon me as if I looked at the sun itself. The sun was portrayed as a semicircle with tentacles growing from it, and a wide smiling mouth. What had I been afraid of? So this was the sun, the picture of benevolence; it had not even eyes to see me. Perhaps the smile was too wide giving its face a suggestion of falseness but there seemed to be no doubt about the sun's kind nature.

'Do these newspaper shelters often happen to snowmen?'

'You are a fool of course. As self-centred as any human being. You imagine that newspapers are printed to shelter you from the sun.'

'I don't need shelter from the sun. I have seen its kind face.'

'It is worse, Snowman, when you are deceived by your own deceit. Newspapers do make convenient shelters for snowmen; also for cooked fish, dog-meat, and they are useful as blankets for tramps; they protect people from the hot and cold weather; they deaden sound; they are the body and tail of kites, and are made into little dishes with flour-and-water paste; they are the heads of puppets, the bed for the cat to have kittens on; they are wrappers, concealers, warmers; also they bring news, even from Rome, Paris, Marseilles.

'Now a gust of wind is blowing near you, Snowman, and for your sake I hope it does not remove your newspaper shelter for when the sun shines it leans close to the earth and the snow is drawn from the earth like white milk from a white breast and when all the snow has vanished and the sun is satisfied the earth lies dry, wrinkled, folded with a dull brown stain spreading through its skin, but you will never see so much, Snowman, nor the change that follows, it is other seasons.'

The gust of wind came near me but it did not blow away my newspaper shelter, and toward evening the tears stopped flowing down my cheeks and a cloud of snow fell from the sky but I could see nothing until a blackbird, going home, stopped to rest on the tree, and seeing me standing forlorn, thin, blind, with the world's news clinging to my stone skull, he flew down and pecked at the newspaper, just a slight stab with his beak, tearing a hole in the paper so that once more I could look at the world with my coal-black pine-forest eye. The blackbird had pierced the word *snowdrops.* When I looked out through the gap in *snowdrops* I could see the blackbird disappearing over the roofs of the buildings and thus I could not ask him whether it was joy or sorrow which had impelled him to stab the chosen word.

Tonight I shall sleep deeply. I feel safe. More snow-armies are arriving upon the earth and all will be as it was on my first day. Snow repairs, cushions, conceals; knives have no blades, mountains have no swords, the yellow earth-cat has white padded claws, and it is people only, those bone-and-flesh scissors snapping in the street, refusing the overcoat of snow which their shadows wear, sneaking faithfully beside them, it is people who change and die. People and birds.

There is a sound at my feet. Something has fallen from the sky. It is not a snowflake, it is a blackbird and it is dead, I know, for I have learned the dispositions of death. Its beak is half-open and quite still and no living blackbird has such a thrust of beak unless it is taking food or attacking the enemy. Its feathers are ruffled about its neck, its body is huddled, and no living blackbird has such an appearance except in a tree in the wind and rain and now that the snow-armies have arrived for the night the wind does not blow, the tree is still, and there is no rain—but what is rain? How quickly I have learned to gather the clues of death! The bird's claws have as much grasping power now as loose pieces of string. Death has stolen the black sheen of his feathery overcoat and there are two round white pieces of skin like tiny portholes fitted and closed over his once bright watchful eyes. There is a snowdrop lying beside him; its neck is twisted and a green liquid oozes from the crushed stem.

'Snowman, Snowman, there is a gap in the sky.'

My sleep is disturbed tonight. I think I must have dozed several times. My newspaper shelter keeps flapping against my face, it seems to have lodged forever upon my head, and I do not really care to harbour or be protected for too long by stale news two sides to him you've had your last chance I'm going to sentence you snowdrops are flowering and crocuses are showing in some places so get ready for spring an unknown boy discovered the fire he was walking past the shop when he thought he saw smoke or steam in the window nobody could talk to them he felt sorry for them because nobody could talk to them they were deaf and dumb.

Stale news. Yet how can I tell whether news is fresh or stale? When the Perpetual Snowflake talks to me of people he brings centuries-old news that is fresh to me, and the stale news of the prompt arrival of each morning brings with it the excitement of fresh news.

A prowling cat has torn the dead blackbird to pieces and eaten him. It is so dark now. I think I will sleep but I am afraid, why am I afraid, I am only a snowman, your last chance I'm going to sentence you two sides to him snowdrops are flowering and crocuses are showing in some places luxury in the sun on the sand by the sea but we do not defeat the sea for we are driven back to the sky or we stay and become what we have tried to conquer, remembering nothing except our new flowing in and out in and out, sighing for one place, drawn to another, wild with promises to white birds and bright red fish and beaches abandoned then longed for.

'Snowman, Snowman.'

Man is simplicity itself. Coal, brass, cloth, wood.

I never dreamed.

9

I believe the armies of snow have deserted me. There are wars of which I know nothing—the wounded and the dead are lying everywhere yet no reinforcements arrive from the sky which I can almost see if I stare through the tiny hole in my newspaper shelter. The clouds are no longer battleships.

'Battleships sail with their crews up and down on the sea and wave golden flags and below deck in the dark places of the ship they fill torpedoes with striped sweets, they press buttons which open snow-white umbrellas above the sea, and certainly it is all most beautiful, Snowman, and artistic, the candy floss of death licked by small boys from the hate and fear blossoming on the tall wooden sticks. Splinter crack, the cost. And the white wood with the sap dried. And the heads of trees hustling rumours out of the long-distance wind on its everlasting runabout ticket got cheap the endless circular limits of life.

'I cannot stare so often now at the clouds but I think I see a streak of red which all knowledgeable people on earth will say is blood from a wound but I cannot tell nor do I know if it is fire I am tired of blood and fire what is it oh what is it? I find that I can scarcely breathe. I wish the reinforcements would arrive. What is the use of conquering the earth with snow if the earth does not stay conquered? Oh there are so many rumours everywhere, there's a gossiping trickle of black blood in the gutter, and through the tiny hole in my newspaper shelter I can see swellings on the twigs and branches of this tree. It must be suffering from a disease; perhaps it is dying. People, birds, trees, everything on earth seems to die. I suppose that before many days have passed everyone in the street will have died and how strange it is to think that I have not yet been told about everyone, that they will die and I shall not have known them, and it will not matter because I am only a snowman. But are knowing and being known the two triumphs which the dead carry with them to their graves, the dead who drop like parachutists to the darkness of memory and survive there because they are buckled and strapped to the white imperishable strength of having known and been known, of having made the leap to darkness surrounded and carried by the woven threads of people whom they greeted, abused, loved, murdered, or heard news from even at a great distance, a voice speaking from Rome, Paris, Marseilles or from the forbidden interior where the ticking sawdust desert is wound and whirled and as you have said, Perpetual Snowflake, men die of thirst with their mouth an O like a spokeless wheel full of the dust and sand and red earth, while tall cactus palms extend their greeting and parry at the sky as if they wore great spiked green boxing-gloves in the whirlwind.'

'There's little more to tell you, Snowman, of the people in the street of the city. You are only a snowman. It is all the same story, in the end. Widows have husbands living, the spinsters are married, the childless have borne children. Rosemary is not dead. She still sleeps late in the morning until her mother climbs the stairs to her bedroom on the top floor (decorated in red for her thirteenth birthday). "Rosemary if you don't get up you'll be late for school." "All right, I'm coming, have I got a clean pair of stockings?" "Yes but hurry." Kath, Harry and Rosemary still drive together in the polished green car which Harry cleans every weekend by removing the little rubber mats and the covers from the covers from the covers of the car seats, shaking everything up and down as if making signals, but that is absurd for you cannot make signals in that way just as you cannot rid the newspaper of its news by shaking it. Snowman, I am not describing a world where a spell has been cast over people forcing them to stay forever within the same moment of time. You saw Rosemary die. Yet she is alive, she goes to school each day, she still dreams of her University student and his long striped scarf. And yet she is also a member of the docile dead who have not yet learned to rebel.

'The idea of rebellion arises in the dead during the first night when they or their ashes lie in their grave and the rain falls all night upon the earth, and the acceptable dampness and darkness where plants thrust and stir and roots are spread with secret buoyancy and warmth like long hair laid softly upon a pillow, change to an uncomfortable wetness with the earth massed in soaking clods knocking and thudding upon the coffin until the rain leaks through to the padded satin, staining it brown, and the stitches decay in the carefully embroidered red-and-white roses, and the ashes and the body whisper with rain and the flesh sinks to accommodate lakes and seas of rain and to make a home for the fugitive creatures which crawl upon the sea bed and are sometimes as brilliantly coloured as earth-flowers; and the pools make rainbows, even in the dark. Or so I believe, Snowman. The first night of rain is the loneliest night the dead will ever endure.

'It is on that night that they rebel, and they never forget their moment of rebellion. They are satisfied no longer to be the calm docile dead with their eyes carefully closed and their hands in an attitude of willing surrender; their toes tied to keep up the orderly lifeless pretence. Rain is terrible, Snowman, the way it affects the dead. A night of ceaseless rain on earth is a night of loneliness for human beings who are alive; they draw their curtains—if they possess curtains, if they possess a home. They huddle together touching skin to skin. Or if they are alone and have no one the rag or dress or shirt which they wear is soaked with rain and clings to their skin; it is a time for clinging and touching. The bare feet sink in the earth and the earth grips them, making a hollow place for them. Birds hide beneath a verandah of leaves, perch on the edge of their nest or sit cosily within it and look out, like early settlers sitting on their homestead porch, at the misty frontier of waterfalls.

'How dark it is, Snowman, when rain falls at night, and how lonely for creatures—beasts and men—who are without shelter! It is worse than cold or thunder and lightning, for though cold cuts the flesh with an axe made of ice, it knows its boundary, it keeps its place in the wound even when it strikes completely through flesh and bone. Thunder and lightning are fearsome to people with homes and people without homes, to those who are loved and those who are unloved, but heartbeats are just as terrifying. What cause have the dead to rebel when their bodies lie night after night in quietness with no sound of knocking, of thunder wanting to get in or heartbeats wanting to get out?

'Until it rains at night. Rain penetrates, the stain of it spreads, it sinks deeper, deeper until it arrives at the dead. But you have never seen rain, Snowman, and as one of the dead Rosemary does not yet know it. Perhaps tomorrow or the next night it may rain, and the rain will continue through the night and Rosemary will lie where she has been buried as one of the dead, and the rain will treat her as earth, making pools in her where little fish swim and insects burrow and skate and new streams form and flow from her body to the clay and back again with circular inclusion flesh clay flesh, and for a while she will submit to the rain, and then suddenly it will be time to rebel both against the living and against her companion dead, and she will rise from her grave and with sympathy for no one but herself and her darkness and loneliness she will teach the living through dreams, nightmares, fantasies, the true discomforts of death.'

'I do not understand. Why is not everyone weeping? Although you have told me of some of the people in the street of the city I cannot remember them or distinguish one from the other. I only know they live in colonies and grow to look alike, but you have said that berries live in colonies and that holly leaves are webbed like bats' wings and the berries are drops of blood at their vampire mouth.'

'I wish you might be, Snowman, when the news arrives.'

'Which news? The news has arrived. You see I am wearing it as a protection against the sky.'

'Not every snowman has the privilege of looking through a gap in a snowdrop.'

I think I have listened to the Perpetual Snowflake for long enough. Since he spoke of the gap in the sky and the sun I have not trusted him. I have become impatient of his stories of the street of the city, and placed here with my feet growing securely in the earth I have no means of deciding whether he has told me the truth. How do I know there are deserts where men die of thirst? The earth is covered with snow; it shall always be covered with snow.

Who is the Perpetual Snowflake? Who is he?

'The wind from the south is blowing and you are disturbed by it, but soon, Snowman, you must have the courage to look up in the sky. There is news of other seasons.'

I wait for the night to come bringing more snow, more and more snow to cover the bare places in the street and on the buildings. The snow has melted from the tree, there is a cancer upon the branches, small swellings that will burst and cause the tree to die. The world is gloom and doom where the only survivors are snowmen. Our limbs are not afflicted with cancers from which burst tiny spears of green disease; our life is not a running sore of sap sealing our eyes and ears from the reality behind the deception. Even though stray newspapers force our gaze to pierce the word and not the perilous flower, we learn enough of life in the street of the city to wish that we were wholly snow, that no one had ever called us Snow-Man.

Even my own creator is dead and her father runs back and forth with his polished earphones trying to get in touch with foreign places but no one listens to him for he cannot make the correct signal. I pity the dead and the living people who possess the gift of sight and hearing and are forbidden to use them, who are born to dance but must be propelled from restricting wall to wall in wheelchairs of their own making. Surely the human eye can see beyond the range of telescopes, and the ear hear the sun growing to the height of day tall against the dark dwarfed hours. I talk of the sun but I do not believe in it. Snow is everlasting. I am a snowman. I feel that tonight and tonight and tonight I shall sleep my deep white sleep surrounded by the calm habitual cold air, soft stirring from corner to corner of the world of the white spiders weaving their webs to shroud the trapped earth forever with snow.

Yet it seems that I may have caught the human habit of deception. Here is a little boy, the Italian Salvatore with hair like black paste. He is out late. I think he is going down to the shops to get some cigarettes for his father and chocolates for his mother and his two small sisters. From the downstairs front room where they live next door to me there is a noise like a market all day, a sound like bargaining and what pleasant bargains they must be, for everyone laughs and seems happy, and then the little girl cries because it is the end of the world, she can see it coming toward her like a terrible dream and it will not stop although she puts up her hands to protect herself oh oh it is the end of the world my lolly on a stick has dropped from its wrapper. When the father is working as a waiter in the West End Salvatore acts as father. He goes shopping. Now he hurries out the door, slithering in the snow at the edge of the pavement. He looks left and right, waits a long time, then he runs across and as he runs he is flapping his right hand against his backside and his legs are galloping and away he goes to the shops. He is a horse galloping through the snow, faster and faster, driving himself gee-up gee-up, and his black paste hair hangs like a mane over his left eye, and he tosses his head, and he snorts with his nose and mouth wrinkled up; away, away he is galloping. His olive skin steams with sweat, he is driven on and on. Suddenly he stoops to the snow, picks up a handful and clamps it in a cold mass in his mouth, drawing his breath sharply. There is the old woman who sweeps the pavement with her silver broom. She scolds him.

'Don't eat snow. It's dirty, it's only dirty water, you'll catch a disease.'

Salvatore thinks, I am eating snow, not dirty water. Besides, I am a horse.

He gives a snort, kicks his legs, taps himself smartly on the rump, and is away flying through the sky.

Five minutes later he is home, outside the window, banging upon the pane, 'Mama, Mama,' to be taken out of the cold into the warm haggling family market that is golden like oranges and yellow and black like ripe bananas.

As I watch Salvatore I think that perhaps people do live forever, their lives are a precious deception which lasts forever. Who dies then? Do snowmen die?

Although I have waited long this evening the reinforcements have not arrived from the sky. I hear something growing, a commotion of roots; it is a disease affecting the earth. I am a mountain, so strong. I am a lamppost with light burning in my head. I am a dragon. I am only a snowman. Now a wind is stirring the sleeping snow; I try to believe that the white mist created by the wind is the reinforcement of flakes from the sky but unlike human beings I am not practised in deception. I know that I am surrounded by tired snow disturbed from sleep and bleeding from its wounds of light. I wish I had the belief of Salvatore that what lies about me is clean white snow, the proper food of creatures who gallop and fly through the clouds in the sky, but again I remain undeceived, the old woman with the silver broom has been whispering in my ear.

The wind has suddenly blown away my newspaper shelter. I can see. But it is too dark now and the street lights are switched on and the cats are lifting the lids of the dustbins and prowling secure and magnificent through their world, the narrow whisker-lane with smells sprouting in the hedgerows.

'It is not true, Snowman, that before people die they experience a flashing vision of their whole lives. It is a myth someone has dreamed in order to soothe the living, to give them the longed-for opportunity to repeat their lives without effort, without trying in vain to dredge the few lost keepsakes of their memory that have perhaps sunk too deep to be shifted, that may not ever be recovered when the energies are so weakened and the sight is failing and the ears are about to be stopped with the black wax of darkness, and the claws that grew as weapons upon the hands have dried and snapped and are no use for scratching and scrabbling in the darkness of the pool. There was never room either during life or before death for the salvage of so much memory.

'When a man is dying he is afraid or is suffering pain or faith and his thought is of the room where he lies and of the people near him, of their shapes and the flapping of their clothes against their bodies. He does not waste the precious moments thinking, When I was a child: when I was a child I flew kites of gull-wide span; I bounced a rubber ball and watched the shadow of it moving like grey sun-bound elastic across the pavement, and my hands were long gloves of grey shadow; I fished in streams and followed them to their source; I stayed away from school, secretly, and was surprised that I did not know how to use the enormous day which the sun and I together were taking care of, with a promise to use it fast until its mass had become threadbare and glowing with night; the sun and I hacked at the hours, but only the sun made any impression and I was lost against the size of the time, and was glad to give up my task and go home; yet I remember that I learned too quickly to sharpen the huge axe of my needs and desires, and too soon without the help of the sun I reduced each day to darkness.

'No, Snowman, dying is a time of greed. There is no leisurely arranging of food upon one's plate when the plate is nearly empty and when what lies there may also be out of reach.'

'Why do you tell me this? I am tired of death. I am not even sure that I believe that people die, not when I see a small boy changing into a horse, galloping through the snow and flying up into the sky while everyone around him thinks that he is still a small boy; not when he tastes a handful of snow and relishes the freshness of it while the old woman with the purple hat and the blue apron and the silver broom whispers in the ears of everyone that new snow is dirty water.'

I have been sleeping and now it is morning. The light is sharper than usual, piercing my coal-black pine-forest eye until it seems to threaten to steal my sight. It is a gorse bush of light, ablaze with golden flowers and thorns dusted with yellow pollen. It is dazzling me, there is a white mist rising from me, the world seems filled with a white glare with the golden bush growing upside down from the sky to meet the earth. Am I only shadow beneath the sea? Or are the sky, the sea, and the golden bush the shadows of myself? It is all the catkin dust in the world swept into a heap in the sky, it is a golden puffball of cloud trampled on my morning with the dust rising and floating and settling upon the earth and the snow, and blown through the air again into the sky. The world is suddenly too old and walked-upon, it is mildewed with gold, soft with gold moss, it has been out in all weathers for too many days and no one has cared to shelter it.

Now the light is dropping bright and sharp and smooth as yellow acorns. They make no sound on the snow.

For so long the snow has lain, the light has settled and been still, and now here is the sun to skim the cream, the top of the light, and spill it everywhere, and the morning laps it up with the wind and the clouds moving their greedy tongues through the sky. The light pours and spills and the first flies are in the air, gummed with sleep.

Oh, oh the sun, see it is a whirling flypaper with the people like new flies clinging to it and drowsy with its dazzle and the syrupy

taste of it. But the sun is poison, why don't they realise that the sun
will cause them to die? Now people are saying At last, At last. What
do they mean? People are opening their front doors and looking
out at the street. They are smiling, they are waving; what are they
saying to each other?

'I knew it would be soon, not last week or even yesterday but I
had an idea today would be the time, I knew it when I looked at the
gap in the sky yesterday. Did you see the gap in the sky, did you
look in the sky? It is all finished now isn't it, it has never seemed so
long, it seems to have been lying here for months and months when
it has only been a few days yet it has seemed so long, I thought it
would last forever, the way it kept falling and drifting and no
sweeping had any effect upon it, and even the traffic did not seem to
shift it, for every morning the cars were white and the street and the
pavement were without foot or wheel mark or even the mark of a
bird or a cat or dog, or even the sign of that death, you heard of the
death in the street, no marks only the tracks of the wind that cold
wind blowing from the ice, from the north, is it Greenland or
Iceland or Spitzbergen, one of those place whose names when you
pronounce them are sharp with icicles for consonants and lakes of
blue ice for vowels, is it, is it really, did you say Iceland is a sunny
place, I had always believed, I had always believed, but it must have
an Arctic climate it can't have green fields and warm days and the
sun if it is up there within the Arctic Circle, did you ever read those
haunting tales of the Northern Gods, of Balder the beautiful is
dead is dead—the voice passed like the mournful cry of sunward-
sailing cranes—that's poetry we had poetry at school once or
twice—Faster than fairies faster than witches bridges and houses
hedges and ditches, "From a Railroad Carriage"—but it's not, true
Iceland's not warm and green, I don't believe it, look at that little
boy at the gate slapping his legs and galloping as if he were a horse.
A cocky little chap. Look at him. Thinks he's a horse. The children
won't like it now it's all over will they? There's been no keeping
them inside even when it's been cold enough to change them into
icebergs but the worst is to come we've seen one death a night or
two of frost and the streets will be treacherous, and it was really so
pretty in a way, I used to think so didn't you. Snowmen and
snowballs and tasting it, like eating white clay or frozen flour and

dew mixed, and it tasted of nothing really, so much of nothing that you could imagine special flavours to it, only the sweetness sourness bitterness which you put there yourself. Snow is a responsibility don't you think? Having no colour too; you have to mix your own colours in it and then it is the most personal weather, it is *you*. We were taught to draw snow at school. We made the grey sky with black and white, Chinese or Ivory white, Indian black, a little water, a wash on white paper and the sky was prepared for the snow to fall but we didn't draw the earth because with the snow there the earth had vanished although sometimes we made threads of grass spiking through the white—didn't snow really taste like grass and roots? And wasn't it always an ingredient of nightmares—don't you remember the times you were lost in a snowstorm in the mountains and the snow was in deep drifts around you and still falling and you were so helpless and so much in despair until you saw the light in the distance, the lantern swaying, and then suddenly your forehead was being licked by the warm tongue of a St Bernard dog and a flask was being uncorked and thrust between your teeth—don't you remember?'

'Snowman, Snowman, the privacy of snow is the privacy of death. Children do not care. They gallop like horses through the streets and fly into the sky.'

While I listen to the people talking I am thinking, It is a great mystery indeed the way they talk of snow, of me. How proud I am! One said, pointing to me, 'Look at him, he has been here ever since it started, every day on my way to catch the bus at the corner I have passed him standing there. The Dincer girl made him. Rosemary Dincer. And now she's dead, and look at him standing there as if he will last forever, as if, when all the people in the world are dead, struck down by their own brewed secret weather, the only man remaining will be a snowman. Did you ever play that game at school, where someone shouted *No Man Standing*, and immediately everyone lay on the ground as if dead and the last person to be standing was counted out and dismissed from the game? What if the last person standing turned out to be a snowman? He seems to think he may have that honour or disgrace, just look at him there so proud with his piece of coal for an eye and the brass buttons in a row down his belly. I believe they photographed him but they say it was too late for the Dincer girl to see the photo but then photos are always too late don't you think? I mean they are *after* the moment, and it used to depend on the sun didn't it, the direction of the sun and the shadow when you took the photo but somehow it doesn't seem to matter now, the sun has no real say in it, why, you can take photos inside with those tiny bulbs that burst in a flash and nearly blind you, certainly it is out of fashion to rely on the sun but there it is, look, look, oh I wish I were living in one of those places where oranges grow, I have seen pictures of such places. One day in summer I will go to France for the day, early morning and home at night. One day in summer I will go—somewhere—out of town where the sky is a blue water-race going so fast above me that it makes me dizzy, look, it isn't even blue today yet there's the sun, look up at the sky, at the gap between the clouds. Goodbye, Snowman!'

They have passed the gate now. They are walking up and down the street. More people have come out, and some are laughing and some are warning each other of the 'treacherous' snow. And all look at me with pity and contempt. Why? Why do they keep saying, One day in Spring, One day in Summer, one day soon. . . ?

I have hunched my shoulders and bowed my head. One of the children passing said, 'Look he's a dirty old polar bear, the kind they keep in a cage with a pond made of concrete and the rocks painted blue and white to cheat him into believing they are ice, he's just a dirty polar bear, gosh it must be beaut to be a real polar bear coming up through the ice with a block of iceberg balanced on your nose!'

'That's a seal.'

'No it's a polar bear. It's tricks.'

'It's a seal.'

'Seals are grey.'

'There are white ones, covered with snow.'

'I mean a polar bear, a real one, diving down under the ice and coming up to do tricks and roaring and growling. With a black nose.'

'Look at the snowman! Hey, you've taken his arm!'

'I didn't. It came away in my hand. Like this, see!'

'You've taken the other arm. You'll cop it. It doesn't belong to us.'

'But it's no good any more, it's melting. Snowmen don't last forever. I bet if I gave it a big push that would be the end of it.'

'You'll cop it if you do. Quick, we'll be in for it if someone catches us.'

'Want me to knock off his head? I bet I could first go!'

Fortunately they have decided not to knock off my head and they have gone up the street, with that loitering lumbering walk of small boys—they are more like polar bears than I; perhaps they have changed into polar bears because they keep talking of them and imitating their roars and one put his head in the air with his nose trying to touch the sky. He balances a block of ice upon his nose, and that is a feat which I myself would be proud to accomplish yet all a passer-by can say to him is, 'Look where you're going, clumsy, you don't want to get yourself a broken arm or leg,' speaking with the certainty which adults seem to possess when they imagine they can divine the wishes of children.

The boy looks contemptusouly at the woman who tells him in a sharper tone, 'You don't want to land up in hospital.'

The little boy is wondering, How does she know I don't? Everybody but me has had a broken arm or leg and been in hospital with dishes of bananas and toffees in coloured paper beside them for helping themselves any time, and people from the BBC coming with a microphone Now little man and how old are you, how long have you been in hospital, what's your favourite subject at school and what record would you like us to play for you? Everyone in the world has been in hospital and had played for them 'My Old Man's A Dustman He Wears A Dustman's Hat he wears gorblimey trousers and he lives in a Council Flat,' or 'There's a hole in my bucket dear Henry dear Henry,' or 'There was an old woman who swallowed a fly oh my she swallowed a fly perhaps she'll die.' Everyone in the world except me. And there's this stupid woman telling me I don't want to have a broken arm or leg! Gosh! Some people!

The two boys look at each other and at the woman and to me their thoughts are as clear as this bright light surrounding me.

They stare at the woman and they burst out laughing, saying in unison, 'Oh my Oh my she's swallowed a fly, perhaps she'll die!'

They look at each other, mirthfully aghast at the suggestion, 'Perhaps she'll die!'

In spite of their laughter echoing merrily around the street, I have an increasing sense of deep gloom. It is fine for the children to be content with being polar bears or horses stabled among the clouds champing the fields of sky, lifting their heads, putting out their tongues, seizing between their teeth a cluster of the million burning straws protruding from the sun. And they are content to break their arms and legs, snap, like striped rock, and to fill the snowy air with sharp menacing cries, being birds now with the quills of their shining black wings digging between their shoulder blades. As yet they are not used to the idea of dying; they have not yet set a place for death at their table in order that it may share their meals, or warmed a hollow in their bed for it to lie there at night with its arm around them, protecting them from the dreams by the living.

But why should I mourn the death of creatures on earth? I am only a snowman. I have no arms to fold across my body or hands to clasp as if in prayer. I am only a snowman. My body seems to be sinking slowly into the earth and I am weeping ceaselessly now and I do not know why, and there is a heaviness upon my shoulders as if an unfamiliar burden had been placed there, but where shall I carry the burden, to whom shall I deliver it, when I cannot move and I am planted forever in this garden? When we flew from the sky we stopped the mouth of the earth, filling it with snow, and all the sound the earth has made has been the distant muffled murmur like streams turning in a long wave of sleep, but now there are sharp subterranean cries, articulate demands which reach up through the snow. The sky, the morning, the light, the sun pay attention. Oh I never heard so much sound in my life, and underneath a hush and white steam rising and blurred creatures moving to and fro, meeting and parting. It seems as if the world were on fire.

Where shall I take my burden? Who has put it upon me? I am only a snowman. I cannot bear the weight for much longer. My body sinks deeper into the earth. I have grown thin with the perplexities of being, of merely standing here in a garden in a street of the city. How much more terrible if I were human, moving, travelling, compelled to catalogue the objects of the world in order that I may have remedies for the distress of living; comparing, creating, destroying; putting all into the picture the birthplace the home the first garden tree house street city. And then to die, to submit to the long night of rain, to become a garden pool reflecting and enclosing the face of darkness.

I am a snowman. My flesh is wasting. If I were wholly human I might deceive myself, I might change to any shape which I cared to name and thus live forever; I might imagine that I am not alone, that I can get in touch with everyone else in the world—in Rome, Paris, Marseilles—although I do not understand the language, although when I tried to learn the alphabet of it I found myself lost among columns and archways of letters with my voice only a small echoless whisper. But I am not wholly human. I am a snowman. Surely I shall live forever!

My flesh is wasting. I cannot deceive myself. I have no treasure-house of time or imagination to provide for my survival after death.

Death? But I am a snowman. I live forever. I am growing thin, I am sinking into the earth, soon I shall be bowed upon my knees. The burden is still upon me driving me deeper to the earth. Another small boy passed me just a moment ago and struck me across the head, knocking off the top of my head, and I begin to be more afraid for my thoughts are exposed to the sun which is probing all my secrets, and a white smoke rises from my head; there's something burning, there is no help for it now, I must influence the sun, I must turn my coal-black pine-forest eye toward the sky, to the widening gap in the clouds, and face the sun. I am brave.

'Do you not think I am brave, Perpetual Snowflake?'

He does not answer. I cannot call in a loud voice for I have no voice. The burden is too much, I cannot bear it, I am down to my knees in the earth, all the creatures arriving in time for spring are piling their luggage upon my shoulders, they think I am a snow-porter, a snow-camel, perhaps it is their responsibilities and not their luggage, or the heaviness of their hearts because they know they shall die whereas I, a snowman, remain forever alive and free.

There is a curtain of fire blowing in a great gale of flame. The pine forest is burning, the pine cones are crackling and sparkling as they are used to doing only when they are ripe and it is time for them to spill their seeds. I have been so afraid of fire. I did not know that I contained it within the sight of my eyes and that when I gazed upon the sun the dreaded fire would originate from myself, that as a snowman I have been deceiving myself into believing I am made wholly of snow when all my life I have carried fire. Is my burden after all the burden of my own fire?

I am weeping now, my cheeks are touched with a red glow, like blood. People looking at me might imagine that I am human. Am I human? Are all other creatures snowmen?

There is no time to think of it, there is no time. I am going to sleep now, and the wall of the sky is patterned with snowdrops, the complete flower and not the broken word or promise.

'Who are you?'

'I am the Perpetual Snowflake.'

'Why do you talk to me? Are you here to explain the world to me because I am only a snowman? I should like to know of the place where I am to live for ever and ever. Tell me.'

I told him. Sometimes I thought of telling him my own story, of when I too was a snowman in a garden in a street in a city, and how I at last faced the sun and was burned by my own fire until all that remained of me was this small Perpetual Snowflake; how another winter came and I watched the children once again making snowmen and flying like horses through the sky. But I kept silent about my life. I do not want to remember the day when I died and yet did not die, for as almost the only snowflake left on that spring morning I whirled suddenly into the air meeting the Perpetual Snowflake who had guided me in my life, and there followed a battle between us two tiny snow-tissues that were so thin the wind could look through us and shadows could signal to each other through our bodies. I survived the battle. I died once yet I survive. I wait for spring, the sun and the snowdrops and the daffodils, with as much fear as when I was a snowman. How is it that I fear death yet I have died? Or is the human deception true, and death is only a dream, it is death that dies?

Oh how I wish now that I had never conquered the earth, for people live on the earth, and animals and birds, and fish live in the sea but we do not defeat the sea for we are driven back to the sky or become what we have tried to conquer, remembering nothing except our new flowing in and out, in and out, sighing for one place, drawn to another, wild with promises to white birds and bright-red fish and beaches abandoned then longed for.

'Snowman, Snowman!'

Man is indeed simplicity. Coal, brass, cloth, wood—I never dreamed.

A Windy Day

When the wind blows in this way the cars bedded in the streets struggle to get free of their green-and-grey canvas or plastic nightshirts; the planes, the new type with their wings down over their hips, rock in the sky. The wind lifts the lids of the dustbins, breaks milk bottles, turns newspapers over and over, around corners, and buffets city sparrows perched in the pruned grey trees.

Spring enters on every gust of wind.

Look at the pearl-coloured sky, the satin clouds ruffled this way and that above the chimney tops! The sun is fresh, never left standing or sour, poured out clean on the stones for the dusty-throated wind to lick.

Trains rattle under dark sagging bridges. People talk from pavement to pavement. Children unwind hair ribbons. The black-and-white tomcat slinks along the crumbling wall.

The motorcyclist, his knees tight against his mount, surges through the tidal streets, riding a seahorse to the lonely shore.

The wind moans near the eaves of the house, Why-do-you? Why-do-you?

Settled pigeons call with folded grey voices, Tear up the eviction order.

Homeless birds, intruders, cry for the sea and the marshland.

The sun burns a transfer of spring on the city.

Do not be afraid of spring.

The Terrible Screaming

One night a terrible screaming sounded through the city. It sounded so loudly and piercingly that there was not a soul who did not hear it. Yet when people turned to one another in fear and were about to remark, Did you hear it, that terrible screaming? they changed their minds, thinking, Perhaps it was my imagination, perhaps I have been working too hard or letting my thoughts get the upper hand (one must never work too hard or be dominated by one's thoughts), perhaps if I confess that I heard this terrible screaming others will label me insane, I shall be hidden behind locked doors and sit for the remaining years of my life in a small corner, gazing at the senseless writing on the wall.

Therefore no one confessed to having heard the screaming. Work and play, love and death, continued as usual. Yet the screaming persisted. It sounded day and night in the ears of the people of the city, yet all remained silent concerning it, and talked of other things. Until one day a stranger arrived from a foreign shore. As soon as he arrived in the city he gave a start of horror and exclaimed to the Head of the Welcoming Committee, 'What was that? Why, it has not yet ceased! What is it, that terrible screaming? How can you possibly live with it? Does it continue day and night? Oh what sympathy I have for you in this otherwise fair untroubled city!'

The Head of the Welcoming Committee was at a loss. On the one hand the stranger was a Distinguished Person whom it would be impolite to contradict; on the other hand, it would be equally unwise for the Head of the Welcoming Committee to acknowledge the terrible screaming. He decided to risk being thought impolite.

'I hear nothing unusual,' he said lightly, trying to suggest that perhaps his thoughts had been elsewhere, and at the same time trying to convey his undivided attention to the concern of the Distinguished Stranger. His task was difficult. The packaging of words with varied intentions is like writing a letter to someone in a foreign land and addressing it to oneself; it never reaches its destination.

The Distinguished Stranger looked confused. 'You hear no terrible screaming?'

The Head of the Welcoming Committee turned to his assistant. 'Do you perhaps hear some unusual sound?'

The Assistant who had been disturbed by the screaming and had decided that very day to speak out, to refuse to ignore it, now became afraid that perhaps he would lose his job if he mentioned it. He shook his head.

'I hear nothing unusual,' he replied firmly.

The Distinguished Stranger looked embarrassed. 'Perhaps it is my imagination,' he said apologetically. 'It is just as well that I have come for a holiday to your beautiful city. I have been working very hard lately.'

Then aware once again of the terrible screaming he covered his ears with his hands.

'I fear I am unwell,' he said. 'I apologise if I am unable to attend the banquet, in honour of my arrival.'

'We understand completely,' said the Head of the Welcoming Committee.

So there was no banquet. The Distinguished Stranger consulted a specialist who admitted him to a private rest home where he could recover from his disturbed state of mind and the persistence in his ears of the terrible screaming.

The Specialist finished examining the Distinguished Stranger. He washed his hands with a slab of hard soap, took off his white coat, and was preparing to go home to his wife when he thought suddenly, Suppose the screaming does exist?

He dismissed the thought. The Rest Home was full, and the fees were high. He enjoyed the comforts of civilisation. Yet supposing, just supposing that all the patients united against him, that all the people of the city began to acknowledge the terrible screaming? What would be the result? Would there be complete panic? Was there really safety in numbers where ideas were concerned?

He stopped thinking about the terrible screaming. He climbed into his Jaguar and drove home.

The Head of the Welcoming Committee, disappointed that he could not attend another banquet, yet relieved because he would not be forced to justify another item of public expenditure, also went home to his wife. They dined on a boiled egg, bread and butter and a cup of tea, for they both approved of simple living.

Then he went to their bedroom, took off his striped suit, switched out the light, got into bed with his wife, and enjoyed the illusion of making uncomplicated love.

And outside in the city the terrible screaming continued its separate existence, unacknowledged. For you see its name was Silence. Silence had found its voice.

The Mythmaker's Office

'The sun,' they said, 'is unmentionable. You must never refer to it.'

But that ruse did not work. People referred to the sun, wrote poems about it, suffered under it, lying beneath the chariot wheels, and their eyes were pierced by the sapphire needles jabbing in the groove of light. The sun lolled in the sky. The sun twitched like an extra nerve in the mind. And the sunflowers turned their heads, watching the ceremony, like patient ladies at a tennis match.

So that ruse did not work.

But the people in charge persisted, especially the Minister of Mythmaking who sat all day in his empty office beating his head with a gold-mounted stick in order to send up a cloud of ideas from underneath his wall-to-wall carpet of skin. Alas, when the ideas flew up they arrived like motes in other people's eyes and the Minister of Mythmaking as an habitually polite occupier of his ceiling-to-floor glass ministry did not care to remove ideas from the eyes of other people.

Instead, he went outside and threw coloured stones against the Office of Mythmaking.

'What are you doing, my good chap?' the Prime Minister asked, on his way to a conference.

'Playing fictional fives,' the Minister of Mythmaking replied, after searching for an explanation.

'You would be better occupied,' the Prime Minister told him, 'in performing the correct duties of your office.'

Dazed, shoulders drooping with care, the Minister of Mythmaking returned to his office where once again he sat alone, staring at the big empty room and seeing his face four times in the glass walls. Once more he took his gold-mounted stick and, beating his head, he sent up another cloud of ideas which had a stored musty smell for they had been swept under the carpet years ago and had never been removed or disturbed until now. One idea pierced the Minister in the eye.

'Ah,' he said. 'Death. Death is unmentionable. Surely that will please all concerned. Death is obscene, unpublishable. We must ban all reference to it, delete the death notices from the newspapers, make it an indecent offence to be seen congregating at funerals, drive Death underground.

'Yes,' the Minister of Mythmaking said to himself. 'This will surely please the public, the majority, and prove the ultimate value of Democracy. All will cooperate in the denial of Death.' Accordingly he drafted an appropriate bill which passed swiftly with averted eyes through the House of Parliament and joined its forebears in the worm-eaten paper territories in panelled rooms.

Death notices disappeared from the newspapers. Periodical raids were carried out by the police upon undertakers' premises and crematoria to ensure that no indecent activities were in progress. Death became relegated to a Resistance Movement, a Black Market, and furtive shovellings on the outskirts of the city.

For people did not stop dying. Although it was now against the law, obscene, subversive, Death remained an intense part of the lives of every inhabitant of the kingdom. In the pubs and clubs after work the citizens gathered to exchange stories which began, 'Do you know the one about . . . ?' and which were punctuated with whispered references to Death, the Dead, Cemeteries, Mortuaries. Often you could hear smothered laughter and observe expressions of shame and guilt as ribaldry placed its fear-releasing hand simultaneously upon Death and Conscience. At other times arguments broke out, fights began, the police were called in, and the next day people were summoned to court on charges relating to indecent behaviour and language, with the witness for the prosecution exclaiming, 'He openly uttered the word . . . the word . . . well I shall write it upon a piece of paper and show it to the

learned judge. . . .' And when the judge read the words 'Death,' 'the
dead' upon the paper his expression would become severe, he
would pronounce the need for a heavy penalty, citizens must learn
to behave as normal citizens, and not flout the laws of common
decency by referring to Death and the practices of burial. . . .

In books the offending five-letter word was no longer written in
full; letters other than the first and last were replaced by dots or a
dash. When one writer boldly used the word Death several times,
and gave detailed descriptions of the ceremonies attending death
and burial, there followed such an outcry that his publishers were
prosecuted for issuing an indecent work.

But the prosecutors did not win their case, for witnesses
convinced the jury that the references to death and its ceremonies
were of unusual beauty and power, and should be read by all
citizens.

'In the end,' a witness reminded the court, 'each one of us is
involved in dying, and though we are forbidden by law to
acknowledge this, surely it is necessary for us to learn the facts of
death and burial?'

'What!' the public in court said. 'And corrupt the rising
generation!' You should have seen the letters to the paper after the
court's decision was made known!

The book in question sold many millions of copies; its relevant
passages were marked and thumbed; but people placed it on their
bookshelves with its title facing the wall.

Soon, however, the outcry and publicity which attended the case
were forgotten and the city of the kingdom reverted to its former
habits of secrecy. People died in secret, were buried in secret. At one
time there was a wave of righteous public anger (which is a
dangerous form of anger) against the existence of buildings such as
hospitals which in some ways cater to the indecencies of death and
are thus an insult to the pure-minded. So effective had been the
work of the Mythmaker's Office that the presence of a hospital, its
evil suggestiveness, made one close one's eyes in disgust. Many of
the buildings were deliberately burned to the ground, during
occasions of night-long uninhibited feasting and revelry where
people rejoiced, naked, dancing, making love while the Watch
Committee, also naked, but with pencils and notebooks,

maintained their vigilance by recording instances of behaviour
which stated or implied reference to the indecencies of Death.

People found dying in a public place were buried in secrecy and
shame. Furtive obscene songs were sung about road accidents,
immodesties such as influenza, bronchitis, and the gross facts of
the sickroom. Doctors, in spite of their vowed alliance with the
living, became unmentionable evils, and were forced to advertise in
glass cabinets outside tobacconists and night clubs in the seedier
districts of the kingdom.

The avoidance of Death, like the avoidance of all inevitability,
overflowed into the surrounding areas of living, like a river laying
waste the land which it had formerly nourished and made fertile.

The denial of Death became also a denial of life and growth.

'Well,' said the Prime Minister surrounded by last week's
wrapped, sliced, crumbling policies, 'Well,' he said proudly to the
Minister of Mythmaking, "you have accomplished your purpose.
You have done good work. You may either retire on a substantial
pension or take a holiday in the South of France, at the kingdom's
expense. We have abolished Death. We are now immortal. Prepare
the country for thousands of years of green happiness.'

And leaning forward he took a bite of a new policy which had
just been delivered to him. It was warm and doughy, with bubbles
of air inside to give it lightness.

'New policies, eaten quickly, are indigestible,' the Minister of
Mythmaking advised, wishing to be of service before he retired to
the South of France.

The Prime Minister frowned. 'I have remedies,' he said coldly.
Then he smiled. 'Thousands of years of green happiness!'

Yet by the end of that year the whole kingdom except for one
man and one woman had committed suicide. Death, birth, life had
been abolished. People arrived from the moon, rubbing their
hands with glee and sucking lozenges which were laid in rows, in
tins, and dusted with sugar.

In a hollow upon dead grass and dead leaves the one human
couple left alive on earth said, 'Let's make Death.'

And the invalid sun opened in the sky, erupting its contagious
boils of light, pouring down the golden matter upon the waste
places of the earth.

The Daylight and the Dust

The Daylight and the Dust were on holiday together with nowhere
to go.

'I might swoop and bury,' the Dust said.

'I might lie between sheets of morning,' the Daylight said.

But they packed a little gold bag and a little grey bag and went on
tour to blind and smother.

The faithless Daylight betrayed the Dust. The Dust was pursued
by his enemies and driven into exile, and to this day the bones of the
dead may or may not lie uncovered in the city.

The Daylight continued his journey alone with his little gold
bag. He walked up and down the sky, upside down, like a fly, and if
you look in the sky you will see him. His little gold bag is the sun.

The sun is a portmanteau of furnaces, boiling remorse, hot
scones, tourist equipment and change of history.

And still the Dust blows homeless, in exile, in hiding, cowers in
crevices and shaded hollows, on ledges and stone faces, and in
anger tears the privacy from impersonal bones and skulls threaded
like identical beads in the jewel case of the dead.

The Dust is Breath. Is not Breath the true and only refugee?

Solutions

This is a story which belongs in the very room in which I am typing. I am not haunted by it, but I shall tell it to you. It happened once—twice, thrice?—upon a time.

A young man was so bedevilled by the demands of his body that he decided to rid himself of it completely. Now this worry was not a simple matter of occasional annoyance. As soon as the man sat down to work in the morning—he was a private student working all day at this very table with its green plastic cover, drop ends, two protective cork mats—he would be conscious perhaps of an itch in his back which he would be forced to scratch, or he would feel a pain in his arm or shoulder and be unable to rest until he had shaken himself free of the pain which would then drop to the carpet and lie there powerless and be sucked into the vacuum cleaner on a Thursday morning when the woman came to clean the house.

Sometimes as the pain lay upon the carpet the man would engage it in conversation; there would be a lively exchange of bitterness and wit, with the man assuring his pain that he felt no ill-will toward it but he wished that its family would cease inhabiting his body just as he was beginning work for the day. But the pain was cunning. It gave no message to its family which returned again and again, and when it was successfully disposed of by the vacuum cleaner and the County Council Dustmen and transported to a County Council grave, another family of pain took its place.

'I must get rid of my body,' the man thought. 'What use is it to me? It interferes with my work, and since my work is concentrated in my head I think I shall get rid of my body and retain only my head.'

Ah, what freedom then!

There was another difficulty. As soon as the young man wanted to begin his work in the morning, all the feelings which he preferred to inhabit his head to nourish and revive his thoughts, would decide to pack their picnic lunches for the day, and without asking permission, they would set out on the forbidden route to the shady spot between the man's legs where his penis lived in a little house with a red roof, a knocker on the front door, and two gothic columns at the front gate. And there, in the little house in the woods, with the penis as a sometimes thoughtful, sometimes turbulent host, the man's feelings would unwrap their picnic lunch and enjoy a pleasant feast, often sitting outside in the shade of the two gothic columns. And how ardently the sun shone through the trees, through the leaves, in a red haze of burning!

Now you understand that the man became more and more distressed at the way his body demanded so much attention. It had also to be washed, clothed, warmed, cooled, scratched, rubbed, exercised, rested; and should it suffer the slightest harm, pain, like a dragonfly, would alight at the spot with its valise full of instruments of torture which dragonflies used to carry (once, twice, thrice upon a time) when they were the envoys of genuine dragons.

The man grew more and more depressed. He felt himself becoming bankrupt—with his feelings engaged hour after hour in extravagant parties which took no account of the cost, so that bills mounted and could not be paid, and strange authorities intruded to give orders and confuse the situation. And with so little work being done the man did not know where he would find money for rent and food. Sometimes he was so depressed and alone that he wept. His feelings did not seem to care. Whenever he glanced at the little house in the woods he could see at once that all the lights in the house were blazing; he could hear the boisterous singing at night, and witness the riotous carousing during the day under the melting indiarubber sun.

'What shall I do?' the man cried when he woke one morning feeling tired and discouraged. 'Shall I rid myself of my body?'

He decided to rid himself of his body, to keep only his head which, he was convinced, would work faithfully for him once it was set free.

Therefore, the same morning, feeling lighthearted and singing a gay song, the man sharpened his kitchen knife which he had bought at Woolworths for two and eleven and which had grown blunt from much use as a peeler of vegetables, spreader of marmalade on toast, cutter of string on mysterious packages from foreign countries, whittler of wood on pencils; and, unfolding a copy of the *Guardian*, the man laid it on the kitchen floor, leaned forward, applied the knife to his throat, and in a moment his head had been cut off and the blood was seeping through the Editorial, Letters to the Editor, and the centre news page.

The problem which confronted the man's head now was to get rid of the body, and to clean the blood from the kitchen floor. The head had rolled, its face rather pale with the excitement of its new freedom, as far as the fireplace. Now the man knew of three little mice who lived behind the screen which covered the disused fireplace, and who emerged on expeditions during the night and during the day when they supposed that all the people in the house were at work. The three mice had survived many attempts to kill them. One of the lodgers from upstairs had shaken three little heaps of poisoned cereal on a strip of hardboard in front of the fireplace and had waited in vain for any sign that the mice had been tempted. She did not know that the young man had warned them. He had been in the kitchen one evening making himself a cup of tea, and he was just about to take a slice of bread from his wrapped sliced white loaf when he saw one of the mice sniffing at the poisoned cereal.

'I wouldn't eat it, if I were you,' the young man said. 'Appearances are deceptive you know. Even I have to be careful with every slice of my wrapped sliced white loaf.'

'Why are you warning me?' the little mouse asked. 'Don't you want to poison me? I thought everybody wanted to poison little mice like me.'

'Don't touch that heap of cereal,' the young man said melodramatically.

The mouse was formal. 'I am grateful sir,' he said, and disappeared.

But naturally the mice were grateful, following the tradition of all rescued animals in fairy stories, and as the young man had indeed been living in a fairy story of despair he had no difficulty now, when he had freed himself from his body, in asking and receiving help from the three mice. They were willing to dispose of the body and to clean the kitchen until the floor was without a trace of blood. In their turn, the mice asked the help of the dustbin downstairs, and because the dustbin had often acted as a gay restaurateur serving delectable suppers to the three mice, and because he did not wish to lose his reputation—for reputations are valuable property and must be stored in a safe place (the dustbin kept his just inside the rim of his grey tin hat) he agreed to come into the house, climb the stairs, remove the body, help to clean away the mess, and put all the refuse and the information concerning it, beneath his tin hat. And all this he accomplished with swiftness and agility which won praise and applause from the three mice. Also, with a kindly impulse, the dustbin carried the man's head to his room and even gave it lessons in flying, for the dustbin lid was a relative of the flying carpet and knew the secrets of flight, and that was why he had been so agile in climbing the stairs and moving in and out of the kitchen.

How patiently he taught the head to fly! He waited so courteously and sympathetically until the art was mastered, and then bidding the head goodbye returned downstairs (conscious of his new reputation as a hero), out the back door, to his home in the tiny backyard where he lived in the company of a shelf of plant pots and a string bag of clothes pegs which continually quarrelled amongst themselves about who were superior, the plastic clothes pegs or the wooden clothes pegs. These quarrels were all the more bitter because they took place among the older generation of clothes pegs; the younger had forgotten or did not know how to quarrel; they were intermarrying and shared shirt flats on the same clothesline; together they topped the country spaces of blankets, and holidayed near the ski slopes of sheets and pillowcases. . . .

Meanwhile, upstairs, the head was flying rapturously to and fro in the bed-sitting-room, and it continued thus in wild freedom all morning and afternoon.

Once it stopped flying and looked thoughtful. 'Am I a man?' it asked itself.

'Or am I a head? I shall call myself a man, for the most important part of me remains.'

'I'll have one day free,' the man said, 'to think things over, and then I'll start my intellectual work with no dictation or interference ever again from my presumptuous imperious body. Oh I feel as if I could fly to the sky and circle the moon; thoughts race through me, eager to be set down upon paper and studied by those who have never had the insight or strategy to rid themselves of their cumbersome bodies. My act has made my brain supreme. I shall work day and night without interruption. . . .'

And on and on the man flew, round and round the room in his dizzy delight. Once he flew to the window and looked out, but fortunately no one in the street saw him or there might have been inquiries. Then in the evening, to his surprise, he began to feel tired.

'It seems that sleep is necessary after all,' he said. 'But only a wink or two of sleep, and then I daresay I shall wake refreshed.'

So he lay down beneath the top blanket of his bed, closed his eyes, and slept a deep sleep, and when he woke next morning his first thought almost set him shouting with exhilaration,

'How wonderful to be free!'

That morning the landlady remarked to her husband, 'The man in the upstairs room seems to have gone away. I'm sure he did not come home last night. The room is so quiet. His rent is due this morning, and we need the money. I'll give him a few days' grace, and then if we are not paid we shall have to see about finding a new lodger—for this one doesn't seem to do any work really, does he? I mean any real work where you catch the bus in the morning and come home tired at night with your *Evening News* under your arm, and you are too tired to read it.'

Also that morning the woman lodger remarked to the other lodger who lived in the small room upstairs, 'The man who shares the kitchen with us has not used his milk—see it's still in the bottle.

I was curious and peeped in the door this morning (I was only wondering about the milk, it might go sour, in this heat) and his bed is unruffled, it's not been slept in. Perhaps I should tell the landlady. She likes to know what goes on. He seems to have vanished. There's no sign of him.'

'Ah,' the man was saying at that very moment as he flew about the room, 'I don't need to eat now, yet I am full of vigour and excitement. My former despair has vanished. I will start work as soon as I hear the two lodgers and the landlady and landlord bang the front door as they go out on their way to work.'

He heard the two lodgers in the kitchen, washing up their breakfast dishes. He heard the landlady putting her clothes through the spin-drier. He heard the landlord go out and start the car.

Then he heard the front door bang, once, twice, three, four times. The house was quiet at last. The man gave a long sigh of content, and prepared to work.

The house was indeed quiet. In the kitchen the three mice emerged from their hiding place to explore and examine the turn of events, for events are like tiny revolving wheels, and mice like to play with them and bowl them along alleyways of yellow light where dustbins glitter and the hats of dustbins shine with pride in their distant relation, the Magic Carpet. . . .

The three mice pattered around the kitchen, and then curious about their friend who had rid himself of his body, they came— one, two, three—into the man's room where they were surprised to observe, on the green plain of the table, the man resting in an attitude of despair.

'Alas,' he was murmuring. 'Where are my fingers to grasp my pen or tap my typewriter, and my hand to reach books from the shelf? And who will comb my hair and rub the hair tonic into my scalp? Besides, my head itches, there is wax in my ears, I need to keep clearing my throat; how can I blow my nose with dignity? And as for shaving every morning, why, my beard will grow and grow like clematis upon a rotten tree.' Tears trickled from the man's eyes.

The three mice felt very sad. 'We could help you,' they suggested, 'by bringing books to you; but that is all. You need arms, hands, fingers.'

'I need much more,' the man replied. 'Who will listen to my words and love me? And who will want to warm an absent skin or picnic in a deserted house, in darkness, or drink from rivers that have run dry?

'Still,' the man continued, 'my thoughts are free. I have sacrificed these comforts for my thoughts. Yet although I am no longer a slave to my body I am even now subject to irritations. My vanity demands that I rub hair tonic into my scalp to postpone my baldness, for baldness comes early to our family. My need for relief demands that I scratch a spot just above my right ear. My training in hygiene insists that I blow my nose with a square white handkerchief which has my name—MAN—embroidered in one corner! Oh if only I could escape from the petty distractions of my head! Then I would indeed do great work, think noble thoughts. Even my head offends me now. If only I did not possess my head, if I could rid myself of it, if I could just keep my brain and the protective shell enclosing it, then surely I could pursue my work in real freedom!'

Then the idea came to him. Why not ask the mice to fetch the knife from the kitchen (they could carry it easily, one taking the blade, the second the handle, the third acting as guide) and remove all parts of my head except the little walnut which is my brain? It could easily be done. If the mice hurry, the man thought, and set my brain free, no one knows what great work I might accomplish even today before the sun goes down!

So the mice offered to help. They performed the cutting operations and once again the dustbin and the dustbin lid agreed to collect and conceal the remains. Then, when the task was finished the mice laid what was left of the head, upon the table, and silently (for the man could not communicate with them any more) they and the dustbin and the dustbin lid went from the room, the mice to their corner by the fireplace, the dustbin to his place beneath the shelf where the pot plants lived and the older generation of plastic clothes pegs and wooden clothes pegs continued their quarrels in the string bag where they lived.

Blind, speechless, deaf, the man lay upon the table beside his blank writing paper, his books, his typewriter. He did not move. No one could have divined his thoughts; he himself could no longer communicate them.

That night when the lodger returned from work she peered into the room, and seeing no one there, she reported the fact to the landlady who only that afternoon had replied to inquiries for a rented room.

'The man must have flitted,' the landlady said, opening the door and gazing around the room. 'The bed has not been slept in. His luggage is still here. But I think he has flitted because he could not pay his rent. I think he was the type. No regular work. No getting up in the morning to catch the bus and coming home at night with the *Evening News* in his pocket and being too tired to read it.'

Then the landlady gave a slight shiver of anticipation. 'Now I can come into the room and scour it out, wash the curtains, clean the linoleum and the chair covers, redecorate. I'll move the furniture, too, repair the damages he is sure to have done—look, no casters on the chairs, and the spring of that armchair broken, and the cord hanging from the window, and look at the soot on the window sill!'

Then the landlady glanced at the table and noticed the shrivelled remains of the man.

'Just look!' she exclaimed to the lodger. 'An old prune left lying around. Eating prunes no doubt while he worked; or pretended to work. Such habits only encourage the mice. No wonder they haven't been tempted by the poison I left out for them if they have been living on titbits from this man!' And with an expression of disgust the landlady removed the deaf, blind, speechless, wrinkled man, took him downstairs and threw him into the dustbin, and not even the dustbin recognised him, for he could never any more proclaim his identity—Man; nor could he see that he was lying in a dustbin; nor could he feel anything except a roaring, like the sound in an empty shell which houses only the memory of the tide within its walls.

And the next morning when the three mice were up early and down to the dustbin for breakfast, one saw the shrivelled man, and not recognising him, exclaimed, 'A prune! I've never tasted prunes, but I can always try.' And so the three mice shared the prune, spitting out the hard bits.

'It wasn't bad,' they said. 'It will do for breakfast.'

Then they hurried downstairs to hide while the landlady who was not going to work that day prepared the man's empty room for its new tenant, a clean businessman who would work from nine till five and bring inconvenience upon no one, least of all upon himself.

Two Sheep

Two sheep were travelling to the saleyards. The first sheep knew that after they had been sold their destination was the slaughterhouse at the freezing works. The second sheep did not know of their fate. They were being driven with the rest of the flock along a hot dusty valley road where the surrounding hills leaned in a sun-scorched wilderness of rock, tussock and old rabbit warrens. They moved slowly, for the drover in his trap was in no hurry, and had even taken one of the dogs to sit beside him while the other scrambled from side to side of the flock, guiding them.

'I think,' said the first sheep who was aware of their approaching death, 'that the sun has never shone so warm on my fleece, nor, from what I see with my small sheep's eye, has the sky seemed so flawless, without seams or tucks or cracks or blemishes.'

'You are crazy,' said the second sheep who did not know of their approaching death. 'The sun is warm, yes, but how hot and dusty and heavy my wool feels! It is a burden to go trotting along this oven shelf. It seems our journey will never end.'

'How fresh and juicy the grass appears on the hill!' the first sheep exclaimed. 'And not a hawk in the sky!'

'I think,' replied the second sheep, 'that something has blinded you. Just look up in the sky and see those three hawks waiting to swoop and attack us!'

They trotted on further through the valley road. Now and again the second sheep stumbled.

'I feel so tired,' he said. 'I wonder how much longer we must walk on and on through this hot dusty valley?'

But the first sheep walked nimbly and his wool felt light upon him as if he had just been shorn. He could have gambolled like a lamb in August.

'I still think,' he said, 'that today is the most wonderful day I have known. I do not feel that the road is hot and dusty. I do not notice the stones and grit that you complain of. To me the hills have never seemed so green and enticing, the sun has never seemed so warm and comforting. I believe that I could walk through this valley forever, and never feel tired or hungry or thirsty.'

Whatever has come over you?' the second sheep asked crossly. 'Here we are, trotting along hour after hour, and soon we shall stand in our pens in the saleyards while the sun leans over us with its branding irons and our overcoats are such a burden that they drag us to the floor of our pen where we are almost trampled to death by the so dainty feet of our fellow sheep. A fine life that is. It would not surprise me if after we are sold we are taken in trucks to the freezing works and killed in cold blood. But,' he added, comforting himself, 'that is not likely to happen. Oh no, that could never happen! I have it on authority that even when they are trampled by their fellows, sheep do not die. The tales we hear from time to time are but malicious rumours, and those vivid dreams which strike us in the night as we sleep on the sheltered hills, they are but illusions. Do you not agree?' he asked the first sheep.

They were turning now from the valley road, and the saleyards were in sight, while drawn up in the siding on the rusty railway lines, the red trucks stood waiting, spattered inside with sheep and cattle dirt and with white chalk marks, in cipher, on the outside. And still the first sheep did not reveal to his companion that they were being driven to certain death.

When they were jostled inside their pen the first sheep gave an exclamation of delight.

'What a pleasant little house they have let to us! I have never seen such smart red-painted bars, and such four-square corners. And look at the elegant stairway which we will climb to enter those red caravans for our seaside holiday!'

'You make me tired,' the second sheep said. 'We are standing inside a dirty pen, nothing more, and I cannot move my feet in their nicely polished black shoes but I tread upon the dirt left by sheep which have been imprisoned here before us. In fact I have never been so badly treated in all my life!' And the second sheep began to cry. Just then a kind elderly sheep jostled through the flock and began to comfort him.

'You have been frightening your companion, I suppose,' she said angrily to the first sheep. 'You have been telling horrible tales of our fate. Some sheep never know when to keep things to themselves. There was no need to tell your companion the truth, that we are being led to certain death!'

But the first sheep did not answer. He was thinking that the sun had never blessed him with so much warmth, that no crowded pen had ever seemed so comfortable and luxurious. Then suddenly he was taken by surprise and hustled out a little gate and up the ramp into the waiting truck, and suddenly too the sun shone in its true colours, battering him about the head with gigantic burning bars, while the hawks congregated above, sizzling the sky with their wings, and a pall of dust clung to the barren used-up hills, and everywhere was commotion, pushing, struggling, bleating, trampling.

'This must be death,' he thought, and he began to struggle and cry out.

The second sheep, having at last learned that he would meet his fate at the freezing works, stood unperturbed now in the truck with his nose against the wall and his eyes looking through the slits.

'You are right,' he said to the first sheep. 'The hill has never seemed so green, the sun has never been warmer, and this truck with its neat red walls is a mansion where I would happily spend the rest of my days.'

But the first sheep did not answer. He had seen the approach of death. He could hide from it no longer. He had given up the struggle and was lying exhausted in a corner of the truck. And when the truck arrived at its destination, the freezing works, the man whose duty it was to unload the sheep noticed the first lying so still in the corner that he believed it was dead.

'We can't have dead sheep,' he said. 'How can you kill a dead sheep?'

So he heaved the first sheep out of the door of the truck onto the rusty railway line.

'I'll move it away later,' he said to himself. 'Meanwhile here goes with this lot.'

And while he was so busy moving the flock, the first sheep, recovering, sprang up and trotted away along the line, out the gate of the freezing works, up the road, along another road, until he saw a flock being driven before him.

'I will join the flock,' he said. 'No one will notice, and I shall be safe.'

While the drover was not looking, the first sheep hurried in among the flock and was soon trotting along with them until they came to a hot dusty road through a valley where the hills leaned in a sun-scorched wilderness of rock, tussock, and old rabbit warrens.

By now he was feeling very tired. He spoke for the first time to his new companions.

'What a hot dusty road,' he said. 'How uncomfortable the heat is, and the sun seems to be striking me for its own burning purposes.'

The sheep walking beside him looked surprised.

'It is a wonderful day,' he exclaimed. 'The sun is warmer than I have ever known it, the hills glow green with luscious grass, and there is not a hawk in the sky to threaten us!'

'You mean,' the first sheep replied slyly, 'that you are on your way to the saleyards, and then to the freezing works to be killed.'

The other sheep gave a bleat of surprise.

'How did you guess?' he asked.

'Oh,' said the first sheep wisely, 'I know the code. And because I know the code I shall go around in circles all my life, not knowing whether to think that the hills are bare or whether they are green, whether the hawks are scarce or plentiful, whether the sun is friend or foe. For the rest of my life I shall not speak another word. I shall trot along the hot dusty valleys where the hills are both barren and lush with spring grass.

'What shall I do but keep silent?'

And so it happened, and over and over again the first sheep escaped death, and rejoined the flock of sheep who were travelling to the freezing works. He is still alive today. If you notice him in a flock, being driven along a hot dusty road, you will be able to

distinguish him by his timidity, his uncertainty, the frenzied
expression in his eyes when he tries, in his condemned silence, to
discover whether the sky is at last free from hawks, or whether they
circle in twos and threes above him, waiting to kill him.

The Reservoir

It was said to be four or five miles along the gully, past orchards and farms, paddocks filled with cattle, sheep, wheat, gorse, and the squatters of the land who were the rabbits eating like modern sculpture into the hills, though how could we know anything of modern sculpture, we knew nothing but the Warrior in the main street with his wreaths of poppies on Anzac Day, the gnomes weeping in the Gardens because the seagulls perched on their green caps and showed no respect, and how important it was for birds, animals and people, especially children, to show respect!

And that is why for so long we obeyed the command of the grownups and never walked as far as the forbidden Reservoir, but were content to return 'tired but happy' (as we wrote in our school compositions), answering the question, Where did you walk today? with a suspicion of blackmail, 'Oh, nearly, nearly to the Reservoir!'

The Reservoir was the end of the world; beyond it, you fell; beyond it were paddocks of thorns, strange cattle, strange farms, legendary people whom we would never know or recognise even if they walked among us on a Friday night downtown when we went to follow the boys and listen to the Salvation Army Band and buy a milk shake in the milk bar and then return home to find that everything was all right and safe, that our Mother had not run away and caught the night train to the North Island, that our Father had not shot himself with worrying over the bills, but had in fact been downtown himself and had bought the usual Friday night treat, a bag of liquorice allsorts and a bag of chocolate roughs, from Woolworths.

The Reservoir haunted our lives. We never knew one until we came to this town; we had used pump water. But here, in our new house, the water ran from the taps as soon as we turned them on, and if we were careless and left them on, our Father would shout, as if the affair were his personal concern, 'Do you want the Reservoir to run dry?'

That frightened us. What should we do if the Reservoir ran dry? Would we die of thirst like Burke and Wills in the desert?

'The Reservoir,' our Mother said, 'gives pure water, water safe to drink without boiling it.'

The water was in a different class, then, from the creek which flowed through the gully; yet the creek had its source in the Reservoir. Why had it not received the pampering attention of officialdom which strained weed and earth, cockabullies and trout and eels, from our tap water? Surely the Reservoir was not entirely pure?

'Oh no,' they said, when we inquired. We learned that the water from the Reservoir had been 'treated.' We supposed this to mean that during the night men in light-blue uniforms with sacks over their shoulders crept beyond the circle of pine trees which enclosed the Reservoir, and emptied the contents of the sacks into the water, to dissolve dead bodies and prevent the decay of teeth.

Then, at times, there would be news in the paper, discussed by my Mother with the neighbours over the back fence. Children had been drowned in the Reservoir.

'No child,' the neighbour would say, 'ought to be allowed near the Reservoir.'

'I tell mine to keep strictly away,' my Mother would reply.

And for so long we obeyed our Mother's command, on our favourite walks along the gully simply following the untreated cast-off creek which we loved and which flowed day and night in our heads in all its detail—the wild sweet peas, boiled-lolly pink, and the mint growing along the banks; the exact spot in the water where the latest dead sheep could be found, and the stink of its bloated flesh and floating wool, an allowable earthy stink which we accepted with pleasant revulsion and which did not prompt the 'inky-pinky I smell Stinkie' rhyme which referred to offensive human beings only. We knew where the water was shallow and could be paddled in, where forts could be made from the rocks; we knew the frightening deep places where the eels lurked and the weeds were tangled in gruesome shapes; we knew the jumping places, the mossy stones with their dangers, limitations, and advantages; the sparkling places where the sun trickled beside the water, upon the stones; the bogs made by roaming cattle, trapping some of them to death; their gaunt telltale bones; the little valleys with their new growth of lush grass where the creek had 'changed its course', and no longer flowed.

'The creek has changed its course,' our Mother would say, in a tone which implied terror and a sense of strangeness, as if a tragedy had been enacted.

We knew the moods of the creek, its levels of low-flow, half-high-flow, high-flow which all seemed to relate to interference at its source—the Reservoir. If one morning the water turned the colour of clay and crowds of bubbles were passengers on every suddenly swift wave hurrying by, we would look at one another and remark with the fatality and reverence which attends a visitation or prophecy,

'The creek's going on high-flow. They must be doing something at the Reservoir.'

By afternoon the creek would be on high-flow, turbulent, muddy, unable to be jumped across or paddled in or fished in, concealing beneath a swelling fluid darkness whatever evil which 'they', the authorities, had decided to purge so swiftly and secretly from the Reservoir.

For so long, then, we obeyed our parents, and never walked as far as the Reservoir. Other things concerned us, other curiosities, fears, challenges. The school year ended. I got a prize, a large yellow book the colour of cat's mess. Inside it were editions of newspapers, *The Worms' Weekly*, supposedly written by worms, snails, spiders. For the first part of the holidays we spent the time sitting in the long grass of our front lawn nibbling the stalks of shamrock and reading insect newspapers and relating their items to the lives of those living on our front lawn down among the summer-dry roots of the couch, tinkertailor, daisy, dandelion, shamrock, clover, and ordinary 'grass'. High summer came. The blowsy old red roses shed their petals to the regretful refrain uttered by our Mother year after year at the same time, 'I should have made potpourri, I have a wonderful recipe for potpourri in Dr Chase's Book.'

Our Mother never made the potpourri. She merely quarrelled with our Father over how to pronounce it.

The days became unbearably long and hot. Our Christmas presents were broken or too boring to care about. Celluloid dolls had loose arms and legs and rifts in their bright pink bodies; the invisible ink had poured itself out in secret messages; diaries frustrating in their smallness (two lines to a day) had been filled in for the whole of the coming year.... Days at the beach were tedious, with no room in the bathing sheds so that we were forced to undress in the common room downstairs with its floor patched with wet and trailed with footmarks and sand and its tiny barred window (which made me believe that I was living in the French Revolution).

Rumours circled the burning world. The sea was drying up, soon you could paddle or walk to Australia. Sharks had been seen swimming inside the breakwater; one shark attacked a little boy and bit off his you-know-what.

We swam. We wore bathing togs all day. We gave up cowboys and ranches; and baseball and sledding; and 'those games' where we mimicked grownup life, loving and divorcing each other, kissing and slapping, taking secret paramours when our husband was working out of town. Everything exhausted us. Cracks appeared in the earth; the grass was bled yellow; the ground was littered with beetle shells and snail shells; flies came in from the unofficial rubbish-dump at the back of the house; the twisting flypapers hung from the ceiling; a frantic buzzing filled the room as the flypapers became crowded. Even the cat put out her tiny tongue, panting in the heat.

We realised, and were glad, that school would soon reopen. What was school like? It seemed so long ago, it seemed as if we had never been to school, surely we had forgotten everything we had learned, how frightening, thrilling and strange it would all seem!

Where would we go on the first day, who would teach us, what were the names on the new books?

Who would sit beside us, who would be our best friend?

The earth crackled in early-autumn haze and still the February sun dried the world; even at night the rusty sheet of roofing-iron outside by the cellar stayed warm, but with rows of sweat-marks on it; the days were still long, with night face to face with morning and almost nothing in-between but a snatch of turning sleep with the blankets on the floor and the windows wide open to moths with their bulging lamplit eyes moving through the dark and their grandfather bodies knocking, knocking upon the walls.

Day after day the sun still waited to pounce. We were tired, our skin itched, our sunburn had peeled and peeled again, the skin on our feet was hard, there was dust in our hair, our bodies clung with the salt of sea-bathing and sweat, the towels were harsh with salt.

School soon, we said again, and were glad; for lessons gave shade to rooms and corridors; cloakrooms were cold and sunless. Then, swiftly, suddenly, disease came to the town. Infantile Paralysis. Black headlines in the paper, listing the number of cases, the number of deaths. Children everywhere, out in the country, up north, down south, two streets away.

The schools did not reopen. Our lessons came by post, in smudged print on rough white paper; they seemed makeshift and false, they inspired distrust, they could not compete with the lure of the sun still shining, swelling, the world would go up in cinders, the days were too long, there was nothing to do, there was nothing to do; the lessons were dull; in the front room with the navy-blue blind half down the window and the tiny splits of light showing through, and the lesson papers sometimes covered with unexplained blots of ink as if the machine which had printed them had broken down or rebelled, the lessons were even more dull.

Ancient Egypt and the flooding of the Nile!

The Nile, when we possessed a creek of our own with individual flooding!

'Well let's go along the gully, along by the creek,' we would say, tired with all these.

Then one day when our restlessness was at its height, when the flies buzzed like bees in the flypapers, and the warped wood of the house cracked its knuckles out of boredom, the need for something to do in the heat, we found once again the only solution to our unrest.

Someone said, 'What's the creek on?'

'Half-high flow.'

'Good.'

So we set out, in our bathing suits, and carrying switches of willow.

'Keep your sun hats on!' our mother called.

All right. We knew. Sunstroke when the sun clipped you over the back of the head, striking you flat on the ground. Sunstroke. Lightning. Even tidal waves were threatening us on this southern coast. The world was full of alarm.

'And don't go as far as the Reservoir!'

We dismissed the warning. There was enough to occupy us along the gully without our visiting the Reservoir. First, the couples. We liked to find a courting couple and follow them and when, as we knew they must do because they were tired or for other reasons, they found a place in the grass and lay down together, we liked to make jokes about them, amongst ourselves. 'Just wait for him to kiss her,' we would say. 'Watch. There. A beaut. Smack.'

Often we giggled and lingered even after the couple had observed us. We were waiting for them to do it. Every man and woman did it, we knew that for a fact. We speculated about technical details. Would he wear a frenchie? If he didn't wear a frenchie then she would start having a baby and be forced to get rid of it by drinking gin. Frenchies, by the way, were for sale in Woolworths. Some said they were fingerstalls, but we knew they were frenchies and sometimes we would go downtown and into Woolworths just to look at the frenchies for sale. We hung around the counter, sniggering. Sometimes we nearly died laughing, it was so funny.

After we tired of spying on the couples we would shout after them as we went our way.

> *Pound, shillings and pence,*
> *a man fell over the fence,*
> *he fell on a lady,*
> *and squashed out a baby,*
> *pound, shillings and pence!*

Sometimes a slight fear struck us—what if a man fell on us like that and squashed out a chain of babies?

Our other pastime along the gully was robbing the orchards, but this summer day the apples were small green hard and hidden by leaves. There were no couples either. We had the gully to ourselves. We followed the creek, whacking our sticks, gossiping and singing, but we stopped, immediately silent, when someone— sister or brother—said, 'Let's go to the Reservoir!'

A feeling of dread seized us. We knew, as surely as we knew our names and our address Thirty-three Stour Street Ohau Otago South Island New Zealand Southern Hemisphere The World, that we would some day visit the Reservoir, but the time seemed almost as far away as leaving school, getting a job, marrying.

And then there was the agony of deciding the right time—how did one decide these things?

'We've been told not to, you know,' one of us said timidly.

That was me. Eating bread and syrup for tea had made my hair red, my skin too, so that I blushed easily, and the grownups guessed if I told a lie.

'It's a long way,' said my little sister.

'Coward!'

But it *was* a long way, and perhaps it would take all day and night, perhaps we would have to sleep there among the pine trees with the owls hooting and the old needle-filled warrens which now reached to the centre of the earth where pools of molten lead bubbled, waiting to seize us if we tripped and then there was the crying sound made by the trees, a sound of speech at its loneliest level where the meaning is felt but never explained, and it goes on and on in a kind of despair, trying to reach a point of understanding.

We knew that pine trees spoke in this way. We were lonely listening to them because we knew we could never help them to say it, whatever they were trying to say, for if the wind who was so close to them could not help them, how could we?

Oh no, we could not spend the night at the Reservoir among the pine trees.

'Billy Whittaker and his gang have been to the Reservoir, Billy Whittaker and the Green Feather gang, one afternoon.'

'Did he say what it was like?'

'No, he never said.'

'He's been in an iron lung.'

That was true. Only a day or two ago our Mother had been reminding us in an ominous voice of the fact which roused our envy just as much as our dread, 'Billy Whittaker was in an iron lung two years ago. Infantile paralysis.'

Some people were lucky. None of us dared to hope that we would ever be surrounded by the glamour of an iron lung; we would have to be content all our lives with paltry flesh lungs.

'Well are we going to the Reservoir or not?'

That was someone trying to sound bossy like our Father, 'Well am I to have salmon sandwiches or not, am I to have lunch at all today or not?'

We struck our sticks in the air. They made a whistling sound. They were supple and young. We had tried to make musical instruments out of them, time after time we hacked at the willow and the elder to make pipes to blow our music, but no sound came but our own voices. And why did two sticks rubbed together not make fire? Why couldn't we ever *make* anything out of the bits of the world lying about us?

An airplane passed in the sky. We craned our necks to read the writing on the underwing, for we collected airplane numbers.

The plane was gone, in a glint of sun.

'Are we?' someone said.

'If there's an eclipse you can't see at all. The birds stop singing and go to bed.'

'Well are we?'

Certainly we were. We had not quelled all our misgiving, but we set out to follow the creek to the Reservoir.

What is it? I wondered. They said it was a lake. I thought it was a bundle of darkness and great wheels which peeled and sliced you like an apple and drew you toward them with demonic force, in the same way that you were drawn beneath the wheels of a train if you stood too near the edge of the platform. That was the terrible danger when the Limited came rushing in and you had to approach to kiss arriving aunts.

We walked on and on, past wild sweet peas, clumps of cutty

grass, horse mushrooms, ragwort, gorse, cabbage trees; and then, at
the end of the gully, we came to strange territory, fences we did not
know, with the barbed wire tearing at our skin and at our skirts put
on over our bathing suits because we felt cold though the sun
stayed in the sky.

We passed huge trees that lived with their heads in the sky, with
their great arms and joints creaking with age and the burden of
being trees, and their mazed and linked roots rubbed bare of earth,
like bones with the flesh cleaned from them. There were strange
gates to be opened or climbed over, new directions to be argued and
plotted, notices which said TRESPASSERS WILL BE PROSECUTED BY
ORDER. And there was the remote immovable sun shedding
without gentleness its influence of burning upon us and upon the
town, looking down from its heavens and considering our
infantile-paralysis epidemic, and the children tired of holidays and
wanting to go back to school with the new stiff books with their
crackling pages, the scrubbed ruler with the sun rising on one side
amidst the twelfths, tenths, millimetres, the new pencils to be
sharpened with the pencil shavings flying in long pickets and
light-brown curls scalloped with red or blue; the brown school, the
bare floors, the clump clump in the corridors on wet days!

We came to a strange paddock, a bull-paddock with its occupant
planted deep in the long grass, near the gate, a jersey bull polished
like a wardrobe, burnished like copper, heavy beams creaking in
the wave and flow of the grass.

'Has it got a ring through its nose? Is it a real bull or a steer?'

Its nose was ringed which meant that its savagery was tamed, or
so we thought; it could be tethered and led; even so, it had once
been savage and it kept its pride, unlike the steers who pranced and
huddled together and ran like water through the paddocks, made
no impression, quarried no massive shape against the sky.

The bull stood alone.

Had not Mr Bennet been gored by a bull, his own tame bull, and
been rushed to Glenham Hospital for thirty-three stitches?
Remembering Mr Bennet we crept cautiously close to the paddock
fence, ready to escape.

Someone said, 'Look, it's pawing the ground!'

A bull which pawed the ground was preparing for a charge. We escaped quickly through the fence. Then, plucking courage, we skirted the bushes on the far side of the paddock, climbed through the fence, and continued our walk to the Reservoir.

We had lost the creek between deep banks. We saw it now before us, and hailed it with more relief than we felt, for in its hidden course through the bull-paddock it had undergone change, it had adopted the shape, depth, mood of foreign water, foaming in a way we did not recognise as belonging to our special creek, giving no hint of its depth. It seemed to flow close to its concealed bed, not wishing any more to communicate with us. We realised with dismay that we had suddenly lost possession of our creek. Who had taken it? Why did it not belong to us any more? We hit our sticks in the air and forgot our dismay. We grew cheerful.

Till someone said that it was getting late, and we reminded one another that during the day the sun doesn't seem to move, it just remains pinned with a drawing pin against the sky, and then, while you are not looking, it suddenly slides down quick as the chopped-off head of a golden eel, into the sea, making everything in the world go dark.

'That's only in the tropics!'

We were not in the tropics. The divisions of the world in the atlas, the different coloured cubicles of latitude and longitude fascinated us.

'The sand freezes in the desert at night. Ladies wear bits of sand. . . .'

'grains . . .'

'grains or bits of sand as necklaces, and the camels . . .'

'with necks like snails . . .'

'with horns, do they have horns?'

'Minnie Stocks goes with boys . . .'

'I know who your boy is, I know who your boy is. . . .'

> *Waiting by the garden gate,*
> *Waiting by the garden gate . . .*

'We'll never get to the Reservoir!'

'Whose idea was it?'

'I've strained my ankle!'

Someone began to cry. We stopped walking.

'I've strained my ankle!'

There was an argument.

'It's not strained, it's sprained.'

'strained.'

'sprained.'

'All right sprained then. I'll have to wear a bandage, I'll have to walk on crutches . . . .'

'I had crutches once. Look. I've got a scar where I fell off my stilts. It's a white scar, like a centipede. It's on my shins.'

'Shins! Isn't it a funny word? Shins. Have you ever been kicked in the shins?'

'shins, funnybone . . .'

'It's humerus . . .'

'knuckles . . .'

'a sprained ankle . . .'

'a strained ankle . . .'

'a whitlow, an ingrown toenail the roots of my hair warts spinal meningitis infantile paralysis . . .'

'Infantile paralysis, Infantile paralysis you have to be wheeled in a chair and wear irons on your legs and your knees knock together. . . .'

'Once you're in an iron lung you can't get out, they lock it, like a cage . . . .'

'You go in the amberlance . . .'

'*ambulance* . . .'

'amberlance . . .'

'ambulance to the hostible . . .'

'the *hospital*, an *amberlance to the hospital* . . .'

'Infantile Paralysis . . .'

'Friar's Balsam! Friar's Balsam!'

'Baxter's Lung Preserver, Baxter's Lung Preserver!'

'Syrup of Figs, California Syrup of Figs!'

'The creek's going on high-flow!'

Yes, there were bubbles on the surface, and the water was turning muddy. Our doubts were dispelled. It was the same old creek, and there, suddenly, just ahead, was a plantation of pine trees, and already the sighing sound of it reached our ears and troubled us. We approached it, staying close to the banks of our newly claimed creek, until once again the creek deserted us, flowing its own

private course where we could not follow, and we found ourselves
among the pine trees, a narrow strip of them, and beyond lay a vast
surface of sparkling water, dazzling our eyes, its centre chopped by
tiny grey waves. Not a lake, nor a river, nor a sea.

'The Reservoir!'

The damp smell of the pine needles caught in our breath. There
were no birds, only the constant sighing of the trees. We could see
the water clearly now; it lay, except for the waves beyond the shore,
in an almost perfect calm which we knew to be deceptive—else why
were people so afraid of the Reservoir? The fringe of young pines
on the edge, like toy trees, subjected to the wind, sighed and told us
their sad secrets. In the Reservoir there was an appearance of
neatness which concealed a disarray too frightening to be
acknowledged except, without any defence, in moments of deep
sleep and dreaming. The little sparkling innocent waves shone
now green, now grey, petticoats, lettuce leaves; the trees sighed,
and told us to be quiet, hush-sh, as if something were sleeping and
should not be disturbed—perhaps that was what the trees were
always telling us, to hush-sh in case we disturbed something which
must never ever be awakened?

What was it? Was it sleeping in the Reservoir? Was that why
people were afraid of the Reservoir?

Well we were not afraid of it, oh no, it was only the Reservoir, it
was nothing to be afraid of, it was just a flat Reservoir with a fence
around it, and trees, and on the far side a little house (with wheels
inside?) and nothing to be afraid of.

'The Reservoir, The Reservoir!'

A noticeboard said DANGER, RESERVOIR.

Overcome with sudden glee we climbed through the fence and
swung on the lower branches of the trees, shouting at intervals,
gazing possessively and delightedly at the sheet of water with its
wonderful calm and menace,

'The Reservoir! The Reservoir! The Reservoir!'

We quarrelled again about how to pronounce and spell the
word.

Then it seemed to be getting dark—or was it that the trees were
stealing the sunlight and keeping it above their heads? One of us
began to run. We all ran, suddenly, wildly, not caring about our

strained or sprained ankles, through the trees out into the sun where the creek, but it was our creek no longer, waited for us. We wished it were our creek, how we wished it were our creek! We had lost all account of time. Was it nearly night? Would darkness overtake us, would we have to sleep on the banks of the creek that did not belong to us any more, among the wild sweet peas and the tussocks and the dead sheep? And would the eels come up out of the creek, as people said they did, and on their travels through the paddocks would they change into people who would threaten us and bar our way, TRESPASSERS WILL BE PROSECUTED, standing arm in arm in their black glossy coats, swaying, their mouths open, ready to swallow us? Would they ever let us go home, past the orchards, along the gully? Perhaps they would give us Infantile Paralysis, perhaps we would never be able to walk home, and no one would know where we were, to bring us an iron lung with its own special key!

We arrived home, panting and scratched. How strange! The sun was still in the same place in the sky!

The question troubled us, 'Should we tell?'

The answer was decided for us. Our Mother greeted us as we went in the door with, 'You haven't been long away, kiddies. Where have you been? I hope you didn't go anywhere near the Reservoir.'

Our Father looked up from reading his newspapers.

'Don't let me catch you going near the Reservoir!'

We said nothing. How out-of-date they were! They were actually afraid!

A Sense of Proportion

The sun's hair stood on end. The sky accommodated all visiting darkness and light. Leaves were glossy green, gold, brown, dried, dead and bleached in drifts beneath the trees. Snow fell in all seasons, white hyphens dropping evenly, linking syllables of sky and earth. Flowers bloomed forever, spinning their petal-spokes like golden wheels, sucking the sun like whirlpools. Black-polished, brick-dusted, spotted ladybirds big as airplanes with pleated wings like sky-wide curtains parting, flew home to flame and cinders.

Houses had painted roofs of red and yellow with tall chimneys emitting scribbles of pale blue smoke. All houses had gardens around them, paths with parallel sides enclosing pebbles; gates were five-barred, with children swinging from them. The children wore red stockings. They had ribbons tied in their hair. Their eyes were round and blue, their eyebrows were arched, their lips were rosy. Their hands displayed five fingers for all to see, their feet pointed the same way, left or right, in gaudy shoes with high heels. The ocean was filled with sailing boats, the sky was filled with rainbows, suns, scalloped clouds.

Coats had many buttons, intricate collars with lace edges. The bricks of houses were carefully outlined. Front doors had four panels and a knocker in its exact position.

Winds were visible, fat men or witches with puffed cheeks in the four corners of the sky. The trees leaned with their skirts up over their heads.

The streets were full of painted rubber balls divided carefully into bright colours.

Men wore hats placed firmly upon their heads.

Dogs walked, their tails like masts in the air.

Cats had mile-long whiskers like rays of the sun. They sat, their tails curled about them, containing them. Their ears were pricked, forever listening.

The moon, like the sun, had a face, a smile, eyes, teeth. The moon journeyed on a cloud convoyed by elaborately five-pointed stars.

There was no distance or shade in our infant drawing. Everything loomed close to the eye; rainbows in the heavens could be clutched as securely as the few blades of bright green grass (the colour of strong lemonade) growing symmetrically in the lower right-hand corner of the picture.

Some years passed during which we learned to draw and paint from a small tin of Reeve's Water Colours: Chinese White, Gamboge Tint, Indigo, Yellow Ochre (which I pronounced and believed to be *Yellow Ogre*), Burnt Sienna: the names gave excitement, pain, wonder. We were shown how to paint a sunset in the exact gradations of colour, to make blue water-colour sky, a scientific rainbow (Read Over Your Greek Book In Verse) receding into the distance. The teacher placed an apple and a pear in a glass bowl upon the table. We drew them, making careful shading, painstakingly colouring the autumn tints of the apple.

We did not paint the worm inside it.

We drew vases of flowers, autumn scenes, furniture which existed merely to cast a perfect shadow to be portrayed by a B.B. pencil. The Art lessons were long and tedious. I could never get my shadow or my distance correct. My rainbows and paths would not recede, and my furniture, my boats at anchor, my buildings stood flat upon the page, all in a total clamour of foreground.

'You must draw things,' said Miss Collins the Art Teacher, 'as they seem. Notice the way the path narrows as it approaches the foothills.'

'But it is the same breadth all the way!'

'No,' Miss Collins insisted. 'You must learn to draw these tricks of the eye. You must learn to think in terms of them.'

I never learned to draw tricks of the eye. My paint refused to wash in the correct proportion when I was trying to fill the paper sky with sunrises, sunsets, and rainbows. My garden spades were without strength or shape; their shadows stayed unowned, apart, incredible, more like stray tatters shed from a profusion of dark remnants of objects. My vases had no depth, and their flowers withered in their laborious journey from the table to the page of my scholastic Drawing Book Number Three.

The classroom was dusty and hot and there was the soft buzz of talking, and people walking to and fro getting fresh water and washing brushes; and Miss Collins touring the aisles, giving gentle but insistent advice about colours and shadows. Her hair was in plaits, wound close to her head. In moments of calm or boredom the fact or fancy rippled about the classroom, lapping at our curiosity, Miss Collins wears a wig. Once, long ago, in the days of the Spartans and Athenians, someone had observed Miss Collins in the act of removing her wig.

'She is quite bald,' the rumour went.

Like so many of the other teachers Miss Collins lived with her mother in a little house, a woven spider's nest with the leaves and rain closing in, just at the edge of town. She cherished a reputation as a local painter and at most exhibitions you could see her poplar trees, tussock scenes, mountains, lakes, all in faded colours, with sometimes in the corner, or looking out of the window of a decayed farmhouse, the tiny fierce black lines that were the shape of people.

Every term she gave us examinations which were days of flurry and anxiety when we filed into the Art Room and took our places at the bare desks and gazed with respectful awe at the incongruous display on the table—fruit, a vase of flowers, perhaps a kettle or similar utensil whose shape would strain our ability to 'match sides'. And for the next forty minutes our attention would be fixed upon the clutter of objects, the submissive Still Life which yet huddled powerfully before us, preying upon us with its overlapping corners and sides and deceptive shadows.

How I envied Leila Smith! Leila Smith could draw perfect kettles, rainbows, cupboards. Her pictures always showed the exact number of strokes of rain, when rain fell, and snowflakes when the scene required them. By instinct Leila Smith *knew*. On those days when the gods attended the classroom, penetrating the dust-layered windows hung with knotted cords so complicated that a special Window Monitor was needed to operate them, and the window sills ranged with dead flowers and beans in water—when the gods walked up and down the aisles at our Art Examination they showed extra care for Leila Smith, they guided her hand across the page. When they passed my desk, alas, they vindictively jogged my elbow. Miss Collins despaired of ever teaching me.

'How's your drawing?' my Father would say, who had spent the winter evenings painting in oils from a tiny cigarette card the ship that carried him to the First World War. His sisters painted as well; their work hung in the passage—roses, dogs, clouded ladies, and one storm at sea.

'I can't draw,' I said. 'I can't paint.'

Miss Collins readily agreed with me. 'Your perspective and proportion are well below average. Your shading is poor.'

The obsession with shading fascinated me. All things, even kettles and fire shovels, stood under the sun complete and unique with their shadows, fighting to preserve them. It was an act of charity for us to draw the shadow with as much love (frustration, despair) as we gave to drawing the shape itself. In the world of Miss Collins, morning and evening were perpetual, with the shadows spread beautifully alongside each object, their contours matching perfectly, a mirror image of the body. Why was it that in my world the sun stood everlastingly at noon; objects were stripped of their shadows, forced to stand in brilliant light, alone?

In the end Miss Collins gave up trying to teach me to draw and paint. She spent her time giving hints to Leila Smith. Oh how wonderful were Leila's flowers and fire shovels, garden spades and kettles!

Sometimes Miss Collins would ask us to paint things 'out of our head.'

It showed, she said, whether we had any imagination.

I had no imagination. My poverty could not even provide shadows or proportionate rainbows. The paths in my head stayed the same width right to the foothills and over the mountains which were no obstacles to vision, as mountains are agreed to be; they were transparent mountains, and there was the path, the same width as before, annihilating distance, at last disappearing only at the boundary of the picture.

Distance did not cloud the outline of objects; trees were not blurred; you could count the leaves upon the trees, even on the slopes of the mountain you could count the pine needles hanging in their green brushes.

Yes, it was true; I had no sense of proportion.

When I last saw Miss Collins she had been taken to the hospital after a stroke, and was lying quietly in the hospital bed. She was dying. The torment of the unshaded world lay before her, the sun in her sky stood resolutely at noon, her life was out of proportion, there was no distance, the foreground blazed with looming and light.

She closed her eyes and died.

Her life, in its spider's web, had absorbed her. She had been aided, comforted, made less lonely, by acknowledging and yielding to a trick of the eye. How does one learn to accept that trick and its blessings before it is too late, before the shadows are razed and the sun stands pitiless at perpetual noon?

The Bull Calf

'Why do I always have to milk the cows?' Olive said. 'Couldn't the others do it for a change?' But no, it is always me. Up early and over the hills to find Scrapers. At night home from school and over the hills again to find Scrapers, to bring her down across the creek (here it is difficult; I tie a rope over her horns and make my leap first; she follows, if she is willing) through the gate that hangs on one hinge, into the cow byre with its cracked concrete floor. Pinning her in the bail. Putting on the leg rope. Day after day rain shine or snow.

'I'm tired of milking the cows,' Olive said. 'Beauty, Pansy, and now Scrapers who is bony like bare rafters and scaffolding. One day I will refuse.'

Sometimes she did refuse, in the early morning with sleep gumming her eyes, her body sticky with night, her hair tangled.

'Milk your own cows!' she cried then, retreating to the bedroom and sitting obstinately on the bed, chanting rhymes and French verbs which her Mother could not understand because she had left school at sixteen to go to service. . . .

But the thought of Scrapers waiting haunted Olive, and soon she would get up from the bed, clatter to the scullery, bumping furniture on the way to show her resentment of everything in the world including corners and walls and doors, take the bucket with a swill of warm water in the bottom for washing the teats, and climb the hill in search of Scrapers who, if her bag was full, would be waiting mercifully not far away.

Olive went to High School. In the morning she worried about being late. And every morning when the teacher called suddenly, 'Form Twos, Form Twos,' Olive worried in case no one formed twos with her. Very often she found herself standing alone. Is it because I stink? she thought. Then she would press the back and front of her uniform, down below, to smooth away the bulge of the homemade sanitary towel, layers of torn sheet sewn together with the blood always leaking through. The other girls used bought towels which were safe and came in packets with tiny blue-edged notices inside the packet, WEAR BLUE LINE AWAY FROM THE BODY. The other girls did not seem to mind when in Drill, which was later called Physical Education to keep up with the times, the teacher would command sharply, 'Uniforms Off, Come on Everybody, Uniforms Off!' Why should they mind when they were using towels which did not show, or even the new type where the advertisement had a picture of a woman in a bathing suit, shouting with rapture from the edge of a high-diving board, 'No Belts, No Pins, No Pads!' But on the days when Olive wore her homemade towel she would ask, blushing, 'Please can I keep my uniform on?'

'Oh,' Miss Copeland said. 'Yes.'

And Olive and one or two other girls with their uniforms on would huddle miserably on the end seat, by the bar stools, out of everybody's way.

Olive and her sisters had hickies on their chins and foreheads. The advertisements warned them never to wear 'off-the-face' hats. Whole pages of the newspapers were devoted to the picture-story of the disasters which befell Lorna, Mary or Marion who continued to wear off-the-face hats in spite of having hickies on their chins and foreheads. Lorna, Mary, Marion were lonely and unwanted until they used Velona Ointment. Olive and her sisters used Velona Ointment. It had a smell like the oil of a motorcar engine and it came off in a sticky grass-green stain on the pillowcase.

But mostly Olive was tired. She stayed up late working on mathematical problems, writing French translations and essays, and in the morning she was up so early to go over the hill and find Scrapers. There were so many trees and hollows on the hill, and often it was in these hollows where the grass was juiciest, nourished by the pools of yesterday's rain or the secret underground streams, that Scrapers would be hiding. Sometimes Olive had to walk to the last Reserve before she found Scrapers. Then there was the problem of tying the rope across her horns and leading her home.

Sometimes Scrapers refused to cooperate. Olive would find her dancing up and down, tossing her horns and bellowing.

'Scrapers, Scrapers, come on, be a good cow!'

Still Scrapers refused, Olive could not understand why. I'll be late for school, she thought, after struggling with and trying to chase the entranced cow. But it was no use. Olive would hurry down the hill, across the creek, through the broken-hinged gate and up the path to the house where the family, waiting for breakfast, would ask, 'Where's the milk?' while Olive in turn confronted them with her question, 'What's the matter with Scrapers? She's dancing and tossing her horns and refusing to be milked.'

Her Mother received the news calmly. 'Leave the cow. She'll be all right in a few days.'

Nobody explained. Olive could not understand. She would pour stale milk on her Weet-Bix, finish her breakfast, brush the mud from her shoes, persuade the pleats into her uniform, and hurry away to school.

It was always the same. She stood alone in Assembly, concealing herself behind the girl in front who was taller, Captain of the 'A' Basketball Team, Holder of a Drill Shield. Olive did not want the teachers on the platform to see her standing alone, hiding behind the girl in front of her.

> *Peace perfect peace in this dark world of sin*
> *the cross of Jesus whispers Peace within*

she sang, sensing the mystery. Her heart felt heavy and lonely.

When she climbed the hill in search of the cow she always stopped in the paddock next door to pat the neighbour's bull calf which was growing plumper and stronger every day. Everyone knew what happened to bull calves. They were taken to the slaughterhouse while they were still young, or they became steers journeying from saleyard to saleyard until they grew old and tough and despised, without the pride and ferocity of bulls and the gentleness and patience of cows. If you were caught in a paddock with them and they attacked you it was in bursts of irritation which left them standing as if bewildered, half-afraid at their own daring. They did not seem able to decide; they panicked readily; they had no home, they were forever lost in strange surroundings, closed in by new fences and gates with unfamiliar smells, trees, earth; with dogs snapping at their heels, herding them this way and that, in and out, up and down. . . .

Olive knew that one day Ormandy's bull calf would be a steer. 'Calfie, calfie,' she would whisper, putting her flattened palm inside the calf's mouth and letting it suck.

Night came. The spotted grey cockabullies in the creek wriggled under the stones to sleep, and soon the birds were hushed in the willow trees and the hedge and the sighing pines. This evening Olive was late in fetching Scrapers. She was late and tired. Her best black stockings, cobbled at the back of the leg, were splashed with mud, there were no clean ones for tomorrow; her stockings never lasted, all the other girls bought their stockings at Morton's, and theirs were cashmere, with a purple rim around the top, a sign of quality, while Olive's were made of coarse rayon. She was ashamed of them, she was ashamed of everything and everyone. She kicked her shoes against a clump of grass. Toe and heel plates! Why must she always have toe and heel plates on her shoes? Why must they always be lace-ups? She yawned. Her skin felt itchy. The pressure of her tight uniform upon her breasts was uncomfortable. Why hadn't Auntie Polly realised, and made the seams deeper, to be let out when necessary? Olive's sisters wore uniforms made by real dressmakers. Her sisters were lucky. How they teased her, pointing to the pictures in the *True Confession* magazines, digging their elbows slyly at each other and murmuring, 'Marylin's breasts were heavy and pendulous.'

'That means you,' they said to Olive. 'You'll be like Mum with two full moons bobbing up and down, moons and balloons and motor tyres.'

Yes, her sisters were lucky.

'Why don't they help with the cow?' Olive asked. 'Why don't they milk the cow for a change?'

She walked slowly up the hill, keeping to the path worn by herself and Scrapers; it was rucked with dry, muddy hoofprints and followed along the edge of the pine plantation. When she reached the top of the hill and there was still no sign of Scrapers she went to the fence bordering the native plant reserve and looked out over the town and the sea and the spilled dregs of light draining beyond the horizon. The silver-bellied sea turned and heaved in the slowly brightening moon-track, and the red and green roofs of the town were brushed with rising mist and moon. She identified objects and places: the Town Clock; the main street; the houseboat down at the wharf; the High School, and just behind the trees at the corner, next to the bicycle sheds, the little shop that sold hot mince pies and fish and chips at lunchtime. Then she gazed once more at the sea, waiting for the Sea-Foam-Youth-Grown-Old to appear. It was her secret dream. She knew he would never reach her. She knew that his bright glistening body became old, shrivelled, yellow, as soon as he touched the sand; it was the penalty. She sighed. The grieving hush-hush of the trees disturbed her. Their heads were bowed, banded with night. The wind moved among them, sighing, only increasing their sorrow. It came to her, too, with its moaning that she could not understand; it filled the world with its loneliness and darkness.

Olive sighed again. What was the use of waiting for the Sea-Foam-Youth-Grown-Old? What was the use of anything? Would the trees never stop saying Why, Why?

She was Olive Blakely going to milk Scrapers. She was Olive Blakely standing on the hill alone at night. The cutty grass and the tinkertailor were brushing against her black stockings; there was bird dirt on the fence post; the barbed wire had snapped and sagged.

That evening she milked Scrapers on the hill. What a miracle! The cow stood motionless for her and did not give those sudden sly kicks which she practised from time to time. Scrapers was an expert at putting her foot in the bucket.

Olive patted the velvety flank. Scrapers was standing so calmly. Why was she so calm when a few days ago she had danced, tossed, bellowed, jumping fences and running with her tail high in the air? Now she stood peacefully chewing, seeming to count the chews before each swallow, introducing a slight syncopation before returning the cud to her mouth which she opened slowly once or twice in a lazy yawn releasing her warm grassy-smelling breath on the cool air. Her teeth were stained and green, her eyes swam and glistened like goldfish. She let down her milk without protest.

Leaning to one side to balance the full bucket with its froth of creamy milk, Olive walked carefully down the hill. Damn, she thought. I will have to iron my uniform tonight, and sponge it to remove the grass stains. And damn again, I have trodden in cow muck. Cow muck, pancakes, cowpad . . .

She mused on the words. The Welsh children up the road said *cowpad*. They were a compact, aloof, mysterious family with the two girls going to High School. They had a cousin called Myfanwy. Olive wished that she were called Myfanwy. Or Eitne. Or anything except plain pickled Olive.

She crossed the creek. The milk slopped against her legs, dampening her stockings and staining the hem of her uniform.

'Damn again,' she said. She would have to look in Pear's *Dictionary*, 'Household Hints,' to find how to remove milk stains; she never remembered.

Then just as she was approaching the gate she noticed two men leaning over the bull calf in the corner of the paddock, near the hedge. 'Mr Ormandy, Mr Lewis,' Olive said to herself. 'Old Ormandy.'

He had been named *Old Ormandy* when he stopped people from picking his plums but there was no law against picking them, was there, when the tree hung over the fence into the road, inviting anyone to take the dusty plums split and dark blue with pearls of jelly on their stalk and a bitter, blighted taste at the centre, near the stone.

Old Ormandy. The girl Ormandy picked her nose and ate it. Their uncle had been in court for sly-grogging.

Olive watched the two men. What were they doing to the bull calf? It was so dark. What were they doing in the dark? She waited until they had left the bull calf before she went over to say good night to it.

'Calfie, calfie,' she whispered. It was lying outstretched. She bent over it, seeking to pat its face and neck. Its nose felt hot and dry, its eyes were bright, and between its back legs there was blood, and a patch of blood on the grass. The calf had been hurt. Old Ormandy and Lewis were responsible. Why hadn't they noticed the calf was ill? Or perhaps they had deliberately been cruel to it?

'I wouldn't put it past them,' Olive said aloud, feeling strangely satisfied that she was expressing her indignation in the very words her Father used when he became suspicious. 'I wouldn't put it past them.'

She trembled and patted the calf.

'Calfie, calfie,' she whispered again. 'Sook sook. Never mind, calfie, I'll get someone to help you.'

But her heart was thudding with apprehension. Supposing the calf were to die? She had seen many animals die. They were not pampered and flattered in death, like human beings; they became immediate encumbrances, threats to public health, with neighbours and councillors quarrelling over the tedious responsibility of their burial. Or were dead human beings—in secret of course—regarded in this way also, and was their funeral procession a concealment, with flowers, of feelings which the living were afraid to admit? Olive's thoughts frightened her. She knew that all things dead were in the way; you tripped over them, they did not move, they were obstacles, they were no use, even if they were people they were no use, they did not complain or cry out, like sisters, if you pinched them or thumped them on the back, they were simply no use at all.

She did not want the bull calf to die. She could see its eyes glistening, pleading for help. She picked up the milk bucket and hurried through the gate to the house and even before she reached the garden tap (she had to be careful here for the tap leaked, the earth was bogged with moss and onion flower) she heard her Father's loud voice talking.

His friends, the Chinese people, had come to visit him, and he was telling the old old story. His operation. He had been ill with appendicitis and while he was in hospital he had made friends

with the Chinese family who came often now to visit him, filling
the house with unfamiliar voices and excitements, creating an
atmosphere that inspired him to add new dimensions of peril to his
details of the operation.

'Going gangrene . . . they wheeled me in . . .'

Almost running up to the house, fearing for the life of the bull
calf, Olive had time only to hear her Father's loud voice talking to
the visitors before she opened the kitchen door. She was almost
crying now. She was ashamed of her tears in front of the visitors.
She tried to calm herself. Everyone looked up, startled.

'It's calfie, Ormandy's bull calf, it's been hurt, there's all blood
between its legs and its nose is hot!'

Olive's Mother glanced without speaking at her Father who
returned the glance, with a slight smile at the corner of his mouth.
The Chinese visitors stared. One of them, a young man, was
holding a bowl with a flower growing in it, a most beautiful water
narcissus whose frail white transparent petals made everything else
in the room—the cumbersome furniture, the heavy-browed
bookcase, the chocolate-coloured panelled ceiling, the solid black-
leaded stove—seem like unnecessary ballast stored beyond, and at
the same time within, people to prevent their lives from springing
up joyfully, like the narcissus growing out of water into the clear
sky.

'The bull calf, what will we do about it?' Olive urged, breaking
the silence, and staring at the flower because she could not take her
eyes from its loveliness and frailty.

Her Mother spoke. 'It's all right,' she said. 'There's nothing the
matter with the calf.'

Olive stopped looking at the flower. She turned to her Mother.
She felt betrayed. Her Mother, who took inside the little frozen
birds to try to warm them back to life, who mended the rabbit's leg
when it was caught in the trap, who fed warm bran to the sick horse
that was lying on its side, stretched out!

'But it's bleeding! The calf might die! I saw Mr Ormandy with it,
Old Ormandy and another man!'

She knew the man had been Mr Lewis, yet she said 'another man'
because it seemed to convey the terrible anonymity which had

suddenly spread over every person and every deed. Nobody was responsible; nobody would own up; nobody would even *say*.

'The bull calf's all right, I tell you,' her Father said, impatient to return to his story of the operation. 'Forget it. Go and do your homework.'

Olive sensed embarrassment. They seemed ashamed of her. They were ashamed of something. Why didn't they tell her? She wished she had not mentioned the bull calf.

'But I saw it with my own eyes,' she insisted, in final proof that the calf was hurt and needed help.

Again everybody was silent. She could not understand. Why were they so secretive? What was the mystery?

Then her Father swiftly changed the subject.

'Yes, they wheeled me in . . . going gangrene . . . I said to Lottie, I said, on the night . . .'

Olive was about to go from the room when the young man in the corner beckoned to her. He smiled. He seemed to understand. He held out the bowl with the narcissus in it, and said, 'You have it. It is for you.'

Gratefully she took the bowl, and making no further mention of the sick calf she went to her bedroom. She put the narcissus on her dressing table. She touched the petals gently, stroking them, marvelling again at the transparency of the whole flower and the clear water where every fibre of the bulb seemed visible and in motion as if brushed by secret currents and tides. She leaned suddenly and put her cheek against the flower.

Then she lay down on her bed and with her face pressed to the pillow, she began to cry.

The Teacup

When he came to live in the same house she hoped that he would be friendlier, take a deeper interest in her, invite her to the pictures or to go dancing with him or in the summer walking arm in arm in the park. They might even go for a day to the seaside, she thought, or on one of those bus tours visiting Windsor Castle, London Airport, or the Kentish Hopfields. How exciting it would be!

He had been working at the factory for over two years now, since he came out of the Army, and they had often spoken to each other during the day, shared football coupons and bets in the Grand National, lunched together at the staff canteen where you could get a decent meal for two and ten, extra for tea, coffee, and bread and butter. He had talked to her of his family, how they were all dead except his brother and himself; of his life in the Army, travelling the world, a good life, India, Japan, Germany. Once or twice he had mentioned (this was certain and had made her heart flurry) that he would like to 'find someone and settle down.'

He needs someone, she thought. He is quite alone and needs someone.

She told him of her own life, how she had thought of emigrating to Australia and had gone to Australia House where an official asked her age and when she told him he said sharply, 'We are looking for younger people; the young and the skilled.'

She was forty-four. They did not want people of forty-four in Australia. Not single women.

'They wouldn't take me either,' he had said, and, quick with sympathy she had exclaimed, 'Oh, Bill!'

She had never called him by his first name before. He had always been Mr Forest. He addressed her as Miss Rogers, but she knew that if they became closer friends he would call her Edith, that is, Edie. She told him that she was staying in South London, living in a room in a house belonging to this family; that she knitted jerseys for the little girl, helped the landlady with the washing and sewing, and looked after the bird and the cat when the family went on holiday. She told how regularly every second weekend she stayed with her sister at Blackheath, for a change; how her other sister had emigrated years ago to Australia and now was married with three children and a house of her own, she sent photos of the family, you could see them outside in the garden in the sun and how brown the children looked and the garden was bright with flowers, tropical blooms that you never see in England except in Kew Gardens, and wasn't it hot there under glass among the rubber plants? But the photos never showed her sister's husband, for they were separated, he had left her; her other sister's husband had gone too, packed up and vanished, even while his daughter still suffered from back trouble and now she was grown up and crippled, lying on the sofa all day, but managing wonderfully with the district nurse coming on Wednesday afternoons, no, Tuesdays, Wednesday was early closing. And her sister's son had a grant to study accountancy, he would qualify, there was a future ahead of him. . . .

So they talked together, and soon it was commonplace for him to call her Edith (not Edie, not yet) and her to say Bill, though in front of the others at work they still said Miss Rogers and Mr Forest. Then one night she invited him home for tea, and he accepted the invitation. How happy she was that evening! How she wished it had been her own home with her own furniture and curtains and not just one room and the small shared kitchen but two or three or four rooms to walk in and out of, opening and closing the doors, each room serving its purpose, one for visitors, another . . .

She bought extra food that evening, far too much, and it turned out that he didn't care for what she had bought, and he didn't mind

saying so, politely of course, but he had been in the Army and was
used to speaking his mind.

'There's no fuss in the Army. You say what you think.'

'Of course it's best,' she said, trying not to sound disappointed
because he did care for golden sponge pudding and had preferred
not to sample the peeled shrimps, cocktail brand.

But on the whole they spent a pleasant evening. She knitted, and
showed him photographs of her family. They went for a short
walk in the park and while they were walking she linked her arm
with his, as she had seen other women do, and her eyes were bright
with happiness. She mentioned to him that a small room was
vacant on the top floor where she stayed, and that if ever he decided
to change his lodging wouldn't it be a good idea if he took the
room?

She could manage things for him; she could arrange meals, see
to shopping and washing; he would be independent of course. . . .

A few weeks later when he had been on holiday at his brother's
and had arrived back at his lodgings only to find that the two
women of the house, having decided after waiting long enough
that he was definitely not going to ask one of them to marry him,
had given him notice to leave, he remembered the vacancy that
Miss Rogers—Edith—had mentioned, and one week later he had
come to live in the house, half a flight of stairs up from her own
room.

She helped to prepare his room. She cleaned the windows and
drew the curtains wide to give him full advantage of the view—the
back gardens of the two or three adjacent houses, the road beyond,
with the Pink Paraffin lorries parked outside their store; the garden
of the large house belonging to the County Councillor.

She made the bed, draping the candlewick bedspread, shelving it
at the top beneath the pillows, shifting the small table from the
corner near the door to a more convenient position near the head of
the bed.

A reading lamp? Would he need a reading lamp?

With a tremble of excitement she realised that she knew nothing
about him, that from now on, each day would be filled to the brim
with discovery. Either he read in bed or he didn't read in bed. Did
he like a cup of tea in the early morning? What did he do in the

evenings? What did he sound like when he coughed in the middle of the night when all was quiet?

Downstairs in the small kitchen which she shared with Jean, another lodger in the house, an unmarried woman a few years younger than herself, she segregated on a special shelf covered by half a yard of green plastic which hung, scalloped at the edge, the utensils he would need for his meals; his own special spoon, knife, fork. On the top shelf there were two large cups, one with the handle broken. Jean had broken it. She had confessed long ago but the subject still came up between her and Edith and always served to discharge irritation between them.

As Edith was choosing the special teacup to be used solely by Bill, she picked up the handleless one, and remarked to Jean, 'These are nice cups, they hold plenty of tea, but that woman from Australia who used to stay in the room before you came, she broke the handle off this cup.'

'No, I broke it,' Jean confessed again.

'No. It was that woman from Australia who stayed here in the room before you came. I was going to emigrate to Australia once. I went as far as getting the papers and filling them in.'

The woman from Australia had also been responsible for other breakages and inconveniences. She had never cleaned the gas stove, she had blocked the sink with vegetables, she hadn't fitted in with arrangements for bathing and washing, and the steam from her baths had peeled the wallpaper off the bathroom wall, newly decorated too. She had left behind a miscellany of objects which were labelled as 'belonging to the woman from Australia' and which Edith carefully preserved and replaced when the cupboards were cleaned out, as if the woman from Australia were still a needful presence in the house.

Attached to the special shelf prepared for Bill there was a row of golden cuphooks; upon one of them Edith hung the teacup she had chosen for him; a large deep cup with a gold, green and dark-blue pattern around the rim and the words ARKLOW POTTERY EIRE DONEGAL, encircled by a smudged blue capital *E*, printed underneath. In every way the teacup seemed specially right for Bill. How Edith longed for him to be settled in, having his tea, with her pouring from the new teapot warmed under its new cosy, into his special teacup!

He took two heaped spoons of sugar, she shivered with excitement at remembering.

On Bill's first night she could not disguise her happiness. They left work together that night, they came home sitting side by side on the top deck of the bus, they walked together from the bus stop down and along the road to the house. His luggage had already been delivered; it stood in the corridor, strapped and bulging, mysterious, exciting, with foreign labels.

And now there was the bliss of showing him his room, the ins and outs of his new lodgings—the bathroom, telling him on which day he could bathe, showing him how to turn on the hot water.

'Up is on, Down is off. . . .'

Explaining, pointing out, revealing, with her cheeks flushed and her breast rising and falling quickly to get enough breath for speech because the details, all the pointing out and revealing were fraught with so much excitement.

At last she led him to the cupboard in the kitchen.

'This is your shelf. Here is your knife, fork, spoon. Of course you can always take anything, anything you want from my shelf, here, this one here, but not from Jean's.'

'Anything you want,' she said again, urgently, 'take from my shelf, won't you?'

Then she paused.

'And this is your special cup and saucer.'

She detached the cup from its golden hook and held it to the light. He looked approvingly at it.

'Nice and big,' he said.

She glowed.

'That's why I chose it from the others. There used to be two of them, but that woman from Australia who stayed here broke the handle of one.'

She still held the teacup as if she were reluctant to return it to its place on the hook.

'Isn't it roomy?' she said, seeking, in a way, for further acknowledgement from him.

But he had turned his attention elsewhere. He was hungry. He sniffed at the food already cooking.

They had dinner then. She had prepared everything—the stewed beef, potatoes, carrots, onions, cabbage. His place was laid at the small table which was really a cabinet and was therefore awkward to sit at, as one's knees bumped into its cupboard door. She apologised for the table, and thought, I'll have to look around for a cheap table, perhaps one with a formica top, easily cleaned, Oh dear there is so much furniture we need, and those lace curtains need renewing, just from where I am sitting I can see they are almost in shreds.

And she sighed with the happy responsibility of everything.

After dinner she washed the dishes, showed him where to hang his bath towel, and where to put his shaving gear, before he went upstairs to lie on his bed and read the evening paper. Then, sharp at half-past eight, she put the kettle on (she hadn't noticed before how furred it was, and dented at the sides, she would have to see about a new kettle) and when the water was boiling she made two cups of tea, taking one up to his room and knocking gently on the door.

'Can I come in, Bill?'

'Yes, come in.'

He was rather irritated at being interrupted, and showed his irritation by frowning at her, for he had of course been in the Army and he believed in directness, in speaking out.

She stood a moment, timidly, in the doorway.

'I've brought you a cup of tea.'

She handed him his special teacup on its matching saucer.

'That's good of you.'

He took it, and blew the parcels from the top. She stayed a while, talking, while he drank his tea. She asked him how he liked his new lodging. She told him there were a few shops around the corner, two cinemas further down the road 'showing nice programmes of an evening,' and that in summer the park nearby was lovely to sit and walk in.

Then he told her that he was tired, all this changing around, that he was going to bed to get some sleep.

'See you in the morning,' she said.

She took the cups and went downstairs to the kitchen to tidy up for the night. Jean was in the kitchen filling her hot-water bottle. Edith glanced at her, not being able to conceal her joy. Jean had no friend to stay, she had no one to cook for, to wash for. Edith began to talk of Bill.

'I'll be up earlier than usual tomorrow,' she said. 'There's Bill's breakfast to get. He has two boiled eggs every morning,' she said, pausing for Jean to express the wonder which should be aroused at the thought of two boiled eggs for breakfast.

'Does he?' Jean exclaimed, faintly admiring, envious.

'I'm calling him in the morning as he finds it difficult to wake up. Some men do, you know.'

'Yes,' Jean said. 'I know.'

Early next morning Edith was bustling about the kitchen attending to Bill and his toilet and breakfast needs—putting on hot water for the shave, boiling the two eggs, and then sharp at twenty to eight they set out together to catch the bus for work, walking up the road arm in arm. Bill wore a navy-blue duffle coat and carried a canvas bag. The morning light caught the sandy colour of his thinning hair, and showed the pink baldness near his temples and the pink confectionery tint of his cheeks. She was wearing her heavy brown tweed coat and the fawn flowerpot hat which she had bought when her sister took her shopping at Blackheath. Clothes were cheaper yet more attractive in Blackheath; the market was full of bargains—why was it not so, Edith wondered, in her home territory, why did other people always live where really good things were marked down, going for a song, though the flowerpot hat was not cheap. Edith had long ago given up worrying over the hat. She had felt uneasy about it—perhaps it would go suddenly out of fashion, and although she never kept consciously in fashion, whenever there was a topsy-turvy revolution with waists going up or down and busts being annihilated, Edith had the feeling that the rest of the world had turned a corner and abandoned her. She felt confused, not knowing which track to follow; people were pressing urgently forward, their destinations known and planned, young girls too, half her age . . . .

Edith felt bitter toward the young girls. Why, the tips of their shoes were like hooks or swords, anyone could see they were a danger.

But everything was different now: there was Bill.

Each night they walked home, again arm in arm, separating at the shops where Edith bought supplies for their dinner while Bill went on to the house, put his bag away, had a wash, and sat cosily on a chair in the kitchen, reading the evening paper and waiting for his dinner to be prepared. They had dinner, sitting awkwardly at the table-cabinet, with Edith each night apologising, remarking that one weekend she would scout around at Blackheath for a cheap table.

'The wallpaper wants doing, too,' she said one evening, looking thoughtfully at the torn paper over the fireplace. To her joy Bill took the hint.

'I'm not bad at decorating,' he said. 'Being in the Army, you know.'

She laughed impatiently and blushed.

'But you're not in the Army now, you're settling down!'

He agreed. 'Yes, it's time I settled down.'

He spent the following weekend papering the kitchen, and although it was Edith's usual time for visiting her sister, she did not go to Blackheath but stayed in the kitchen, making cups of tea for Bill, fetching, carrying, admiring, talking to him, holding equipment for him, and by Sunday evening when the job was finished and the kitchen cupboard had been painted too, and the window sills, and even new curtains hung on plastic hooks which were rustpoof and could be washed free of dust and soot, the two sat together, in deep contentment, drinking their cups of tea and eating their slices of white bread and apricot jam, homemade.

But Edith's satisfaction was chilled by the persistent thought, It isn't even my own home, it isn't even my own home. Still, she consoled herself, in time, who knows?

Their routine was established. Every evening it was the same— dinner, apologies over the awkward shape of the table (but why, she thought, should I spend money on a table when it isn't even my own home?), meagre conversation, a few exclamations, statements, revival of rumours; the newspapers to read. . . . They

each bought their own evening paper, and after they both had
finished reading they exchanged papers, with a dreamlike
movement, for they were at the same time concentrating on their
stewed beef or fried chops or fish.

'There's the same news in both, really.'

'Yes, there's not much difference.'

Nevertheless they exchanged papers and settled once more to eat
and read. When they had finished she would say, 'I'll do the dishes.'

At first Bill used to walk around with a tea towel hanging over
his arm. Later, when he realised that his help was not needed, he
didn't bother to remove the towel from the railing behind the
kitchen door. There were three railings, one each for Edith, Jean,
and Bill. Edith had bought Bill a special tea towel, red and blue
(colourfast) with a matador and two bulls printed on it.

One evening when Edith was not feeling tired she said she would
like to go to the pictures, that there was a good one showing down
the road, and if they hurried they would get in at the beginning of
the main picture, or halfway through *Look at Life*.

Bill was not interested.

'Not for me, not tonight.'

He went upstairs to make the final preparations and judgements
for the filling-in of the football coupon, while Edith retired to her
room, switched on the electric fire, and sat in her armchair,
knitting. The glow from the fire sent bars of light, like burns,
across her face. Her eyes watered a little as she leaned forward to
follow the pattern. The wool felt thick and rough against her
fingers.

I must be tired after all, she thought, and put down her knitting.

At half-past eight she went to the kitchen to make the usual cup
of tea, and as she said good night to Bill she thought, He's tired
after that heavy packing at work all day. Maybe in the weekends
we'll go out together somewhere, to the pictures or the park.

The next morning when it was time to set out for work it seemed
that Bill was not quite ready, there were a few things to see to, he
said. So Edith went alone up the road to the bus stop, and later Bill
set out for work alone. And that night they came home separately.
And after that, every morning and evening they went to and from
work alone.

In the weekend Bill mentioned that he knew friends who kept a pub in Covent Garden, that he would be spending the weekend there. Soon he spent every weekend there. At night he still came home for meals, but sometimes he neglected to say that he wasn't coming home, and Edith would make elaborate preparations for dinner, only to find that she had to eat it alone.

'If only he would tell me,' she complained to Jean. 'I see him at work during the day, and for some reason he's even ashamed to let on that he stays here. Afraid the others will tease him.'

She smiled wistfully, a little secretively, as if perhaps there might be cause for teasing.

Well, she thought, at least he sleeps here.

And was there not all the satisfying flurry in the morning of heating his shaving-water, putting the two eggs to boil, leaving the kettle on low gas in case he needed it, setting his place at the table with his plate, his knife, and, carefully at the side, his special teacup and saucer? And then taking possession of details concerning him, as if they were property being signed to her alone? He eats far too much salt. One drum of salt lasts no time with him. How can he eat so much black pudding? He's fond of sugar, too.

He likes, he prefers, he would rather have . . .

He'd be lost without his cup of tea.

Yes, that was one thing he was always ready for, she could always make him a cup of tea.

And then there were his personal habits which she treasured as legacies, as if his gradual withdrawal from her had been concerned, in a way, with death, wills and next-of-kin, with her being the sole beneficiary.

'Why, oh why, does he leave all his pairs of socks to be washed at once?'—said in a voice at the same time complaining and proud— 'I've told him to bring his dirty clothing down for me to wash, but he persists in leaving it in his room, and there I have to go and search about in his most private clothing, and I never know where he keeps anything!'—said in a voice warm with satisfaction.

It was true that her washing seemed endless, and lasted all Saturday morning, and the ironing took all Sunday morning or Monday evening. She liked ironing his shirts, underclothes and handkerchiefs. She tried to accept the fact that he was not inclined to take her out anywhere, not even to the pictures or the park, that he did not care to accompany her to or from work. Once or twice she reminded him that he was getting old, that he was forty-seven, that she was about the same age . . . perhaps they could spend the rest of their lives together, life was not all dizzy romance, perhaps they could marry . . . she would look after him, see to him. . . .

'But I like my freedom,' he said.

Then she tried to frighten him into thoughts of himself as a lonely old man with no one to care for him and no one to talk to.

'If it happens,' he said, 'it happens. I've been in the Army, you know, around in Japan, India, Germany, I've seen a thing or two.'

As if being in the Army had provided him with special defences and privileges. And it had, hadn't it? He could speak his mind, he knew what he was up to. . . .

So the wonderful hopes which had filled Edith's mind when Bill had first come to stay, began to fade. Why won't he see? she thought. I'm trying to do my best for him. It would be nice, in summer, to walk arm in arm in the park.

Meanwhile her stated attitude became, I don't care, it doesn't worry me.

The Council were starting a course of dancing lessons for beginners over thirty. She began to go dancing in the evenings, and when she came home she would tell Jean about the lovely time she had enjoyed.

'I go with the girl from work. Her father has that grey Jaguar with the toy leopard in the back.'

'You want to go dancing,' she suggested one night to Jean.

'Oh,' Jean replied. 'I had a friend to visit me.'

'A friend? A man?'

'Yes. A man.'

'I didn't see him.'

'Oh, he came to visit me.'

Sometimes Edith went dancing twice a week now, and Bill came home or didn't come home to dinner. Still, rather wistfully, Edith prepared food for him, peeled the potatoes (he was fond of potatoes), cleaned the Brussels sprouts, or left little notes with directions in them: 'The sausages from yesterday are in the oven if you care for them. There's soup in the enamel jug. There are half a dozen best eggs on my shelf . . . or if you fancy baked beans . . .'

Edith noticed that Jean's new friend seemed to bring her a plentiful supply of food. Why, sometimes her shelf was filled to overflowing. She hoped that Bill had remembered not to touch anything upon Jean's shelf.

'My friend's good that way,' Jean said. 'And he always lets me know when he is coming to visit me.'

Edith flushed.

'Bill would let me know about dinner and suchlike, but I don't see him much during the day, not now he's working upstairs. He's very thoughtful underneath, Bill is.'

'My friend bought me underwear for Christmas. Do you think I should have accepted it?'

'It's rather personal isn't it?'

Bill had not given Edith a present.

'Oh there's nothing between us,' Jean assured her.

'Bill wanted to give me something but I wouldn't have it. I said I enjoy what I'm doing for him and that's that. You say your friend came on Saturday? I've never seen him yet.'

'You always miss him, don't you?'

That was Monday.

That night when Bill had come home, eaten his dinner, and gone to his room, and Edith had put the kettle on the gas and was setting out the cups for tea, she noticed that Bill's cup was missing, the big teacup with the gold, dark-blue and light-green decorations and the words printed at the bottom, the big teacup, Bill's cup, that hung always on the golden hook.

With a feeling of panic she searched Bill's shelf, Jean's, her own, and the cupboards underneath, removing the grater and flour sifter, the cake tins, and the two battered saucepans which had belonged to the woman from Australia.

She could not find the teacup.

She hurried from the kitchen and up to Bill's room.

'Bill,' she called, 'your cup's missing!'

A sleepy voice sounded, 'My what?'

She opened the door. He was lying fully dressed on the bed. He sat up.

Edith's voice was trembling, as if she were bringing him bad news which did not affect him as much as it affected herself, yet which she needed to share.

'Your big teacup that hangs on the hook on your shelf. Have you seen it?'

He spoke abruptly. 'No, I haven't seen it.'

She looked at him with all the feelings of the past weeks and months working in her face, and her eyes bright. Her voice implored him, 'Now Bill, just stay there quietly and try to remember when you last saw your cup!'

He got up from the bed. 'What the hell?' he shouted. 'What the hell is the fuss about?'

He lowered his voice. 'Well I last saw it on the ledge by the cupboard. I had a cup of tea in it,' he said guiltily.

Then he saw the marks where his shoes had touched the end of the bed. He brushed at the counterpane. 'I should have taken my shoes off, eh?'

Edith was calm now. 'So you haven't seen your teacup?' she said, but she could not bear to dismiss the subject, to make an end of it all, without saying, 'Your teacup, Bill, the one with the gold, dark-blue and green that hangs on the hook on your shelf?'

Then she suddenly left him, and hurried down the stairs, and knocked sharply on Jean's door, and almost before she was invited, she opened the door and looked searchingly around the room. Her face was flushed. Her eyes were glistening as if she had been leaning too close to the fire. At first she did not speak but glanced meaningly at one of the kitchen cups which Jean had borrowed for a drink of water.

'Have you seen Bill's cup?' Edith asked, staring hard at the cup of water as if to say, 'If you borrow this you might surely have borrowed Bill's cup!'

Jean felt a pang of guilt. She had not seen or borrowed the cup but she felt sure that suspicion rested on her.

'No,' she said. 'I haven't seen it. Isn't it in the kitchen?'

'No, it's not there.'

Edith's voice had a note of desperation, as if the incident had brought her suddenly to the limit of her endurance.

'No, it's not there,' she said. She felt like weeping, but she was not going to break down, she had her suspicions of Jean. She looked once more around Jean's room, as if trying to uncover the hiding-place.

'I last saw it,' she said, 'on Saturday at lunchtime when I washed it. Then I went away to my sister's at Blackheath, as you know, and Bill went away for the weekend, and the family was away. That means you were the only one in the house.'

'My friend came,' Jean reminded her.

Edith pounced. 'Perhaps he used Bill's cup?'

No, Jean told her, he hadn't.

'Well you were the only one in the house from Saturday at lunchtime.'

'Perhaps Bill knows where it is?' Jean asked.

Edith's voice quavered. 'He doesn't. I've asked him. I said to him, "Now just sit quietly and remember when you last saw it."'

'What did he say?'

'He said when he last saw it, there were dregs of tea in it, and it was on the ledge by the cupboard in the kitchen. And that's correct,' Edith said triumphantly, 'for I washed it—you were the only one in the house with it until Monday, today, and between Saturday and today it vanished. There was your friend of course,' she said accusingly.

'Oh, he didn't touch it. I don't know what to do with him, he brings me so much food. And he always writes to tell me when he is visiting me.'

'Bill is a typical man,' Edith said coldly. 'He has no idea what food we (he and I) need. If he did he would buy it, and see to things. And now that he's upstairs at work during the day he can't see me to say whether or not he's coming home to dinner.'

Then she made a stifled sound, like a sob. 'I don't know where his cup has got to, his teacup.'

It seemed that the teacup hanging on its golden hook had contained the last of Edith's hope, and now it was gone, someone had taken it. She suspected Jean. Who was this mysterious friend who came to visit Jean? Jean hadn't discovered this friend until Bill had come to stay in the house. It was all Jean's fault, everything was Jean's fault, Jean was jealous of her and Bill, she has stolen Bill's teacup, his special teacup with the gold, dark-blue and green decorations, and the writing underneath. . . .

For the next few days there was tension between the two women.

Edith left a note before she went to work, 'Dear Jean, If you are ironing please will you run over Bill's two towels?'

Jean forgot to iron the towels.

Each evening the same questions and answers passed between them.

'Bill's cup must be somewhere. It just can't vanish. You didn't break it by chance, and put it in the rubbish tin?'

'If I had broken it I would have said.'

'That woman from Australia broke the handle of the other one, if that woman from Australia hadn't broken the other one Bill could be using it now.'

'*I* broke the other one.'

'Then you could have broken this one as well. But I thought . . . that handle . . . I thought it was the woman from Australia. I tried to emigrate to Australia once. I went as far as getting papers and filling them in . . .'

She spoke longingly as if emigrating to Australia were another of the good things in life which had been denied her at the last moment, as if it were somehow concerned with the affair of Bill and the lost teacup and never ever walking arm in arm in the park, in summer.

By the fourth day the kitchen had been thoroughly searched and the cup was nowhere to be found. Bill was now spending many of his week-nights away from the house, and the two women found themselves often alone together. They spoke little. They glanced grimly at each other, accusingly.

Sometimes at night in her room in the middle of reading her romantic novel from the library (*Set Fair For France, All My Own, Love and Ailsa Dare*), Edith would break down and weep, she could not explain it, but the disappearance of the teacup was the last straw. She said the phrase to herself, drying her eyes, 'The last straw.'

Then she chided herself, 'Don't be silly. What's the use?' But the people in the novels had everything so neatly provided for them. There was this secretary with the purple eyes and trim figure, and she dined by candlelight with the young director, the youngest and wealthiest director of the firm; everybody was jealous of this secretary; all the men made excuses to visit her at her desk, to invite her out. . . .

Edith was heavily built; she bought a salmon-pink corset once a year; she needed to wear it. Her eyes were grey and chipped, like a pavement. Her back humped.

'I'm ugly of course,' she said, as she closed *Love and Ailsa Dare*. 'I don't mind that so much now I'm used to it, but the teacup, Bill's cup, who has taken it?'

After the week had passed and the cup had still not been found, and there was no clue to its hiding-place, Edith gave up preparing meals for Bill. She even neglected to go to his room to collect what he referred to as his 'mid-week smalls'. And the following week, in an effort to cheer herself, she went dancing three times to the Council class, but she found little pleasure in it. She had tried to buy a pair of white satin shoes such as everyone else wore, and when she did find a pair they nipped and cramped her two toes, causing a pain which was so prolonged that she visited the doctor (the one around the corner with his house newly decorated, and his smart car standing outside the gate; everyone went to him) who said to her, 'I can do nothing about it, it's your age, Miss Rogers, the best thing is for you to have a small operation which will remove those two toes; it's arthritis, it attacks the toes first, with some patients; the operation is quite quick and harmless.'

When Edith came home from the doctor's she burst into tears. Two toes removed, just like that! It was the beginning of the end. They would soon want permission to remove every part of her, they did that sort of thing, gradually, once they began they never knew where to finish.

She stopped going to dancing class. She stayed inside by the electric fire, knitting, and sewing at the sewing machine, pedalling fiercely until her legs ached and she was forced to rest them.

One weekend when she returned from her sister's at Blackheath she found that Bill had changed his lodging, had gone to stay with his friends who kept the pub in Covent Garden. He had gone without telling her, without a word. But he never told people things, he was secretive, he didn't understand, he had been in the Army. . . .

That Monday evening on her way past the shops Edith saw Jean in the grocer's; she was buying food, mountains of it. So much for her mysterious friend, Edith thought, as she hurried home.

The two met later in the kitchen, filling their hot-water bottles.

'Have you been dancing lately?' Jean asked.

'Yes,' Edith said. 'I go often. In fact I went during the weekend. I had a wonderful time. Smashing. Did your friend come?'

'Yes, my friend came, with stacks of food, look!'

Jean pointed to the bread, fruit salad, ham, which she had just bought at the grocer's.

Then, without speaking much—for what was there to say?—they filled their hot-water bottles and said good night.

And no one ever found the dark-blue, gold, green teacup with the writing ARKLOW POTTERY EIRE DONEGAL underneath, that used to hang—an age ago, it seemed—in the kitchen on the special shelf on the shining golden hook!

The Advocate

If you stop Ted in the street and ask him the way he is always eager
to direct you. He helps the aged, the blind, the crippled. He will
rescue children in distress separated from their mothers in a crowd.
At the scene of an accident he is among the first to restore calm, to
comfort people, ring for ambulances, distribute hot sweet tea.

He will reprimand or report to the police anyone making
himself a public nuisance or breaking the law. Ted has deep
respect for the law.

If you say good morning to him he returns your greeting with a
cheerful smile.

That is Ted.

At work he is willing, eager; he goes out of his way to please, he
stays behind in the evenings to give extra attention to his tasks and
prepare for the following day. How courteous he is, how efficient.

In his conversation he refers to his many friends, to his
popularity among them.

'They will do anything for me,' he says.

He tells you of the liftman at work who is always ready to take
him to any floor, to give him service before all others; of the
manager who calls him by his Christian name and gives him a
friendly wink from time to time, there being definite
understanding between them; of the Director who chats intimately
with him in a manner which he does not adopt with the other
members of the staff; of the shy young office girls who are delighted

to be taken 'under his wing'; of the Chief Security Officer who, relaxing the principle of keeping aloof from the staff, invites him to his room for coffee, talking to him as an equal.

He likes to make it known that he is given certain privileges: he is allowed free time whenever he chooses; he is trusted, taken into the confidence of others, consulted on personal problems. He has so many friends. If you spend enough time with him you soon learn that he seems to have more friends than most people; you learn too of his illustrious relatives, of famous people who have spoken to him or corresponded with him, of high-ranking officials in other countries whom he has known intimately. In case you do not believe him (but who would doubt his word?) he has a supply of anecdotes, dates, Christian names. And in all his stories he features as the man with many friends, the man to whom people turn for advice and comfort.

Then why is he so alone? Why does he go to bed each night hoping for immediate sleep to ward off his loneliness? Why does he go every Sunday afternoon to the pictures and sit alone in the dark through two showings of the programme, and then return to his deserted flat and once more go to bed, trying to evade the loneliness?

He hasn't a friend in the world, and he knows it.

When his back is turned they label him bumptious, over-bearing, conceited, nosey-parker, poke-nose, opinionated, bigot-ed. . . .

Over his dead body, before he is taken to be buried in the grave of a suicide, they praise him as helpful, kind, courteous, willing, conscientious, a noble and good man. . . .

Which judgement is correct? Is there a correct one? How can one be judged truly unless, like Ted, one hires the services of the Advocate Death?

The Chosen Image

In late winter when the seed catalogues were thrust through the letter box, the poet, having a spare hour or two, gathered them upon his table, studied them carefully, and from the many magnificent illustrations he chose the bloom which he had decided to plant in a wooden box upon his window sill, for he did not possess a garden. That same afternoon he went to the local post office and after waiting in the queue which extended from the stationery beyond the frozen foods to the cheeses which were next to the door, the poet bought a postal order for two and threepence, put it in an envelope with the number of the packet of seed, and sent it to the seed company. Then he returned home and for three days waited impatiently for the seed to arrive. At night after he had gone to bed he would take the catalogue and read it, and on the third night when he was gazing at the picture of his chosen seed which he already loved very dearly, he happened to read the small print beneath the advertisement.

'Hothouse bloom only,' he read.

For a moment he was alarmed. He knew that his room would not provide much warmth for the plant, because he did not earn much money as a poet, in spite of the occasional television interviews where he was asked, What do you think of the world situation? Do you think Success comes too early in this modern age? If you had to live your life over again which one thing would you change? And in spite of the occasional poem printed in a literary journal, and the advertisement jingle which he wrote for a friend in an agency, his slight income did not allow for central heating. How would a hothouse bloom ever survive? he wondered.

'Well,' he said at last to himself, 'I will breathe on it. My body is warm, well stoked, blood flows from rafter to basement and even the rats have been driven inside this winter to seek shelter in me. By the way, one day when I am free of dreams and light, hawkers, carrion crows and enchantments I shall take time to sprinkle an appetising sweet poison for the rats in my sealed cabinet. In the meantime I shall await my packet of wonderful blossom.'

So he waited, sitting down to work the next morning with his mind continually straying to the thought of growing a hothouse bloom upon his window sill.

In due course the packet of seed arrived. The poet planted it, following the instructions as carefully as his individual temperament would allow. He resolved to breathe upon the soil, the seed and the resulting plant as often as he remembered or was free to do so when he took time from writing his poems to walk about the room counting the faded leaves upon the carpet or looking from the window at the man in the battered grey cap who walked from door to door asking,'Have you any old watches, old gold, bracelets, wedding rings?'

The poet was not married, although like all poets he possessed an invisible muse, a mistress and wife to him, and a wedding ring with which he pledged his devotion to the Chosen Image. Unfortunately, when he turned the wedding ring three times upon his finger it did not provide him with a poem. There had been much controversy. Some poets had said that the wedding ring should provide poems in this way.

Nor could the poet give to the man in the grey battered cap any old watches, old gold or bracelets. How could he possess such valuables? He lived in a small flat where his only treasures which were yet not his alone but were accessible to all, lay arranged in dictionaries and grammars upon his bookshelves. Strange, wasn't it, that no burglar had been known to raid the premises in order to steal suitcases of words?

As for old watches, well, the poet owned a wrist watch which he preferred to keep in his pocket or upon his table. Strapped on his wrist it reminded him of a too genial handcuff to which he had no key, for which no key had yet been made.

Did I tell you that he was a poet who could not write good poetry (there are many such) but unearthed cliche[1]s as if they were archaeological treasures arranged on a silver spade? After he had written each poem he was pleased with it, he confused the warmth and excitement which the act of writing gave him with the feelings naturally provided by a thing of beauty; therefore he thought his poem beautiful, and was most distressed and could not understand when later, from somewhere in the cave roof, the dampening idea leaked through that his poem was bad. Yet he could not stop writing just as he could not stop counting the leaves on the carpet or looking from his window at the man calling for Old Watches, Old Gold, Bracelets; or breathing warmth upon the tender leaves that had sprung from his chosen seed.

One evening when he looked at the plant he noticed a tiny bud with its petals beginning to open, and he knew that when morning came the plant would be in full blossom. So he went quickly to bed, pulling the blankets well over him in the belief that concealment means escape and acceleration of time, and soon he was fast asleep and dreaming, but the anonymous voices which inhabit all dreams said to him, 'What can you call entirely your own? You cannot write a poem without using the words, often the thoughts, of others. The words of the world lie like stagnant water in the ponds for the poets masquerading as the sun to quench their thirst, spitting out the dead tadpoles and the dry sticks and stones and bones. If ever you have precious thoughts of your own which do not lie accessible to all beneath the sky, how can you safeguard them? Where are your security measures for putting thoughts under lock and key?

'But then no thoughts belong entirely to you. You have no talent for your work. Your only talent and personal possession is breath, and yet since late winter when the seed catalogues were thrust through your letter box you have bestowed your breath upon a mere plant in order that it should give you pleasure by blossoming on your window sill. Do you think that is wise? Should you not conserve your breath, issue it according to a planned system of economy, and not waste it upon objects like flowers which perish almost as soon as they have bloomed?'

The poet heeded the voices in his dream and the next morning when he looked at the plant, although he knew that the flower was almost in blossom, he refused to breathe upon it, and all day it shivered upon the window sill, feeling for the first time the bitterness of the March winds that moaned up and down the street, and the chill touch of the tendrils of frost and fog that crept down the chimney, under the door, and through the top of the window into the poet's room. And the petals of the flower never opened, their promise was never fulfilled. By nightfall the leaves had blackened at the edges and the bud was a shrivelled silken cocoon of nothing.

The saddened poet gazed at the corpse of his Chosen Image, then uprooting it from the window box and taking it outside onto the landing, he thrust the plant and flower down the chute which extended from the top floor to the basement and which carried away all the refuse of the block of flats where he lived—cataracts of detergent packets, drums, soup tins, sardine keys, torn letters, parcel wrappings, newspapers, ends of bread, eggshells, orange peel, used cotton wool. Sorrowfully the poet watched the plant join its travelling companions, finding its place almost is if it belonged there, taking up the new rhythm of its journey, jostling, struggling in the narrow chute, being trampled and crushed by overbearing jam jars, bottles, and a rusted paraffin container.

For a moment the poet regretted his action. He longed to be in his room again with the plant there on the window sill, almost in blossom, and with him breathing tenderly upon it to provide it with the warmth it needed in order to survive.

Then he shrugged, and smiled cheerfully. What was the use of feeling dejected when one had only done what was right, and refused to waste one's breath upon a negligible hothouse bloom which had been deceitful anyway as its real nature had not been known until the small print of the contract was studied?

'I will forget the whole episode,' the poet said.

And he tried to forget.

He returned to his room and began to write his new poem. Now and again he glanced at the empty window box and sighed. The poem refused to be composed. The poet turned his wedding ring three times. Still the poem refused to be composed.

Well, that was nothing unusual.

He glanced once again at the empty window box and stilled his conscience by remarking to himself, 'Anyway it was a hothouse bloom and would never have survived the rigours of this climate; not even if it had been allowed to blossom. It was not selfish of me to deny it my breath, to dispose of it. Rather was it an act of thoughtfulness which is rare these days.'

He smoothed the paper before him, ready to imprint his poem.

Then a fit of coughing seized him, and he died.

In her silk and ivory tower the Muse turned from her window. 'He was a hothouse plant, anyway. I chose him at random without reading the small print at the bottom of the contract. He would never have blossomed. In future I shall keep my breath to myself— well at least I shall not be tempted when aspiring poets thrust their souls catalogued, numbered, illustrated, through my letter box.'

The Linesman

Three men arrived yesterday with their van and equipment to repair the telephone lines leading to the house opposite. Two of the men stayed at work in the house. The third carried his ladder and set it up against the telegraph pole twenty-five yards from the house. He climbed the ladder and beyond it to the top of the pole where, with his feet resting on the iron rungs which are embedded at intervals in the sides of the pole, he began his work, his hands being made free after he had adjusted his safety harness. He was not likely to fall. I did not see him climb the pole. I looked from my window and saw him already working, twisting, arranging wires, screwing, unscrewing, leaning back from the pole, dependent upon his safety belt, trusting in it, seeming in a position of comfort and security.

I stared at him. I was reluctant to leave the window because I was so intent upon watching the linesman at work, and because I wanted to see him descend from the pole when his work was finished.

People in the houses near the telegraph pole had drawn their curtains; they did not wish to be spied upon. He was in an excellent position for spying, with a clear view into the front rooms of half a dozen houses.

The clouds, curds and whey, were churned from south to north across the sky. It was one of the first Sundays of spring. Washing was blowing on the clotheslines in back gardens; youths were lying in attitudes of surrender beneath the dismantled bellies of scooters; women were sweeping the Saturday night refuse from their share of the pavement. Perhaps it was time for me to have something to eat—a cup of coffee, a biscuit, anything to occupy the ever marauding despair.

But still I could not leave my position at the window. I stared at the linesman until I had to screw up my eyes to avoid the bright stabs of spring light. I watched the work, the snipping, twisting, joining, screwing, unscrewing of bolts. And all the time I was afraid to leave the window. I kept my eyes fixed upon the linesman slung in his safety harness at the top of the telegraph pole.

You see, I was hoping that he might fall.

The Bath

On Friday afternoon she bought cut flowers—daffodils, anemones, a few twigs of a red-leaved shrub, wrapped in mauve waxed paper, for Saturday was the seventeenth anniversary of her husband's death and she planned to visit his grave, as she did each year, to weed it and put fresh flowers in the two jam jars standing one on each side of the tombstone. Her visit this year occupied her thoughts more than usual. She had bought the flowers to force herself to make the journey that each year became more hazardous, from the walk to the bus stop, the change of buses at the Octagon, to the bitterness of the winds blowing from the open sea across almost unsheltered rows of tombstones; and the tiredness that overcame her when it was time to return home when she longed to find a place beside the graves, in the soft grass, and fall asleep.

That evening she filled the coal bucket, stoked the fire. Her movements were slow and arduous, her back and shoulder gave her so much pain. She cooked her tea—liver and bacon—set up knife and fork on the teatowel she used as a tablecloth, turned up the volume of the polished red radio to listen to the Weather Report and the News, ate her tea, washed her dishes, then sat drowsing in the rocking chair by the fire, waiting for the water to get hot enough for a bath. Visits to the cemetery, the doctor, and to relatives, to stay, always demanded a bath. When she was sure that the water was hot enough (and her tea had been digested) she ventured from the kitchen through the cold passageway to the colder bathroom. She paused in the doorway to get used to the chill of the air then she walked slowly, feeling with each step the pain in her back, across to the bath, and though she knew that she was gradually losing the power in her hands she managed to wrench on the stiff cold and hot taps and half-fill the bath with warm water. How wasteful, she thought, that with the kitchen fire always burning during the past month of frost, and the water almost always hot, getting in and out of a bath had become such an effort that it was not possible to bath every night or even every week!

She found a big towel, laid it ready over a chair, arranged the chair so that should difficulty arise as it had last time she bathed she would have some way of rescuing herself; then with her nightclothes warming on a page of newspaper inside the coal oven and her dressing-gown across the chair to be put on the instant she stepped from the bath, she undressed and pausing first to get her breath and clinging tightly to the slippery yellow-stained rim that now seemed more like the edge of a cliff with a deep drop below into the sea, slowly and painfully she climbed into the bath.

I'll put on my nightie the instant I get out, she thought. The instant she got out indeed! She knew it would be more than a matter of instants yet she tried to think of it calmly, without dread, telling herself that when the time came she would be very careful, taking the process step by step, surprising her bad back and shoulder and her powerless wrists into performing feats they might usually rebel against, but the key to controlling them would be the surprise, the slow stealing up on them. With care, with thought. . . .

Sitting upright, not daring to lean back or lie down, she soaped herself, washing away the dirt of the past fortnight, seeing with satisfaction how it drifted about on the water as a sign that she was clean again. Then when her washing was completed she found herself looking for excuses not to try yet to climb out. Those old woman's finger nails, cracked and dry, where germs could lodge, would need to be scrubbed again; the skin of her heels, too, growing so hard that her feet might have been turning to stone; behind her ears where a thread of dirt lay in the rim; after all, she did not often have the luxury of a bath, did she? How warm it was! She drowsed a moment. If only she could fall asleep then wake to find herself in her nightdress in bed for the night! Slowly she rewashed her body, and when she knew she could no longer deceive herself into thinking she was not clean she reluctantly replaced the soap, brush and flannel in the groove at the side of the bath, feeling as she loosened her grip on them that all strength and support were ebbing from her. Quickly she seized the nail-brush again, but its magic had been used and was gone; it would not adopt the role she tried to urge upon it. The flannel too, and the soap, were frail flotsam to cling to in the hope of being borne to safety.

She was alone now. For a few minutes she sat swilling the water against her skin, perhaps as a means of buoying up her courage. Then resolutely she pulled out the plug, sat feeling the tide swirl and scrape at her skin and flesh, trying to draw her down, down into the earth; then the bathwater was gone in a soapy gurgle and she was naked and shivering and had not yet made the attempt to get out of the bath.

How slippery the surface had become! In future she would not clean it with kerosene, she would use the paste cleaner that, left on overnight, gave the enamel rough patches that could be gripped with the skin.

She leaned forward, feeling the pain in her back and shoulder. She grasped the rim of the bath but her fingers slithered from it almost at once. She would not panic, she told herself; she would try gradually, carefully, to get out. Again she leaned forward; again her grip loosened as if iron hands had deliberately uncurled her stiffened blue fingers from their trembling hold. Her heart began to beat faster, her breath came more quickly, her mouth was dry. She moistened her lips. If I shout for help, she thought, no one will hear me. No one in the world will hear me. No one will know I'm in the bath and can't get out.

She listened. She could hear only the drip-drip of the cold water tap of the wash-basin, and a corresponding whisper and gurgle of her heart, as if it were beating under water. All else was silent. Where were the people, the traffic? Then she had a strange feeling of being under the earth, of a throbbing in her head like wheels going over the earth above her.

Then she told herself sternly that she must have no nonsense, that she had really not tried to get out of the bath. She had forgotten the strong solid chair and the grip she could get on it. If she made the effort quickly she could first take hold on both sides of the bath, pull herself up, then transfer her hold to the chair and thus pull herself out.

She tried to do this; she just failed to make the final effort. Pale now, gasping for breath, she sank back into the bath. She began to call out but as she had predicted there was no answer. No one had heard her, no one in the houses or the street or Dunedin or the world knew that she was imprisoned. Loneliness welled in her. If John were here, she thought, if we were sharing our old age, helping each other, this would never have happened. She made another effort to get out. Again she failed. Faintness overcoming her she closed her eyes, trying to rest, then recovering and trying again and failing, she panicked and began to cry and strike the sides of the bath; it made a hollow sound like a wild drum-beat.

Then she stopped striking with her fists; she struggled again to get out; and for over half an hour she stayed alternately struggling and resting until at last she did succeed in climbing out and making her escape into the kitchen. She thought, I'll never take another bath in this house or anywhere. I never want to see that bath again. This is the end or the beginning of it. In future a district nurse will have to come to attend me. Submitting to that will be the first humiliation. There will be others, and others.

In bed at last she lay exhausted and lonely thinking that perhaps it might be better for her to die at once. The slow progression of difficulties was a kind of torture. There were her shoes that had to be made specially in a special shape or she could not walk. There were the times she had to call in a neighbour to fetch a pot of jam from the top shelf of her cupboard when it had been only a year ago that she herself had made the jam and put it on the shelf. Sometimes a niece came to fill the coal-bucket or mow the lawn. Every week there was the washing to be hung on the line—this required a special technique for she could not raise her arms without at the same time finding some support in the dizziness that overcame her. She remembered with a sense of the world narrowing and growing darker, like a tunnel, the incredulous almost despising look on the face of her niece when in answer to the comment 'How beautiful the clouds are in Dunedin! These big billowing white and grey clouds—don't you think, Auntie?' she had said, her disappointment at the misery of things putting a sharpness in her voice, 'I never look at the clouds!'

She wondered how long ago it was since she had been able to look up at the sky without reeling with dizziness. Now she did not dare look up. There was enough to attend to down and around—the cracks and hollows in the footpath, the patches of frost and ice and the potholes in the roads; the approaching cars and motorcycles; and now, after all the outside menaces, the inner menace of her own body. She had to be guardian now over her arms and legs, force them to do as she wanted when how easily and dutifully they had walked, moved and grasped, in the old days! They were the enemy now. It had been her body that showed treachery when she tried to get out of the bath. If she ever wanted to bath again—how strange it seemed!—she would have to ask another human being to help her to guard and control her own body. Was this so fearful? she wondered. Even if it were not, it seemed so.

She thought of the frost slowly hardening outside on the fences, roofs, windows and streets. She thought again of the terror of not being able to escape from the bath. She remembered her dead husband and the flowers she had bought to put on his grave. Then thinking again of the frost, its whiteness, white like a new bath, of the anemones and daffodils and the twigs of the red-leaved shrub, of John dead seventeen years, she fell asleep while outside, within two hours, the frost began to melt with the warmth of a sudden wind blowing from the north, and the night grew warm, like a spring night, and in the morning the light came early, the sky was pale blue, the same warm wind as gentle as a mere breath, was blowing, and a narcissus had burst its bud in the front garden.

In all her years of visiting the cemetery she had never known the wind so mild. On an arm of the peninsula exposed to the winds from two stretches of sea, the cemetery had always been a place to crouch shivering in overcoat and scarf while the flowers were set on the grave and the narrow garden cleared of weeds. Today, everything was different. After all the frosts of the past month there was no trace of chill in the air. The mildness and warmth were scarcely to be believed. The sea lay, violet-coloured, hush-hushing, turning and heaving, not breaking into foamy waves; it was one sinuous ripple from shore to horizon and its sound was the muted sound of distant forests of peace.

Picking up the rusted garden fork that she knew lay always in the grass of the next grave, long neglected, she set to work to clear away the twitch and other weeds, exposing the first bunch of dark blue primroses with yellow centres, a clump of autumn lilies, and the shoots, six inches high, of daffodils. Then removing the green-slimed jam jars from their grooves on each side of the tombstone she walked slowly, stiff from her crouching, to the ever-dripping tap at the end of the lawn path where, filling the jars with pebbles and water she rattled them up and down to try to clean them of slime. Then she ran the sparkling ice-cold water into the jars and balancing them carefully one in each hand she walked back to the grave where she shook the daffodils, anemones, red leaves from their waxed paper and dividing them put half in one jar, half in the other. The dark blue of the anemones swelled with a sea-colour as their heads rested against the red leaves. The daffodils were short-stemmed with big ragged rather than delicate trumpets—the type for blowing; and their scent was strong.

Finally, remembering the winds that raged from the sea she stuffed small pieces of the screwed-up waxed paper into the top of each jar so the flowers would not be carried away by the wind. Then with a feeling of satisfaction—I look after my husband's grave after seventeen years. The tombstone is not cracked or blown over, the garden has not sunk into a pool of clay. I look after my husband's grave—she began to walk away, between the rows of graves, noting which were and were not cared for. Her Father and Mother had been buried here. She stood now before their grave. It was a roomy grave made in the days when there was space for the dead and for the dead with money, like her parents, extra space should they need it. Their tombstone was elaborate though the writing was now faded; in death they kept the elaborate station of their life. There were no flowers on the grave, only the feathery sea-grass soft to the touch, lit with gold in the sun. There was no sound but the sound of the sea and the one row of fir trees on the brow of the hill. She felt the peace inside her; the nightmare of the evening before seemed far away, seemed not to have happened; the senseless terrifying struggle to get out of a bath!

She sat on the concrete edge of her parents' grave. She did not want to go home. She felt content to sit here quietly with the warm soft wind flowing around her and the sigh of the sea rising to mingle with the sighing of the firs and the whisper of the thin gold grass. She was grateful for the money, the time and the forethought that had made her parent's grave so much bigger than the others near by. Her husband, cremated, had been allowed only a narrow eighteen inches by two feet, room only for the flecked grey tombstone In Memory of My Husband John Edward Harraway died August 6th 1948, and the narrow garden of spring flowers, whereas her parents' grave was so wide, and its concrete wall was a foot high; it was, in death, the equivalent of a quarter-acre section before there were too many people in the world. Why when the world was wider and wider was there no space left?

Or was the world narrower?

She did not know; she could not think; she knew only that she did not want to go home, she wanted to sit here on the edge of the grave, never catching any more buses, crossing streets, walking on icy footpaths, turning mattresses, trying to reach jam from the top shelf of the cupboard, filling coal buckets, getting in and out of the bath. Only to get in somewhere and stay in; to get out and stay out; to stay now, always, in one place.

Ten minutes later she was waiting at the bus stop; anxiously studying the destination of each bus as it passed, clutching her money since concession tickets were not allowed in the weekend, thinking of the cup of tea she would make when she got home, of her evening meal—the remainder of the liver and bacon, of her nephew in Christchurch who was coming with his wife and children for the school holidays, of her niece in the home expecting her third baby. Cars and buses surged by, horns tooted, a plane droned, near and far, near and far, children cried out, dogs barked; the sea, in competition, made a harsher sound as if its waves were now breaking in foam.

For a moment, confused after the peace of the cemetery, she shut her eyes, trying to recapture the image of her husband's grave, now bright with spring flowers, and her parents' grave, wide, spacious, with room should the dead desire it to turn and sigh and move in dreams as if the two slept together in a big soft grass double-bed.

She waited, trying to capture the image of peace. She saw only her husband's grave, made narrower, the spring garden whittled to a thin strip; then it vanished and she was left with the image of the bathroom, of the narrow confining bath grass-yellow as old baths are, not frost-white, waiting, waiting for one moment of inattention, weakness, pain, to claim her for ever.

Winter Garden

Mr Paget's wife had been in a coma for two months. Every day he visited her in the hospital, sitting by her bed, not speaking except to say, 'Miriam, it's me, Alec, I'm here with you,' while she lay unresponsive, not moving, her eyes closed, her face pale. Usually Mr Paget stayed half an hour to an hour; then he would kiss his wife, return her hand that he'd withdrawn and held, to her side under the bedclothes, pat the clothes into their position, and then, conscious of his own privileged freedom and movement in the afternoon or evening light, he would go home to the corner brick house in the hill suburb, where he would prepare and eat a meal before going outside to work in the garden. Every day in all seasons he found work to do in the garden. His time was divided between visiting the hospital and tending his flowers, lawn and olearia hedge. When the neighbours saw him digging, clipping, or mowing they said, 'Poor Mr Paget. His garden must be a comfort to him.' Later in the evening, when the violet-coloured glare showed through the drawn curtains of the sitting-room as Mr Paget watched television, the neighbours said, 'Poor Mr Paget. The television must be a comfort to him.' Often in the evening he would phone for news of his wife and the answer would be, always, Her condition shows no change. No change, no change. He had learned to accept the words without question. He knew what they meant—that she was no nearer living or dying, that the scarcely perceptible fluctuations he noted in his daily visits were ripples only, this way and that, as the opposing winds blew, but were no indication of the surge of the tide. No change. How intently he watched her face! Sometimes he stroked it; even her eyelids did not blink; they were shut and white like lamp shells.

Mr Paget's garden was admired in the street. His roses were perfect, untouched by blight or greenfly. His lawn shone like fur in the sun. Laid between his lawn and the street his hedge looked like a long smooth plump slice of yellow cake—except that it moved; in the wind it crackled its curly dented leaves with a kindling sound as if small fires were being started; in the morning light it was varnished a glossy green; in the evening it became pale lemon, appearing under the mass of house shadow as lawns do sometimes, seen beneath dark trees at sundown.

In the corner of the garden overhanging the street a rowan tree grew that was Mr Paget's pride. It was now, in autumn, thick with berries suspended from beneath the protecting leaves of each twig like clusters of glistening beads. Everyone admired the rowan tree, and its berries cheered Mr Paget as he trimmed, mowed, staked, planted. In the early days of his wife's illness, depressed by the funereal association of flowers, he made up his mind not to take them to the hospital; but one day, impulsively, he picked a cluster of rowan berries.

He arrived early, before visiting time. He found on his wife's bedside so many instruments, tubes, needles—all the tools necessary to care for an apparently lifeless body—that at first there did not seem to be room for the berries. Hesitating, he put them on the locker next to a brick-coloured gaping-throated tube. Perhaps his wife, lying in the strange secret garden where those instruments tended her, would notice the berries.

A nurse came into the room, 'Oh, Mr Paget, you're early. I'll remove this tray and put these berries in water. Aren't they from your garden?'

Mr Paget nodded.

The nurse leaned over his wife, tucking in the bedclothes as if to arrange a blanket defence against the living, speaking creature who had invaded her vegetable peace. Then taking her silver tray of tools and the twig of berries she went from the room, and only when she had gone did Mr Paget say, 'Miriam, it's me, Alec,' taking her hand in his. He could feel a faint pulse like a memory gone out of reach, not able to be reclaimed. He stroked the fingers. He was overwhelmed by the familiar hopelessness. What was the use? Would she not be better dead than lying silent, unknowing in a world where he could not reach her?

The nurse came back. She put the berries on the window sill, where they made a splash of colour. The slim skeleton-shaped leaves soared, like spears, against the glass.

'With winter coming and the leaves turning, there'll soon be only the late berries.'

'Yes,' Mr Paget said.

The nurse looked at him, answering his unspoken question, her face warm with sympathy. 'There's been no change, Mr Paget. But she's not suffering at all.'

'No,' Mr Paget said.

He waited for the nurse to say what everyone was saying to him now, beating the words about his ears until he wanted to cry out for mercy, 'It will be a happy release for her when it comes.'

The nurse did not say it and he was glad. She smiled and left the room, and he sat watching the narrow ribbon of afternoon light that had bound itself across the window pane and the sill and the berries, surging in their glass like tiny bubbles of blood. Mr Paget shivered. He began to feel afraid. What will it be like, he wondered, when death comes and I am with her?

He looked again at his wife's hand, at the wrinkled soft skin; new skin. He stroked her fingers and his heart quickened and a warmth of joy spread through him as he realised her skin was new; and of course her fingernails had been cut; and if they had been cut they had also been growing; her hair, too. Her hair had been cut. Quickly he leaned to touch her damp mouse-coloured hair. It had grown and been cut. They had cut her hair! Then the wild joy began to ebb as he remembered that even after death the hair and fingernails may grow and need to be cut. Was this growth then more a sign of death than of life?

'Oh no, oh no,' Mr Paget said aloud.

For while his wife lay in a coma, again and again they would need to cut her fingernails and hair, to bathe her, to take from her each day the waste of the food they had given her, and each day was different, had been different all the weeks she had been ill; and he had not dreamed, they had not told him, he thought bitterly. They had said, 'No change, no change,' when each day one speck more or less of dust had to be washed away, one ounce more or less of food was stored, rejected; and one day the wide blade of sunlight pressed burning and sharp upon her face while another day she lay in cool dark shade. She was alive, in the light. In the grave there was no sun, no shadow, touching of hands, washing of body.

When Mr Paget smiled happily as he said goodbye to his wife, the nurse looked startled. Poor Mr Paget, she said to herself.

That evening, Mr Paget took special care in trimming the hedge, stepping back to admire its evenness, putting the clippings into a neat pile. He felt quite frivolous as he ran the old-fashioned mower over the lawn; chatter-chatter it gossiped throatily, spewing out the green minus-marks of grass. Then, before he went inside to phone the hospital and watch television, in a spurt of extravagant joy he picked two clusters of rowan berries, and as he was springing back the branch a neighbour passed on her way home.

She saw Mr Paget. Her face assumed the appropriate expression of sympathy. 'And how is Mrs Paget?'

Mr Paget's accustomed answer flowed from him. 'There's been no change.'

He heard the despair in his voice as he spoke. Then, sympathetically, he asked, 'And how's Mr Bambury?'

The neighbour's husband had been ill. She released her news. 'They're stripping his arteries tomorrow.'

There was a jubilant consciousness of action in Mrs Bambury's voice. Mr Paget groped from a dark void of envy to his new joy: no change, no change indeed!

He smiled at Mrs Bambury. He wanted to comfort her about her husband and his arteries but he knew nothing about the stripping of a person's arteries: the resulting nakedness seemed merciless; he was grateful that his wife lay enclosed in sleep, her arteries secret and unyielding.

'I hope everything will be all right with Mr Bambury,' he said at last.

'Oh, there's a risk but a very strong chance of recovery. I do hope there'll be a change in Mrs Paget's condition.'

'Thank you,' Mr Paget said humbly, playing the game. 'So far there has been no change.'

'No change?'

'No change.'

They said goodbye. On his way to the house he stopped to scan the garden. He looked tenderly at the pile of grass and hedge clippings and the succulent golden hedge with the dark pointed roof-shadow eating into it.

Mrs Paget died in late autumn. It is winter now. The berries are gone from the rowan tree, some eaten by birds, some picked by the wind, others scattered by the small boys switching the overhanging branches up and down as they pass in the street. In a luxury of possession rather than deprivation, Mr Bambury, his arteries successfully stripped, rests in a chair on the front porch of his home, looking across the street at Mr Paget in his garden. Mr Bambury and his wife say to each other, 'Mr Paget is tied to his garden.'

Others notice it, too, for Mr Paget seems now to spend all his waking time in the garden. 'Since his wife's death, he's never out of the garden,' they say. 'Why? Nothing grows now but a few late berries. Nothing grows in the garden in winter.'

They wonder why Mr Paget stands for so long looking at the dead twigs, the leafless shrubs, the vacant flower beds set like dark eyes in the middle of the lawn, why he potters about day after day in the dead world where nothing seems to change. And sometimes they think perhaps he is going mad when they see him kneel down and put his cheek against the skin of the earth.

You Are Now Entering the Human Heart

I looked at the notice. I wondered if I had time before my train left Philadelphia for Baltimore in one hour. The heart, ceiling-high, occupied one corner of the large exhibition hall, and from wherever you stood in the hall you could hear its beating, *thum-thump-thum-thump*. It was a popular exhibit, and sometimes, when there were too many children about, the entrance had to be roped off, as the children loved to race up and down the blood vessels and match their cries to the heart's beating. I could see that the heart had already been punished for the day—the floor of the blood vessel was worn and dusty, the chamber walls were covered with marks, and the notice 'You Are Now Taking the Path of a Blood Cell Through the Human Heart', hung askew. I wanted to see more of the Franklin Institute and the Natural Science Museum across the street, but a journey through the human heart would be fascinating. Did I have time?

Later. First, I would go across the street to the Hall of North America, among the bear and the bison, and catch up on American flora and fauna.

I made my way to the Hall. More children, sitting in rows on canvas chairs. An elementary class from a city school, under the control of an elderly teacher. A museum attendant holding a basket, and all eyes gazing at the basket.

'Oh,' I said. 'Is this a private lesson? Is it all right for me to be here?'

The attendant was brisk. 'Surely. We're having a lesson in snake-handling,' he said. 'It's something new. Get the children young and teach them that every snake they meet is not to be killed. People seem to think that every snake has to be knocked on the head. So we're getting them young and teaching them.'

'May I watch?' I said.

'Surely. This is a common grass snake. No harm, no harm at all. Teach the children to learn the feel of them, to lose their fear.'

He turned to the teacher. 'Now, Miss—Mrs—' he said.

'Miss Aitcheson.'

He lowered his voice. 'The best way to get through to the children is to start with teacher,' he said to Miss Aitcheson. 'If they see you're not afraid, then they won't be.'

She must be near retiring age, I thought. A city woman. Never handled a snake in her life. Her face was pale. She just managed to drag the fear from her eyes to some place in their depths, where it lurked like a dark stain. Surely the attendant and the children noticed?

'It's harmless,' the attendant said. He'd been working with snakes for years.

Miss Aitcheson, I thought again. A city woman born and bred. All snakes were creatures to kill, to be protected from, alike the rattler, the copperhead, king snake, grass snake—venom and victims. Were there not places in the South where you couldn't go into the streets for fear of the rattlesnakes?

Her eyes faced the lighted exit. I saw her fear. The exit light blinked, hooded. The children, none of whom had ever touched a live snake, were sitting hushed, waiting for the drama to begin; one or two looked afraid as the attendant withdrew a green snake about three feet long from the basket and with a swift movement, before the teacher could protest, draped it around her neck and stepped back, admiring and satisfied.

'There,' he said to the class. 'Your teacher has a snake around her neck and she's not afraid.'

Miss Aitcheson stood rigid; she seemed to be holding her breath.

'Teacher's not afraid, are you?' the attendant persisted. He leaned forward, pronouncing judgement on her, while she suddenly jerked her head and lifted her hands in panic to get rid of the snake. Then, seeing the children watching her, she whispered, 'No, I'm not afraid. Of course not.' She looked around her.

'Of course not,' she repeated sharply.

I could see her defeat and helplessness. The attendant seemed unaware, as if his perception had grown a reptilian covering. What did she care for the campaign for the preservation and welfare of copperheads and rattlers and common grass snakes? What did she care about someday walking through the woods or the desert and deciding between killing a snake and setting it free, as if there would be time to decide, when her journey to and from school in downtown Philadelphia held enough danger to occupy her? In two years or so, she'd retire and be in that apartment by herself and no doorman, and everyone knew what happened then, and how she'd be afraid to answer the door and to walk after dark and carry her pocketbook in the street. There was enough to think about without learning to handle and love the snakes, harmless and otherwise, by having them draped around her neck for everyone, including the children—most of all the children—to witness the outbreak of her fear.

'See, Miss Aitcheson's touching the snake. She's not afraid of it at all.'

As everyone watched, she touched the snake. Her fingers recoiled. She touched it again.

'See, she's not afraid. Miss Aitcheson can stand there with a beautiful snake around her neck and touch it and stroke it and not be afraid.'

The faces of the children were full of admiration for the teacher's bravery, and yet there was a cruelly persistent tension; they were waiting, waiting.

'We have to learn to love snakes,' the attendant said. 'Would someone like to come out and stroke teacher's snake?'

Silence.

One shamefaced boy came forward. He stood petrified in front of the teacher.

'Touch it,' the attendant urged. 'It's a friendly snake. Teacher's wearing it around her neck and she's not afraid.'

The boy darted his hand forward, rested it lightly on the snake,

and immediately withdrew his hand. Then he ran back to his seat.
The children shrieked with glee.

'He's afraid,' someone said. 'He's afraid of the snake.'

The attendant soothed. 'We have to get used to them, you know.
Grownups are not afraid of them, but we can understand that when
you're small you might be afraid, and that's why we want you to
learn to love them. Isn't that right, Miss Aitcheson? Isn't that right?
Now who else is going to be brave enough to touch teacher's
snake?'

Two girls came out. They stood hand in hand side by side and
stared at the snake and then at Miss Aitcheson.

I wondered when the torture would end. The two little girls did
not touch the snake, but they smiled at it and spoke to it and Miss
Aitcheson smiled at them and whispered how brave they were.

'Just a minute,' the attendant said. 'There's really no need to be
brave. It's not a question of bravery. The snake is *harmless*,
absolutely *harmless*. Where's the bravery when the snake is
harmless?'

Suddenly the snake moved around to face Miss Aitcheson and
thrust its flat head toward her cheek. She gave a scream, flung up
her hands, and tore the snake from her throat and threw it on the
floor, and, rushing across the room, she collapsed into a small
canvas chair beside the Bear Cabinet and started to cry.

I didn't feel I should watch any longer. Some of the children
began to laugh, some to cry. The attendant picked up the snake and
nursed it. Miss Aitcheson, recovering, sat helplessly exposed by the
small piece of useless torture. It was not her fault she was city-bred,
her eyes tried to tell us. She looked at the children, trying in some
way to force their admiration and respect; they were shut against
her. She was evicted from them and from herself and even from her
own fear-infested tomorrow, because she could not promise to love
and preserve what she feared. She had nowhere, at that moment,
but the small canvas chair by the Bear Cabinet of the Natural
Science Museum.

I looked at my watch. If I hurried, I would catch the train from
Thirtieth Street. There would be no time to make the journey
through the human heart. I hurried out of the museum. It was
freezing cold. The icebreakers would be at work on the Delaware

and the Susquehanna; the mist would have risen by the time I arrived home. Yes, I would just catch the train from Thirtieth Street. The journey through the human heart would have to wait until some other time.

Insulation

In the summer days when the lizards come out and the old ewes, a rare generation, a gift of the sun, gloat at us from the television screen, and the country, skull in hand, recites To kill or not to kill, and tomatoes and grapes ripen in places unused to such lingering light and warmth, then the people of Stratford, unlike the 'too happy happy tree' of the poem, do remember the 'drear-nighted' winter. They order coal and firewood, they mend leaks in the spouting and roof, they plant winter savoys, swedes, a last row of parsnips.

The country is not as rich as it used to be. The furniture in the furniture store spills out on the footpath and stays unsold. The seven varieties of curtain rail with their seven matching fittings stay on display, useless extras in the new education of discernment and necessity. The dazzling bathroom ware, the chrome and fur and imitation marble are no longer coveted and bought. For some, though, the time is not just a denial of gluttony, of the filling of that worthy space in the heart and the imagination with assorted satisfied cravings. Some have lost their jobs, their life-work, a process described by one factory-manager as 'shedding'.

'Yes, we have been shedding some of our workers.'

'Too happy happy tree'?

The leaves fall as if from other places, only they fall here. They are brittle in the sun. Shedding, severing, pruning. God's country, the garden of Eden and the conscientious gardeners.

Some find work again. Some who have never had work advertise in the local newspaper. There was that advertisement which appeared every day for two weeks, full of the hope of youth, sweet and sad with unreal assumptions about the world.

'Sixteen year old girl with one thousand hours training at hairdressing College seeks work.' The *one thousand hours* was in big dark print. It made the reader gasp as if with a sudden visitation of years so numerous they could scarcely be imagined, as if the young girl had undergone, like an operation, a temporal insertion which made her in some way older and more experienced than anyone else. And there was the air of pride with which she flaunted her thousand hours. She was pleading, using her richness of time as her bargain. In another age she might have recorded such time in her Book of Hours.

And then there was the boy, just left school. 'Boy, sixteen, would like to join pop group as vocalist fulltime'—the guileless advertisement of a dream. Did anyone answer either advertisment? Sometimes I imagine they did (I too have unreal assumptions about the world), that the young girl has found a place in the local Salon Paris, next to the Manhattan Takeaway, where she is looked at with admiration and awe (one thousand hours!) and I think that somewhere, maybe, say, in Hamilton (which is to other cities what round numbers are to numbers burdened by decimal points), there's a pop group with a new young vocalist fulltime, appearing, perhaps, on *Opportunity Knocks*, the group playing their instruments, the young man running up and down the stairs, being sexy with his microphone and singing in the agony style.

But my real story is just an incident, a passing glance at insulation and one of those who were pruned, shed, severed, and in the curious mixture of political metaphor, irrationally rationalised, with a sinking lid fitted over his sinking heart. I don't know his name. I only know he lost his job and he couldn't get other work and he was a man used to working with never a thought of finding himself jobless. Like the others he had ambled among the seven varieties of curtain rail and matching fittings, and the fancy suites with showwood arms and turned legs, and the second circular saw. He was into wrought iron, too, and there was a wishing well in his

garden and his wife had leaflets about a swimming-pool. And
somewhere, at the back of his mind, he had an internal stairway to
the basement rumpus. Then one day, suddenly, although there had
been rumours, he was pruned from the dollar-flowering tree.

He tried to get other work but there was nothing. Then he
thought of spending his remaining money on a franchise to sell
insulation. It was a promising district with the winters wet and
cold and frosty. The price of electricity had gone up, the
government was giving interest-free loans—why, everyone would
be insulating. At first, having had a number of leaflets printed, he
was content to distribute them in letter boxes, his two school-age
children helping. His friends were sympathetic and optimistic.
They too said, Everyone will be wanting insulation. And after this
drought you can bet on a cold winter. Another thing, there was
snow on Egmont at Christmas, and that's a sign.

He sat at home waiting for the orders to come in. None came. He
tried random telephoning, still with no success. Finally, he decided
to sell from door to door.

'I'm going from door to door,' he told his wife.

She was young and able. She had lost her job in the local
clothing factory, and was thinking of buying a knitting-machine
and taking orders. On TV when they demonstrated knitting-
machines the knitter (it was always a she, with the he
demonstrating) simply moved her hands to and fro as if casting a
magic spell and the machine did the rest. To and fro, to and fro, a
fair-isle sweater knitted in five hours, and fair-isle was coming
back, people said. Many of her friends had knitting-machines, in
the front room, near the window, to catch the light, where, in her
mother's day, the piano always stood, and when she walked by her
friends' houses she could see them sitting in the light moving their
hands magically to and fro, making fair-isle and bulky knit,
intently reading the pattern.

'Yes, door to door.'

The words horrified her. Not in her family, surely! Not door to
door. Her father, a builder, had once said that if a man had to go
door to door to advertise his work there was something wrong with
it.

'If you're reputable,' he said, 'you don't advertise. People just come to you through word of mouth, through your own work standing up to the test.' Well, it wasn't like that now, she knew. Even Smart and Rogers had a full-page advertisement in the latest edition of the local paper. All the same, door to door!

'Oh no,' she said plantively.

'It can't be helped. I have to look for custom.'

He put on his work clothes, a red checkered shirt, jeans, and he carried a bundle of leaflets, and even before he had finished both sides of one street he was tired and he had begun to look worried and shabby.

This is how I perceived him when he came to my door. I saw a man in his thirties wearing a work-used shirt and jeans yet himself looking the picture of disuse, that is, severed, shed, rationalised, with a great lid sinking over his life, putting out the flame.

'I thought you might like to insulate your house,' he said, thrusting a leaflet into my hand.

I was angry. Interrupted in my work, brought to the door for nothing! Why, the electrician had said my house was well insulated with its double ceilings. Besides, I'd had experience of that stuff they blow into the ceiling and every time there's a wind it all comes out making snowfall in the garden, drifting over to the neighbours too.

'No, I'm not interested,' I said. 'I tried that loose-fill stuff once and it snowed everywhere, every time the wind blew.'

'There's a government loan, you know.'

'I'm really not interested,' I said.

'But it's new. New. Improved.'

'Can't afford it, anyway.'

'Read about it, then, and let me know.'

'Sorry,' I said.

My voice was brisk and dismissing. He looked as if he were about to plead with me, then he changed his mind. He pointed to the red print stamped on the leaflet. There was pride in his pointing, like that of the girl with the thousand hours.

'That's my name and phone number, if you change your mind.'

'Thank you, but I don't think I will.'

He walked away and I shut the door quickly. Insulation, I said to myself with no special meaning or tone. How lovely the summer is, how cosy this house is. The people here before me had carpets that will last for ever, the ceiling is double, there are no cracks in the corners, that is, unless the place decides to shift again on its shaky foundations. How well insulated I am! How solid the resistance of this house against the searching penetrating winds of Stratford. The hunted safe from the hunter, the fleeing from the pursuer, the harmed from the harmer.

'How well insulated I am!'

That night I had a curious ridiculous dream. I dreamed of a land like a vast forest 'in green felicity' where the leaves had started to fall, not by nature, for the forest was evergreen, but under the influence of a season that came to the land from within it and had scarcely been recognised, and certainly not ruled against. Now how could that have been? At first I thought I was trapped in a legend of far away and long ago, for the characters of long ago were there. I could see a beggar walking among the fallen leaves. He was the beggar of other times and other countries, and yet he was not, he was new, and he was ashamed. I saw a cottage in the forest and a young woman at the window combing her hair and—a young man with a—lute? No, a guitar—surely that was the prince?—and with the guitar plugged in to nowhere he began to play and sing and as he sang he sparkled—why, it was Doug Dazzle—and he was singing,

> *One thousand hours of cut and set*
> *my showwood arms will hold you yet*
> *baby baby insulate,*
> *apprentice and certificate,*
> *God of nations at thy feet*
> *in our bonus bonds we meet*
> *lest we forget lest we forget*
> *one thousand hours of cut and set. . . .*

The girl at the window listened and smiled and then she turned to the knitting-machine by the window and began to play it as if from a 90 per cent worsted, 10 per cent acrylic score. I could see the light falling on her hands as they moved to and fro, to and fro in a leisurely saraband of fair-isle. Then the beggar appeared. He was carrying a sack that had torn and was leaking insulation, faster and faster, until it became a blizzard, vermiculite falling like snow, endlessly, burying everything, the trees and their shed leaves, the cottage, the beggar, the prince, and the princess of the thousand hours.

The next morning I found the leaflet and telephoned the number on it.

'I'd like to be insulated,' I said.

The man was clearly delighted.

'I'll come at once and measure.'

We both knew we were playing a game, he trying to sell what he didn't possess, and I imagining I could ever install it, to deaden the world. All the same, he measured the house and he put in the loose-fill insulation, and following the Stratford custom, although it was summer, I ordered my firewood against that other 'drear-nighted' winter.

Janet Frame
Living in the Maniototo

Winner of the Fiction Prize, New Zealand Book Awards,
1980

Janet Frame again offers us a richly imagined exploration of
uncharted lands. The path is through the Maniototo, that
'bloody plain' of the imagination which crouches beneath the
colour and movement of the living world. The theme of the
novel is the process of writing fiction, the power,
interruptions and avoidances that the writer feels as she
grapples with a deceptive and elusive reality. We move with
our guide, a woman of manifold personalities, though a
physical journey which is revealed to be a metaphor for the
creative process – on which our own survival depends.

'A many-layered palimpsest of a book, probably as near a
masterpiece as we are likely to see this year' *Daily Telegraph*

'Try it: it could change your unconscious' *Evening Standard*

'Puts everything else that has come my way this year right in
the shade' *Guardian*

Fiction   £3.50

Janet Frame
Faces in the Water

'I will write about the season of peril . . . a great gap opened
in the ice floe between myself and the other people whom I
watched, with their world, drifting away through a violet-
coloured sea where hammer-head sharks in tropical ease
swam side by side with the seals and the polar bears. I was
alone on the ice . . . I traded my safety for the glass beads of
fantasy'

Faces in the Water is about confinement in mental
institutions, about the fear the sensible and sane of this
world have of the so-called mad, the uncontrolled. Banished
to an institution, Istani Mavet lives a life dominated by the
vagaries of her keepers as much as by her own inner world.

Janet Frame's clear and unforgettable prose startles and
evokes. A remarkable piece of writing by New Zealand's
finest living novelist.

'Lyrical, touching and deeply entertaining' John Mortimer,
Observer

Fiction   £2.75

Janet Frame
Scented Gardens for the Blind

'A brilliant outburst of a book' *Kirkus Reviews*

In this haunting novel Janet Frame leads us to inhabit in turn
Vera Glace, the mother who has willed herself sightless;
Erlene, the daughter who has ceased to speak; and Edward,
the husband and father who has taken refuge in a distant
land. She bids us consider the pain – impossibility? – of
closeness, of love, among human beings; and the beauty, and
danger, in the world of the senses. Then, behind this parable
of human relationships, she springs another level of meaning
upon us: a study of a mind that has burst the confines of
everyday individual consciousness and invented its own
colourful and tormented reality.

Fiction   £3.50

Michèle Roberts
A Piece of the Night

Michèle Roberts' first novel was acclaimed as a landmark in feminist fiction. It concerns Julie Fanchot, French born, English convent educated, who has learned to please. The seductive daughter, Virgin Mary, romantic heroine, perfect wife and mother – she knows how to be all of these. But she knows that she is also the witch, the whore, the madwoman, the insatiable, the lesbian.

'Her prose is rich and sinewy and invigorating and her ideas are stimulating and thought provoking' *The Sunday Express*, Dublin

'Uncompromising in its feminism and confident and original in its style . . . Its language is our own – angry, analytic, harsh and poetic' *Women Speaking*

Joint winner of the *Gay News* Book Award, 1979

Fiction £3.95

Michèle Roberts
The Visitation

This rich and mysterious new novel concerns the growing up
of Helen, and the conflict between her need to be a creative
woman, and her desire to love men.

'*The Visitation* has done something so rare it may be unique –
described heterosexual sex from a female point of view with
all the force and lyricism of those male authors, like D H
Lawrence, who have famously falsified the female
experience' *The Guardian*

Fiction   £3.95

Manny Shirazi
Javady Alley

This haunting first novel is set in Iran in the turbulent year of 1953, when working class activists are struggling to wrest the country's oil from the control of foreigners.

But we see events through seven-year-old Homa's eyes. Her world is the intensely private one of childhood, bounded by house, courtyard, and the lives of her mother and grandmother. Her ventures outside are to the women-only baths, a religious pilgrimage, or once, daringly, with neighbourhood children to the railway track.

It is only slowly that the violence of outside events begins to threaten . . .

Full of the sights, smells and sounds of daily life, Manny Shirazi's prose is at once sensuous, and direct.

Manny Shirazi grew up in Iran, and has spent much of her adult life in London, where she now lives. The Women's Press is proud to publish this outstanding new author.

Fiction £3.95

Toni Cade Bambara
The Salt Eaters

Velma Henry finds herself in the Southwestern Community Infirmary facing Minnie Ransom, fabled healer and vehicle of the spirit world, when, falling on hard times, she tries to commit suicide. In facing the responsibilities of health so that she can become whole she delves, with the salt eaters – the black community – into the shared dreams of their past to find a shared vision of the future.

'A book full of marvels' *The New Yorker*

'Swirling, whirling and compelling' *Guardian*

'Toni Cade Bambara's magicians are women. Their words will bathe you in illuminations, and spread balm on bruised spirits' *Morning Star*

Fiction £3.50

Toni Cade Bambara
Gorilla, My Love

From Sister Sugar on sex to young Hazel on survival in Harlem, these sixteen stories explode with humour and energy. Written in Toni Cade Bambara's inimitable style, the effect has been described as 'like reading jazz'. From uptown New York to small-town Carolina, from first love to last wishes, her touch remains absolutely sure.

'Ms Bambara grabs you by the throat. She dazzles, she charms' *Chicago Illinois News*

Fiction £3.95

Alice Walker
The Color Purple
1983 Pulitzer Prize Winner

'Dear God: I am fourteen years old. I have always been a good girl. Maybe you can give me a sign letting me know what is happening to me . . .' So begins Alice Walker's touching, complex and engrossing new novel about two sisters in the Deep South between the wars. Celie, raped by the man she calls her father, her two children taken from her, her sister run away, has no one to talk to but God. Until, forced into an ugly marriage, she meets Shug Avery, the singer, the magic woman; and discovers not the pain of rivalry but the love and support of women.

'A striking and consummately well written novel . . . without doubt her most impressive' *New York Times Book Review*

Fiction   £3.95

Alice Walker
In Search of Our Mothers' Gardens
Womanist Prose

'Womanist is to feminist as purple is to lavender'

This is a phrase from Alice Walker's own definition of the special quality of her 'womanist' prose. The depth of thought it implies is reflected throughout this major collection of the essays, reviews and articles she has written over the last fifteen years.

Non-fiction   £4.95 paperback   £12.95 hard cover

Joanna Russ
How to Suppress Women's Writing

How to suppress women's writing?
Begin by saying/writing/thinking:
She didn't write it.
But if it's clear she did the deed:
She wrote it, but she wrote only one of it (*Jane Eyre. Poor dear, that's all she ever . . .*)
She wrote it, but look what she wrote about (*the bedroom, the kitchen, her family. Other women!*)
She wrote it, but 'she' isn't really an artist, and 'it' isn't really art (*it's a thriller, a romance, a children's book. It's sci fi!*)
She wrote it, but she had help (*Robert Browning, Branwell Brontë. Her own 'masculine side'*).
She wrote it BUT . . . Congratulations! You have just belittled/distorted/neglected/suppressed women's writing. But don't worry. It's a tradition . . .

Joanna Russ has written an explosive, irreverent, angry and very funny book, which rediscovers women's literary heritage. She reveals how it has been belittled in the past, just how impressive the reality is, and how (and why) women's writing is now finding new forms.

'A book of the most profound and original clarity. The study of literature should never be the same again' *Marge Piercy*

Non-fiction   £3.50